# OUT OF HER DEPTH

## BRENDA HIATT

Dolphin Star Press

**OUT OF HER DEPTH**

Copyright 2013 by Brenda Hiatt
Cover art by Fantasia Frog Designs

This is a work of fiction. Names, characters, places and incidents are either the products of the author's imagination or are used fictitiously. Any resemblance to actual persons (living or dead), events or locations is entirely coincidental.

Dolphin Star Press

ISBN: 978-1-947205-41-3

———

# ALSO BY BRENDA HIATT

### The Seven Saints Hunt Club

*Tessa's Touch*

*The Runaway Heiress*

*A Taste for Scandal*

### The Saint of Seven Dials

*Scandalous Virtue*

*Rogue's Honor*

*Noble Deceptions*

*Innocent Passions*

*Saintly Sins*

*Gallant Scoundrel*

### Hiatt Regency Classics

*Gabriella*

*The Cygnet*

*Lord Dearborn's Destiny*

*Daring Deception*

*Christmas Promises* (novella)

*Christmas Bride*

*Azalea*

<u>**Americana Dreaming**</u>

*Azalea*

*Ship of Dreams*

*Bridge Over Time*


<u>**The Starstruck series**</u>

*Starstruck*

*Starcrossed*

*Starbound*

*Starfall*

*Fractured Jewel: A Starstruck Novella*

*The Girl From Mars*

*The Handmaid's Secret*

*Convergent*

*Yuletide Perils: A Starstruck Novella*

*Unraveling the Stars*

*Mindbound*

———

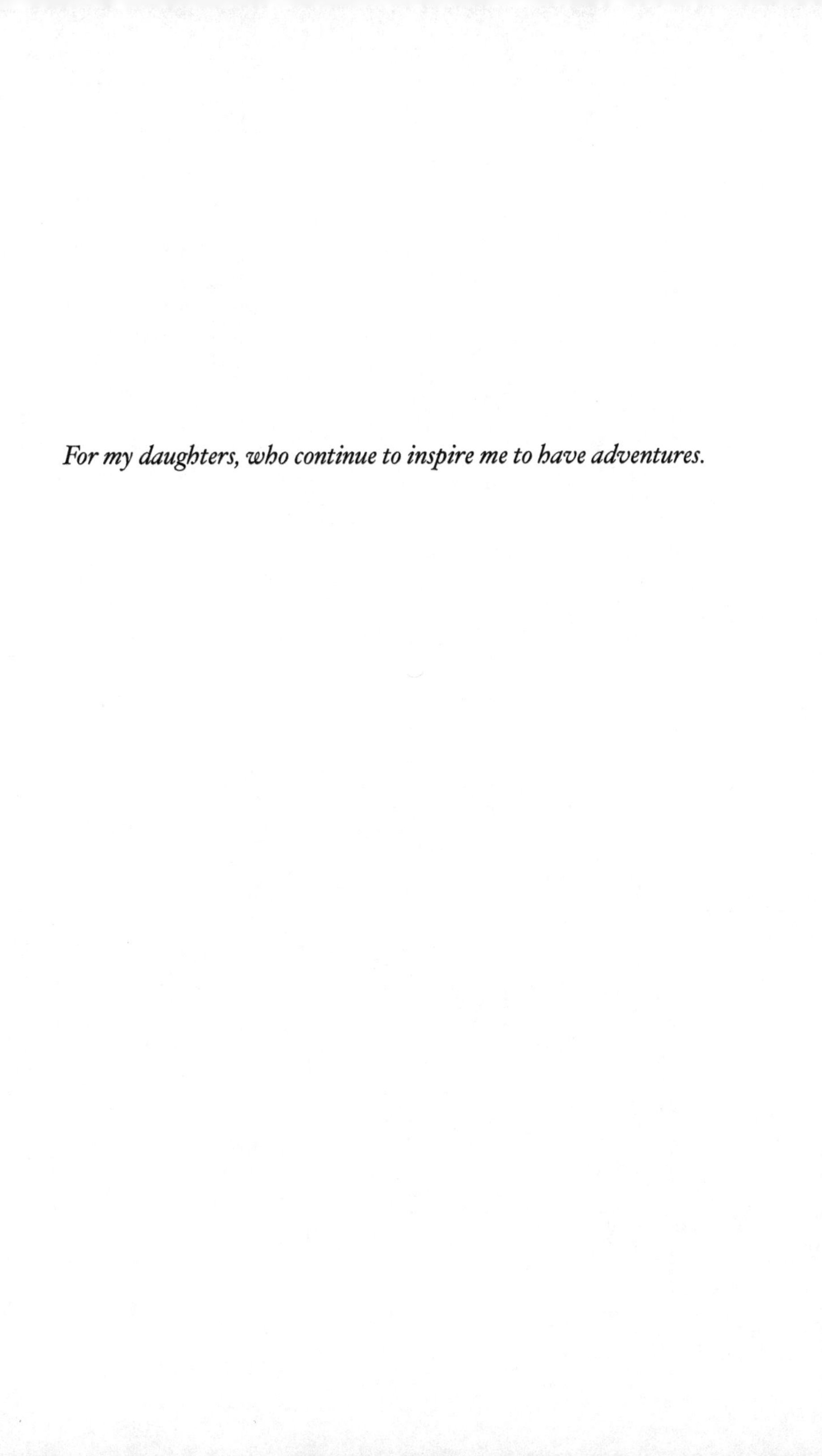

*For my daughters, who continue to inspire me to have adventures.*

# CHAPTER ONE

February—Palm Beach, Aruba

*NO FEAR.*

I read the blood-red lettering, set inside the outline of a shark, on one of the t-shirts adorning the walls of the dive shop. Another shirt proclaimed, *Divers Do It Deeper.* Uh-huh.

Definitely not my kind of place. It was just as well I was only here to cancel the scuba lessons I'd signed up for eight months ago. Before my life was turned upside down.

"May I help you, ma'am?" The girl at the counter couldn't be any older than my younger daughter Debra, though I cynically told myself that her impressive suntan would have her looking forty in another five years.

"Um, yes. I signed up for dive lessons, starting today. But now I—"

"Mrs. Seally?"

I nodded warily, wondering how she knew that.

She must have seen my surprise. "Only three women are signed up for this class, and the other two have already checked in. I've got your forms here." Then, glancing behind me, "Isn't your husband with you?"

"I no longer have a husband."

The girl looked stricken, and I realized with a completely inappropriate spurt of amusement how that must have sounded.

"Oh, I'm terribly sorry, ma'am. Did he...die recently?"

"No, I let him live."

Now she looked confused, so I added, "We're divorced. As of three weeks ago."

Her expression cleared, though she still looked dubious. I couldn't blame her. I was still dubious myself about the wisdom of coming all the way to Aruba alone on what should have been my twenty-fifth anniversary trip. For about the hundredth time, I wondered whether I was crazy.

Probably.

Still, my defiant little burst of irony temporarily restored my confidence, and when the girl shoved a clipboard toward me, I abruptly changed my mind about backing out of the class. Instead, I filled out the form and read the disclaimer that essentially promised that if I were eaten by a shark, I wouldn't sue. I glanced over my shoulder at the *NO FEAR* t-shirt again.

Taking a deep breath, I signed my full name: Wynne Nightingale Seally. Little did I know that I had just set in motion a harrowing adventure that would change my life—permanently.

"The class will be starting in about five minutes, through that door, there." The girl handed me a copy of the form.

Six people were already in the small classroom at the back of the dive shop—five students, sitting in a row of old-fashioned school desks, and a blond, tanned, handsome fellow of perhaps thirty, standing in front of them with an air of authority.

Vainly (in both senses of the word) wishing I were a decade or two younger, I handed him my paperwork. He glanced over it, then checked the list he held.

"Is—?"

"Nope, just me," I replied before he could finish the question and moved to a desk in the second row, behind the others.

"Okay, then," he said, after only the slightest hesitation. "I'm Jason, and I'll be your dive instructor. Before we start, let's go around the room and introduce ourselves." He indicated one of the two dark-haired young men up front. "What's your name and where are you from?"

"I'm Rick, from Texas. Er, in the United States."

The next young guy was Dobry, from Poland, then a very attractive blonde girl, Bebe, from Maine, and a cute couple from Canada, Greg and Linda, in Aruba for their honeymoon. All of them appeared to be in their twenties.

"And I'm Wynne, from Indiana," I said, feeling more strongly than ever that I did *not* belong here.

"Great, let's get started," Jason said briskly before I could give voice to my doubts. "Did you all bring your books?"

I pulled out the handbook I'd been mailed months ago, shortly after signing up for the class, and nodded along with the others.

For once, my insecurities had worked in my favor. On the off chance I'd be foolish enough to go through with this, I had read every word of the book and done all of the quizzes. As Jason asked us questions, it quickly became obvious that I was the only one who had.

"Wynne?" Jason prompted—again—when no one volunteered the atmospheric pressure at a depth of twenty meters.

Feeling like a high school know-it-all, I smiled sheepishly as I answered, "Um, three atmospheres?"

Jason beamed at me. "Very good. Okay, everyone, what's the most important rule in scuba diving?"

Since we'd already gone over this twice, everyone chorused together, "Keep breathing."

"Right. You never, never want to hold your breath. Now, let's watch the first video, and then we'll get you all outfitted and head to the pool for your first taste of the fun stuff." He started the video, dimmed the lights, and left the room.

I had to force myself to focus on the video, simplistic as it was, to keep from panicking. It was just a swimming pool, I told myself. How badly could I embarrass myself in a swimming pool? I wasn't sure I wanted to find out. I'd always done better in academic settings than real-world ones. The fact that I'd been blindsided by my husband's infidelity was proof of that.

Keeping that in mind, I paid close attention to the video demonstration of how to set up all of the gear we'd be using. Even though I'd read the book, it looked complicated—and a little bit scary. I guess they had to point out everything that could possibly go wrong, but it didn't help my confidence any.

In front of me, the newlyweds whispered and giggled together, and Rick and Bebe took turns pantomiming how bored they were. Only Dobry was paying attention to the video, possibly as insecure with his slight language barrier as I was with my advanced age.

Just before the video ended, Jason rejoined us. In spite of my nervousness, the crescendo of dramatic music that ended the video almost made me laugh. We were going to play in a *swimming pool*, for Pete's sake!

"Who already has their own masks, fins, and snorkels?" Jason asked, flicking the lights back on.

Rick, Bebe, and the newlyweds raised their hands.

"BCDs and regulators?"

Only Rick raised his hand.

"I have my own wetsuit," Bebe volunteered.

Jason smiled, and I wondered if I imagined the spark between them. "That's good. You won't need it for the pool, but you'll want it for our open water dives later this week."

My stomach clenched at the words "open water dives," but I trooped gamely back into the dive shop behind the others, where we were fitted for our equipment. On Jason's advice, I went ahead and bought my mask, fins, and snorkel. Even if diving scared me as much as I expected it to, I could still use them for snorkeling.

Forty-five minutes later, the group of us stood beside the swimming pool, awkwardly holding our gear. I wondered if the others felt as silly as I did under the curious stares of the hotel guests on their lounge chairs.

"Okay, let's strip down to bathing suits for the swim test," Jason said. "Two hundred meter swim—that's ten lengths in this pool—and a ten minute float. You can all do it at once."

I was now several zip codes outside my comfort zone. After stepping out of my shorts and peeling off my t-shirt, I crossed my arms over my middle, which was already well covered by my modest one-piece. I couldn't help wishing I'd been a whole lot more faithful about getting to the gym in recent months. The other two women in the group wore bikinis and looked disgustingly good in them.

Not that I'd have worn a bikini even if I were in fabulous shape. I firmly believed there were some things a forty-plus body just shouldn't do, and a bikini was one of them.

"Everyone into the pool," Jason urged.

I had a fleeting worry about what the chlorine might do to my Auburn #6 hair color, then jumped into the pool. What difference did it make, really? It's not like anyone here cared.

Though I'd swum competitively in high school, it had been years since I'd done more than splash around on vacation, since my gym didn't have a pool. I was pleased to discover I could still manage a decent breast stroke. And I could float with the best of them, though I preferred not to think about exactly why that was.

Jason congratulated us all when our ten minutes expired, then told us to get into our dive gear.

My stomach clenched again. This was where I'd either panic and make a complete fool of myself, or prove that an old dog like me really could learn a new trick. I desperately hoped it would be the latter. Pressing my lips together in concentration, I started putting my equipment together exactly the way we'd been shown in the video.

"I learned all this stuff from my cousin on South Padre Island a couple summers ago," Rick was saying loudly to Bebe. "So let me know if you need any help."

"Um, okay." Bebe was already further along in the process than Rick was.

I'm sure I wasn't the only one who had to stifle a laugh when Jason came up to him a moment later to point out that he'd put the first stage onto his air tank backward. "Remember? You want the gauge on your left and your regulator on the right."

"Uh, right." Rick kept his back to us as he fixed it, and didn't make any more offers of help.

I had some difficulty getting my BCD (short for "buoyancy control device," the inflatable vest) strapped tightly enough to my tank, but once Jason showed me how to cinch the strap, I managed everything else on my own.

Reciting the instructions in my head, I clipped one air hose into the BCD, another to the depth and pressure gauge, a third to the regulator, for breathing, and the final one to the "octopus," or backup regulator, which I obediently clipped to the vest to keep it out of the way.

Jason estimated how much weight each of us would need to stay submerged and handed out weight belts, which we all fastened around our middles. Following his directions, I pulled on my fins and mask, snapped myself into my vest, and, with some difficulty, stood up. The tank was a lot heavier than I expected, given that it was full of air, not lead.

"You all look great," Jason told us, though I thought we all looked pretty stupid. "Now, one at a time, do the giant stride you saw on the video to enter the pool. That's exactly how we'll be doing it off the back of the boat in a couple of days."

I refused to think that far ahead, since I was already working hard to keep panic at bay. Instead, I concentrated on shuffling all the way to the edge of the pool in my enormous hot pink flippers without falling on my face.

Greg and Linda stepped into the pool with resounding splashes, and then it was my turn. Swallowing hard, reminding myself yet again that this was just a swimming pool, I scooted the toes of my flippers over the edge.

I was breathing loudly through my regulator, sounding like Darth Vader, when Jason nodded. With one hand on my weight belt and the other spanning my mask and regulator, just like in the video, I swung my right leg forward over the water and pushed off the ledge. I had one frantic moment of terror as the water closed over my head. Then I remembered to breathe.

*Cool!*

The water gently cocooned my whole body as I hung suspended in total silence, except for the sound of my own breathing. It made me think of an astronaut doing a space walk. The weights on my belt let me sink to the bottom of the pool, where I sat cross-legged next to Greg and Linda to wait for the others.

I could see the length of the pool with the help of my mask—much farther than I was used to seeing underwater. Also cool, even though there was nothing to see but some hotel guests' legs at the far end. For the first time since signing in, I was glad I hadn't chickened out.

Once the class was assembled on the bottom of the pool, we followed Jason's lead in removing, replacing and clearing our masks and regulators, and practicing buoyancy control by inflating and deflating our BCD vests while slowly swimming around.

By the time we surfaced for the day, I was feeling pretty pleased with myself. I hadn't panicked, and I hadn't screwed up, which was more than show-off Rick could claim. Twice, he'd had to stand up, gasping, when he'd forgotten to clear his regulator before taking his first breath after recovering it.

But I wasn't about to get cocky. Rick's example showed exactly how easy it would be to do something stupid when it really mattered—like when we were fifty feet under the surface of the ocean. Still, I didn't find that prospect nearly as terrifying as I had that morning.


THE HOT ARUBA wind dried my swimsuit almost instantly, so I pulled my shorts and shirt back on before heading to the poolside grill for a quick lunch. The rest of the class dispersed, but that was fine. Being alone gave me a chance to get my bearings.

I'd assumed Aruba would be tropical, but it was more like a desert—a very windy desert. The previous afternoon, during the drive from Queen Beatrix International Airport through tiny, bustling Oranjestad and on to the high rise hotels of Palm Beach, I'd noticed there were only limited patches of green, mainly in the tourist areas. That is, unless you counted the scattered stands of cactus along the four-lane road that passed for a highway.

Now, as the dry noontime heat seeped into my skin, I began to fully appreciate what a different world this was from the one I'd left behind in Indianapolis. Not only was it at least fifty degrees warmer —it was February—but the whole atmosphere was calmer, slower... less judgmental.

Finishing my burger and diet soda, I entered the hotel and headed across the opulent, open-air lobby. Signs I'd barely noticed last night pointed to a casino at one end, a tiki bar and a boutique at the other.

Near the casino, to my left, was a more upscale bar sporting a grand piano with a huge bird-of-paradise flower arrangement on top. The elevators were just beyond. I stepped in and pushed the button for the fourteenth floor.

Last night I'd been tired and depressed, and the opulence of my room had only made me feel worse. The king-sized bed, whirlpool tub, glassed-in shower, and wide balcony overlooking the beach had reminded me of a honeymoon suite—a thought that had reduced me to tears.

But that was last night. Now, I was able to look at the room with new eyes and appreciate the luxury. *I deserve this*, I told myself, and almost believed it.

I unplugged my cell phone from its charger on the desk and turned it on, wandering out onto the balcony as it powered up. Gazing out at the expanse of white sand and astonishingly blue ocean, I reminded myself that I'd come to Aruba to celebrate my new freedom. In fact, I'd brought along my old wedding ring with a vague idea of symbolically flinging it into the ocean. Maybe I'd—

My cell phone rang in my hand, startling me out of my thoughts. "Hello?"

"Mom?" It was my younger daughter, Debra. "Where have you been? You haven't been home, and your cell phone has been off since yesterday. Did you get my voice mail?"

"Oops, no, sorry." My old cell phone hadn't worked internationally, so I hadn't even thought to turn my new one on until now. "Is something wrong?"

"No, but I was hoping I could come over for dinner tonight. My fridge is empty, and I don't get paid until Friday."

This had become a pattern for Debra, despite the fact she'd landed a plum job with an advertising firm right out of college. She always seemed to end up with more month than money—but no shortage of designer clothes.

"Sorry, sweetie, but I'm out of town and won't be back for a couple of weeks." I waited for the inevitable question, wondering how she'd react to the answer.

"Out of town? Out of town where?"

"Aruba."

"*What?* Oh, wait. There's an Aruba, Indiana, right? Like Peru and Brazil? So where is Aruba?"

"Off the coast of Venezuela. As far as I know, there's no Aruba in Indiana. I'm on the actual island."

There was a long silence. "Why?"

Good question. I'd asked it myself a few hundred times, but the answer seemed even less plausible as I said it out loud to Debra.

"I booked the trip for our twenty-fifth wedding anniversary before...well, you know." In fact, I'd booked it the very same day I'd caught Tom cheating on me, but Deb didn't need to know that. "With everything going on, I forgot to ask for a refund by the deadline, so I decided what the heck."

"What the heck is right. What are you going to do all by yourself in Aruba for two weeks? This is crazy."

Great. Now I had my youngest validating my suspicion that I was crazy. "I plan to relax, away from everyone who knows—or thinks they know—everything about me," I told her, and vowed to make it true. "And I'm learning to scuba dive."

"Okay, now I know you're yanking my chain. If you don't want me there for dinner tonight, just say so."

I had to laugh at her affronted tone, even if her disbelief undermined my new confidence a bit.

"I'm not making any of it up, I promise. Of course, when I signed up for scuba lessons, I didn't think I'd be taking them alone. But they say learning new things helps to stave off Alzheimer's."

"So learning to scuba dive will give you a few more years before Bess and I have to put you in a home?" Now her voice dripped with irony. "Then by all means, go for it, Mom."

"I am. I had my first lesson this morning, so I'm committed now." And I was—though not the way Debra clearly thought I should be.

"No way! Seriously, Mom, I don't think you should try something like this without Dad. I mean, by yourself. I mean, you've never—"

I cut her off. "That's the whole point. There are lots of things I've never done. I've decided to start changing that." I was impressed at how firm I sounded, how sure of myself.

Apparently, so was Debra. At least, she didn't try to argue any further. "Fine. I guess it's your life. Have you told Bess what you're doing yet?"

"Not yet. I only turned on my phone two minutes before you called."

She made a "*hmph*" noise. Debra could be such a mother hen sometimes. "Do you want me to tell her, or will you?"

"I'll call her." I couldn't keep a touch of acid from my tone. "No need for the two of you to start conspiring about how to drag your doddering old mother back to sanity and civilization. I'm only here for two weeks, anyway."

"Bess will probably love what you're doing. She's always pushing us both to walk on the wild side."

"I can only hope. Why don't you get one of your boyfriends to buy you dinner tonight?"

There was that noise again. "They're not boyfriends. Just friends. But yeah, I can do that. I'll talk to you later, Mom." She made it sound like a threat.

"Bye, sweetie." I couldn't help smiling as I hung up.

Who'd have thought I'd ever be in a position to be scolded for recklessness by one of my own daughters? It made me feel...young. And impulsive. Something I hadn't felt in almost twenty-five years —not since Bess was born.

I'd gone from bride at twenty-one to too-young mother at twenty-two. For the next two decades, my life had been defined by the roles of wife and mother. I'd worked part-time to put Tom through his MBA program while juggling the demands of two toddlers. Then I'd finished my own degree so that I could contribute to his startup insurance company. Gradually my role had shifted from business partner to corporate hostess, from mommy to empty-nester.

From wife to ex, traded in for a newer model.

Somewhere along the line, the real me, the real Wynne, had gotten lost. Now, I was determined to find her again.

I just hoped I'd like her when I did.

# CHAPTER TWO

AFTER THREE DAYs in Aruba, I'd achieved my best tan since college, even with constant use of SPF 45 sunscreen. At only twelve degrees above the equator, I wasn't taking any chances on a burn that would ruin the rest of my vacation.

And by lunchtime tomorrow, I'd also achieve my diving certification—assuming, of course, I didn't totally screw up during our first open water dive today.

"Your tanks, weights, BCDs, and wetsuits are already on the boat," Jason told us when we were all assembled on the beach end of the dock near the hotel. "Everyone has masks, fins, and snorkels, right?"

I held mine up, as did the others—except Rick, who was trying to get Bebe's attention, as usual.

"Great. It's time to go have some *fun* diving."

We followed him the length of the dock to the waiting boat, which rocked gently on the bright turquoise water. Colors seemed somehow more vivid in Aruba than anywhere else I'd been. Or maybe I was seeing them with new eyes?

One by one, we stepped onto the *Scubaruba*, a thirty-foot modified cabin cruiser. Benches ran along both sides, from the cabin to the rear platform, with air tanks lined up behind the benches, held in place with thick elastic bands. Jason cast us off, and we headed out to sea.

I'd been on boats before, but only on lakes, unless I counted that cruise Tom and I took for our tenth anniversary. No, I wasn't going to count that. At least I knew I wasn't prone to seasickness, which was definitely a good thing. Though the ocean was smooth, poor Linda was looking a bit green around the gills already. No one else in our group seemed affected—so far.

"This is Ronan Gale, our captain today," Jason said, and the man at the helm half turned with a grin. He was older than Jason, maybe late thirties, and every bit as good looking, but with a more rugged edge. "He's filling in for Bertie, who's sleeping one off—I mean, sick."

We all chuckled along with him. Ronan had already turned back to the wheel.

"We'll reach the *Pedernales* wreck in about ten minutes," Jason continued, "so go ahead and put your equipment together and then get into your wetsuits. I'll tell you about the site and what we'll be doing there while you get ready."

I obediently picked up my regulator and my BCD vest and began connecting everything to an air tank. It was trickier on a moving boat than on the pool deck, but I supposed that was the point.

Next to me, Greg was trying to help Linda attach a hose to her vest, but I could see he had the angle wrong. Since mine was already done, I offered my assistance, which they both seemed relieved to accept.

"See, if you line this end up with this, it just clicks in." I didn't think Jason would appreciate me actually doing it for her, since this was still part of our training. Linda watched my demonstration closely, then did it herself.

"Oh, okay, I think I finally get it now. Thanks, Wynne, that really helped."

"You're welcome." I was absurdly flattered by her words, but I tried not to let it show. My divorce must have destroyed my self-confidence even more thoroughly than I'd realized.

A moment later, struggling into my wetsuit for the first time, I felt inept all over again. Made of neoprene, a thin, rubbery, foam-type material, it had long sleeves but legs that went only to mid-thigh. Jason had called it a "shortie."

Mimicking Bebe, who had her own suit and presumably more experience at putting it on, I first forced my right leg through one leg-hole, then my arms through the sleeves. Next, I tried to engage the zipper that started at the bottom, in the middle of my left thigh, and would—theoretically—finish at my throat.

"Ouch!" I'd managed to pinch my white, fleshy thigh in the zipper. Wincing, I tried again, and this time managed to keep the zipper away from my skin. Pulling the tab upward, I felt like I was squashing myself into a sausage casing. No doubt that was how I looked, too.

Once I was securely zipped into my full-body black girdle, only spilling out a little around the edges, I glanced at the others. All younger and thinner than I, they looked pretty good in their suits. Bebe, I noticed sourly, looked positively sexy in hers. The turquoise styling down the sides helped. I decided right then that if I continued diving after certification, my next purchase would be a decent-looking wetsuit.

"We're almost there," Jason informed us as we strapped our weight belts on over our wetsuits. "Have you all buddied up?"

I glanced at Dobry, since he and I had paired up for most of the pool exercises, but to my surprise, Bebe touched him on the arm.

"Dobry, will you be my buddy?" she asked with a smile guaranteed to make a man agree to anything.

His Adam's apple bobbed visibly as he swallowed. "I, ya, yes of course, Miss Bebe."

Rick had been struggling with the clasp on his weight belt and belatedly looked up with a frown. "But—"

He and Bebe had been partners for the pool dives, and clearly he'd expected they would be again. But it seemed Bebe'd had enough of his macho mess-ups, which left me paired with Rick. Lucky me.

"Guess that leaves us," I forced myself to say brightly, mainly to break the tension, since Rick's face was reddening as Bebe pointedly ignored him.

He seemed to realize how rude it would be to protest. "Uh, yeah. Guess so," he grumped, which wasn't much better.

"Hey, I know I wasn't your first choice, but I won't get in your way or anything." I couldn't quite keep the annoyance out of my voice.

That penetrated. "No, it's—I'm fine with it. Really. You need any help with anything?" After one last glance at Bebe, he gave me his full attention without *too* obvious an effort.

I glanced down at my suit, belt, and vest, all fastened in place. "I think I'm okay for now, but thanks. How about you?"

He gave a derisive snort. "Nah, I've done this before. I'm good."

I watched as he tried to clip his backup regulator—the yellow one called an "octopus"—to the wrong side of his vest. "I, um, think it's supposed to attach to that ring, there." I pointed.

"Yeah, yeah, right. I knew that." He quickly slid the mouthpiece through the flexible rubber ring intended for that purpose, not meeting my eye.

The boat slowed, then stopped, the engine idling while Jason and Ronan attached a line to a mooring ball bobbing on the surface of the nearly smooth sea. Jason turned to us when they were done.

"Okay, fins on. Does everyone have a dive watch?"

Trying to ignore a fresh surge of nervousness, I raised my arm to display my watch, a cheap blue plastic model that was supposedly good to at least 100 feet. The others did likewise.

"Good. I have nine thirty. We're limiting our bottom time to forty-five minutes, which means we'll head back up no later than ten-twenty, but keep an eye on your air pressure. Follow me down the mooring line, and remember to equalize on the way down.

"Once we're all on the bottom, we'll have our first open water class. If anyone has trouble and needs to surface, give the signal, and Ronan will fish you out. Right, Ronan?"

"Right. And if you aren't in trouble, give me the okay sign." Ronan demonstrated the circle with his arms we'd been taught in class. "I hate getting wet when I don't have to." His voice was deeper than I expected, with just a hint of some kind of brogue—Irish or maybe Scottish.

He caught me staring at him and gave me a ghost of a wink that made me quickly look away. It was a good thing I was too old to blush, I told myself as I bent to adjust my fins unnecessarily.

"You ready?" Rick asked, pushing himself to his feet.

I nodded, then noticed that his tank was about to slip free. "Sit down a sec," I told him. "Let me tighten your tank strap."

For a moment he looked like he would refuse, but then he shrugged. "I'm sure it's fine, but go ahead," he said, sitting sideways on the bench with his back toward me.

I released the strap, hoisted the tank a few inches higher, then pulled the strap as tight as I could before re-cinching it. "There. That should hold."

"Yeah. Thanks." His tone made it clear he was humoring me, but I didn't really care. If I had to be his buddy, at least now I wouldn't have to attempt reattaching his tank underwater.

Our four classmates had already entered the water during our delay, and now bobbed on the surface, adjusting the buoyancy of their vests before starting the descent. I'd really wanted to watch how they got off the boat and silently grumbled at Rick for distracting me.

I stood up, surprised again at how heavy a tank filled with compressed air could be. Though the sea was calm, even the gentle rocking of the boat was enough to make shuffling to the back platform tricky. I couldn't imagine doing this in rougher water, though I supposed people must do it all the time.

"Ready, Wynne?" Jason asked, extending his hand to me. I pulled my mask over my eyes and nodded. "Okay, one hand on mask and regulator, the other on your weight belt, then a giant stride off to your left."

For an instant I panicked as he released my hand so that I could grasp my weight belt, sure the rocking of the boat would pitch me sideways, but then I got my balance. Before I could lose it again, I flung my left leg forward, over the deep blue of the ocean, and pushed off.

The water closed over my head, colder than the pool water, at least where the wetsuit didn't cover me. Then I was back on the surface, bobbing around with the others, in time to see Rick hit the water with a terrific splash. With a wave to Ronan, Jason lowered his own mask and hopped in after Rick, creating almost no splash at all.

I wondered if I'd ever look that natural in scuba gear. At the moment, I felt more like a half-mechanical monster of the deep. One that didn't know what the heck she was doing.

Following Jason's lead, I raised my vest's air release out of the water and depressed the end until I started to sink. Suddenly, magically, I was back in the silent world of underwater—and this time it really was a whole world, not just a hotel swimming pool. I could see the bottom, thirty feet away, almost as clearly as if I were looking through air instead of water.

Greg and Linda started down the line, with Bebe and Dobry right behind them. I waited until they'd gone at least ten feet down to follow. Twice, I saw Linda come back up a few feet, pinching her nose, before starting to descend again.

I soon knew exactly how she felt. I was only fifteen feet below the surface, according to my depth gauge, when I felt a pressure in my ears that bordered on pain. Remembering our lessons, I stopped, pinched my nose through the mask, and "blew" without exhaling. My ears popped—first the right one, then the left, with audible squeals—and the pressure was gone.

Twice more, as I made my way to the ocean floor, I had to pause to relieve the pressure in my ears. I realized when I touched bottom that the frequent equalizing had effectively distracted me from the frightening fact that I was now far deeper underwater than I'd ever been before.

Once we were all on the bottom, we sat cross-legged in a circle around Jason, and he led us through our first open water exercises. They were the same ones we'd done in the pool: mask clearing, regulator recovery, etc.

I watched Rick closely as he put his regulator back in his mouth, and, sure enough, he tried to breathe before purging it of seawater. I could see the panic in his eyes as his mouth filled with water.

Even as I reached for him, he pushed off from the bottom, groping for the hose on his vest to inflate it. Though the very real risk of "the bends" from surfacing too quickly had been drilled into us, he was clearly too frantic to consider that now.

Jason was on the opposite side of the circle, too far away to stop him. Shifting instinctively into mom-mode, I lunged after Rick myself and managed to grab his arm before he'd ascended more than ten feet. Digging my fingers into his forearm to force him to look at me, I reached across and pushed the purge button on his regulator. He took a deep breath, then another.

It was hard to tell, with the regulator in his mouth, but I was pretty sure he gave me an apologetic grin as we dropped down to rejoin the others.

Jason met us halfway, questioningly giving both of us the "okay" sign until we echoed it back to him. I noticed he kept Rick next to him as we resumed our lesson.

Fifteen minutes later, the basic drills over, Jason swept his arm out, indicating that we were free to explore the area. Looking around, I saw a couple of half-buried pieces of the torpedoed

German tanker interspersed with coral formations teeming with marine life.

I gave my BCD a little bit of air for buoyancy, then kicked my fins and propelled myself forward, my body parallel to the ocean floor. It was almost like flying.

Keeping half an eye on Rick in case he panicked again, I continued slowly along the bottom. A dull pinging sound made me look up, to see Jason tapping on his tank to get our attention as he pointed at something. We all converged on his position, where he hovered just above the sea bed at the base of a small coral reef.

There, no more than three feet from his outstretched finger, was a green moray eel. I backpedaled, my stomach clenching, and I wasn't the only one. We'd heard how dangerous those things could be if you got too close—they could take a finger or even a hand off a diver.

This one didn't look big enough to do that, but it still looked mean, its mouth opening and closing, its beady little eyes fixed on Jason's hand. Jason didn't seem worried. I wished I'd bought one of those disposable underwater cameras like the one Greg had.

Our time was up long before I was ready to stop exploring. Reluctantly, I followed Jason and the others back to the line. I made sure Rick went ahead of me, and I noticed that Jason kept a close eye on him as well, reminding him to pause for our three minute safety stop at fifteen feet.

When we reached the surface, Rick touched me on the shoulder. "I, uh, want to thank you," he said, quietly so the others couldn't hear. "You kinda saved my bacon down there. I don't know why I keep forgetting to use the purge button."

"I'll bet you won't forget again." I realized I was using my "Mom" voice—but then, Rick couldn't be more than a year older than Bess.

He stared at me for a second, then said, "You know, you're a pretty cool lady. I'm lucky you were my partner." Then, clearly embarrassed, he turned away to remove his fins.

I was reminded of Tom, my ex. He'd have been just as embarrassed to admit to any fault, but probably would have deflected it by finding something to criticize in my own diving or appearance. With a flash of insight, I suddenly realized that I wouldn't have enjoyed this dive half as much if he'd been with me.

I moved closer to the boat, awkwardly trying to pull off my own fins without losing them or drifting away on the gentle swells, waiting my turn to climb the ladder.

Poor Linda needed both her husband's help and Ronan's, and still almost fell backward into the sea. I was torn between feeling sorry for her and worrying that I'd have the same trouble. Rick made it up the ladder and onto the boat without assistance, and then I was next.

I'd managed to get both of my fins off and now handed them up to the waiting Ronan. He set them behind him, then moved to the ladder to reach out a hand as I heaved myself out of the water.

A wet wetsuit weighed a lot more than a dry one, more than making up for my air tank being emptier. It took all my strength to climb the ladder, and I was definitely grateful for Ronan's helping hand.

"Thanks," I panted as I got my feet under me on the deck.

"My pleasure," he replied with a grin that almost made me believe he meant it.

I reined in the little flutter I got from that grin, reminding myself that with someone like Bebe on board, Ronan was hardly likely to be flirting with me.

"You okay?" he asked, and I realized I'd spaced out for a moment.

"Oh, yeah, fine." How smooth was that? Forcing my lips into something I hoped resembled a carefree smile, I made my way back to my spot on the left bench, eager to get the heavy tank off my back.

Jason brought up the rear, folding up the ladder after climbing it with no apparent effort. I found myself envying the guys' strength, which gave them a definite advantage in the out-of-water part of diving.

"So, how did everybody like your first open water dive?" he asked. Everyone, even Linda, managed at least a weak grin for him, while Bebe, Dobry, and I gave him an enthusiastic thumbs-up.

"Great. Our second dive today will be Malmok Reef and the wreck of the *Debbie II*. We're going to almost sixty feet this time, which means the safety stop on the way up is especially important. We'll spend about fifteen minutes exploring the reef, then use our compasses to navigate to the *Debbie II*. This is a pretty cool dive, so those of you with cameras be sure to bring them along."

The boat ride to the next site was only a few minutes, barely giving us time to change air tanks. Since Rick would be my partner again, I swapped mine out as quickly as I could, then watched him finish up his. I was glad to see that he seemed to be taking more care this time. Still, when he bent to put his flippers back on, I quickly reached behind him to double check his hose connections.

I snatched my arm back when he started to sit up, then noticed Ronan watching me from the bridge. Was that a wink, or just wishful thinking?

"Everyone ready?" Jason asked as the boat bobbed gently near the mooring ball.

We all nodded, with varying degrees of enthusiasm.

"All right, same order as before. Masks and fins on and let's go."

I was definitely more eager than nervous this time as I took my big step off the back of the boat, and I felt more natural in the water than I'd have believed possible back on the dock an hour and a half ago. Scuba diving really *was* fun. I couldn't wait to tell my daughters.

Malmok Reef was alive with a fascinating variety of life—fantastic fan and barrel coral in an array of colors, swaying urchins, and dozens of fish. One long, skinny fish seemed to be almost half mouth, looking for all the world like some kind of alien life form. Again, I wished for a camera.

After fifteen minutes, Jason had us consult our compasses to swim south-southwest. The huge hulk of the *Debbie II* loomed above us as we approached, ghostly through the deep blue of the water. Even though Jason had told us the 120-foot-long fuel barge was deliberately sunk, I couldn't suppress a shudder at the sight of its yawning portals.

We swam upward along the hull of the wreck until we reached its deck, complete with railings. I was reminded of the movie *Titanic* and tried to imagine what the *Debbie II* must have looked like with its surfaces intact, its railings polished instead of encrusted with marine life.

Making sure I didn't lose sight of Rick, I moved slowly along the deck with its gaping hatches leading down into darkness. Clouds of tiny silver fish darted in and out of the openings, weaving around the rails. A dull clanging of metal on metal brought my attention back to Jason, who this time motioned us to follow him down the far side of the hull.

When we reached the bottom of the ship, he pointed. Wedged between the base of the wreck and the ocean floor was another green moray eel, this one at least three times the size of the one we'd seen at the *Pedernales* site. I noticed that Jason kept a much more respectful distance from this monster.

Greg snapped a couple of pictures, then everyone moved on—except me. I continued to examine the eel, fascinated that something that size could make its living in such an out-of-the way place. What did it eat? Unwary divers? It seemed almost big enough, more than a foot in diameter behind its tapering head. Impossible to tell how long it was, as its length disappeared beneath the ship. I was guessing at least ten or twelve feet.

As I started to turn away to follow the others, a glint caught my eye. I sharpened my gaze and swam a little—only a little—closer. It looked like a ring, perched on a sandy little shelf jutting out from the wreck, several feet above and to the left of the eel. I gauged my distance to the ring and then the distance from the ring to the enormous moray. Did I dare?

I dared. Maybe I surprised the eel as much as myself, because it didn't make a move toward me until I was already retreating, the ring—and a good bit of sand—clutched in my fist. Then I saw the thing coming at me and flung myself backward, kicking my bright pink flippers toward its gaping mouth, protecting my hands and face.

For a moment I thought it might grab my right fin, so I kicked harder. To my relief, it retreated back into its sanctuary, looking more irritated than ever. My heart was pounding, and I was probably using twice the air I should be, but I was safe—and so was my treasure.

I looked down at the ring in my hand, letting the sand sift away between my fingers. It appeared to be a wedding band, adorned with several respectably-sized stones—diamonds or cubic zirconia. A woman's ring, from the size of it.

Had some woman done exactly what I'd planned and pitched it into the ocean to throw off the bonds of matrimony? Amusing to think so, though more likely it was lost accidentally.

The light was too dim for a thorough examination, so I tucked the ring into one of the zippered pockets of my vest and looked up, to see that the others were almost out of sight.

I hurried after them, my pulse and breathing slowing. I'd done something brave, all on my own, and I had the prize to prove it.

If my life were a movie, ominous music might have warned me right then that this was a major turning point. But since it wasn't, I didn't have even the slightest sense of foreboding to mar my triumph.

# CHAPTER THREE

BY THE TIME I reached the others, they were preparing to surface. They'd been playing with a sea urchin, a thing about six inches in diameter that looked like a little white hedgehog. No one looked around when I joined them, and I wasn't sure whether to be flattered that they weren't worried about me, or insulted that no one had noticed I was missing.

We ascended in the same order as before, and this time Rick did a much better job of controlling his speed. I was proud of him, I realized, as we paused for our fifteen foot safety stop. I still wouldn't wish him on one of my daughters, but maybe he wasn't a complete idiot after all.

I was more prepared for the weight of my suit and tank as I came out of the water this time, but I was also more tired, which meant I was still grateful for Ronan's help getting up the ladder.

We were done for the day, so I wasted no time getting out of my vest and weight belt, then unzipping my wetsuit. The breeze felt chilly on my exposed wet skin, though I knew it was at least eighty degrees. Even as I thought it, my goose bumps started to subside.

"Everyone start breaking down your equipment," Jason told us as Ronan started the boat's engine for the trip back to shore. "Turn off your air first."

I turned around and disconnected the hoses from my tank, remembering to put the dust cover over the regulator opening. Rick actually thanked me when I reminded him of that step.

By the time we reached the dock, we'd all stripped out of our wetsuits and piled our gear near the back of the boat. Belatedly, I remembered the ring I'd found, and fished through the heap of BCDs to find my vest and pull the ring out of the little zippered pocket.

"What have you got there?" Ronan's voice startled me.

I turned to see him standing on the dock just behind me, hauling the rear line to a cleat. With an embarrassed smile—embarrassed mainly because I found the man so darned attractive—I held up the ring.

"Something I found on the bottom. Do you think it's real?"

He shrugged without really looking at it, but then smiled at me before he finished tying up the boat. He had a great smile.

I stuck the ring in my shorts pocket and focused instead on the circus act of carrying all of my wet equipment without dropping anything or soaking my shorts. We paused at the water barrel to rinse the saltwater off of our gear, then continued to the shop, where Jason congratulated us on our performance.

"We had one or two little glitches," he said, glancing at Rick and Linda, "but for a first dive, you all did great. We'll meet back here at nine tomorrow morning for more of the same, then a quick review in the classroom, and then you'll all be certified divers."

Our tired group managed a ragged cheer, and I was surprised to hear myself joining in—a real part of the crowd. It felt good. When they started debating where to have lunch, I was included in the discussion as a matter of course.

Ronan joined us just as we agreed on pizza as something quick and filling. I felt a silly, age-inappropriate thrill when he said he'd come along, and another one when we reached the restaurant and he sat next to me. I was trying to think of something clever but nonchalant to say when Jason spoke from across the table.

"Wynne, did I hear you telling Ronan that you found something during the dive?"

"Oh, yeah. Thanks for reminding me." I dug into my shorts pocket, very aware of Ronan watching and wishing I had it in me to be smooth. "Look, everyone," I said, raising my voice to be heard over the excited babble. "I found this at the end of our dive."

"Cool! Where was it?" Rick asked.

"Ooh, diamonds!" Linda and Bebe chorused.

"That'll be worth something," Greg opined.

For the first time, I was able to take a good look at the ring myself, and I realized Greg was right—if it was real. Together, the seven marquis-cut diamonds had to total more than four carats, and the ring itself looked like white gold or platinum.

I didn't own a lot of jewelry myself, but between avid window-shopping, the few purchases I'd made over the years and Tom's insurance business, I knew enough about it to guess the ring's value at something over twenty thousand dollars—if it was real.

I passed the ring around the table. When it got to him, Ronan held it just a bit longer than the others had, turning it this way and that.

"What?" I asked him.

"Nothing. Just that it's inscribed," he said, handing it back to me.

Holding the ring so the light caught it better, I realized he was right. For a long moment I debated with myself, but curiosity won out over vanity, and I pulled my reading glasses out of my purse.

"Stefan & Melanie 2008," it read—along with a Cartier hallmark. Which meant my estimate had been low. And it almost certainly hadn't been thrown into the ocean on purpose, interesting as that theory had been.

"So, are you going to keep it as a souvenir or sell it?" Linda asked, voicing the very question I'd been asking myself before reading the inscription.

"I'm not sure," I said. "I should probably try to find out who it belongs to first, don't you think?"

"Seriously?" Rick sounded incredulous. "Why bother? Finders keepers." The others nodded their agreement.

I shrugged, not wanting to come across as some kind of goodie-two-shoes. I was just starting to bond with these folks. Odds were no local jewelry store would be able to trace it, so I'd get to keep it anyway.

The pizza arrived then, cutting off further discussion of the ring, which I tucked back into my pocket. I'd planned to tell the story of how I'd snatched it away from the moray eel, but decided against it. I was still more comfortable in the background, I realized, for all the progress I thought I'd made the past few days.

I was content to sit and listen while everyone else shared stories and impressions from our first real dives.

"It was almost like flying underwater," Bebe declared. "Did it seem that way to the rest of you?"

Linda shook her head. "I didn't really notice. I'm still pretty nervous down there—and I thought it would take me forever to *get* down there! Why do I have so much more trouble equalizing than the rest of you?"

Rick, I noticed, kept quiet while the others offered various—and conflicting—bits of advice.

"You just need to blow harder," Greg told her.

"Just think your way through it," Bebe suggested.

"Slow is fine," I said when Linda began to look confused. "Better to have two or three fewer minutes on the bottom than to break an eardrum."

Beside me, Ronan nodded. "Wynne's right. In diving, speed isn't the point. It's about safety and being comfortable in the water. It's supposed to be fun."

"So why don't you come down with us tomorrow?" Bebe asked. I admired—and envied—the forthright, easy way she was able to flirt.

Ronan grinned. "Maybe I will, if Bertie's recovered from his bender. Someone's got to stay on the boat."

I concentrated on how good the pepperoni and mushroom pizza tasted—the first pizza I'd had in months—instead of on how out of practice I was at flirting. Not that I'd been particularly good at it even in my prime. I had other skills to compensate.

Didn't I?

Of course I did. I was an excellent business manager, or had been a dozen years ago. I'd raised two great kids, I was a pretty decent cook. And I was learning to scuba dive. How many women my age did that? Not many, judging by our class and the group I'd seen boarding another dive boat this morning. That made me feel a little better.

We lingered over lunch, commenting on the amazing appetite diving gave us. As we were chipping in on the check, I realized I'd eaten four slices of pizza. Just as well I'd already decided a bikini would never be my style.

As we left the restaurant, Bebe somehow ended up between me and Ronan, talking to him animatedly but still very naturally. I shrugged mentally and waved a cheery goodbye to everyone before heading back to my hotel. It's not like I'd expected anything to come of it, after all. I was only a few weeks divorced and *definitely* not looking for another man.

With that settled, I breathed deeply as I walked through the beautiful open-air lobby to the elevators. Housekeeping had already been to my room—the bed smoothly made and fresh towels in the bathroom, through no effort of my own. I could get used to this sort of life.

I unplugged my cell phone from its charger by the nightstand and woke it up. Two messages. Taking another deep breath, this time in an effort to preserve my contented mood no matter what, I went out onto the balcony to play my voice mail.

The first was from Bess, finally returning the message I'd left her two days ago. I couldn't help grinning as I listened.

"Hey, Mom, I guess Deb wasn't kidding—I got her voice mail before yours. Aruba, huh? I think that's great. Haven't I been saying you need to get out more? I only wish you'd brought me along. But then I'd have missed last night's audition, which went really well. Give me a call, and I'll tell you about it. And have fun!"

That was Bess, my free-spirited firstborn. I wondered if her audition had been for singing or acting, since she was trying to break into both professionally. Or maybe even dancing, which she'd taken up a few months ago. There were times I wanted to be Bess when *I* grew up, she had so much confidence and *joie de vivre*.

Maybe I'd taken my first step by coming to Aruba.

The second message was from my mother—and did not elicit a grin. "Wynne, sweetie, where *are* you? I've been calling your house for two days and finally thought to try your cell phone, but you're not answering that, either. I've got some news you'll want to hear, so please call me when you get this."

I stared at my phone for a long minute, debating. If anyone was likely to spoil my mood, it was Mom, with her sweetly worded suggestions on how I ought to be living my life. She hadn't said whether her news was good or bad. Maybe she'd won the lottery. Or maybe she had cancer. I hit the return call button.

"Mom?"

"Wynne! Where on earth have you been? Debra wouldn't tell me, which seemed terribly odd. You're not in some sort of trouble, are you? This would be such a bad time—"

"No, Mom, I'm not in trouble. I'm just out of town. What's your news?"

She chuckled—that chuckle that always got my back up, for some reason. "It's not *my* news, sweetie. More your news, I'd say. I heard Tom finally dumped that blonde he left you for."

I definitely should have trusted my instincts and not called until I got home. "Lucky her. Are you sure Darlene didn't dump him, instead of the other way around?" Maybe he'd cheated on her, too. I'd already learned that Darlene wasn't his first fling. Just the first I'd found out about.

"*Hmph*. I can't imagine she'd let him go voluntarily. You, of all people, know what he's worth."

"Not much, in my book."

She tsked. "I'm talking about money, Wynne. And influence. Tom Sealy is a mover and shaker in Indianapolis, and you know it."

"He can move and shake whatever he likes, Mom, as long as it isn't me."

"You always were stubborn. But don't you see that this could be your chance to get him back? I knew he'd get tired of that bimbo after a few months. How could he not, when he had you to compare her to? Just call him, see if—"

"No, Mom. It's over."

"Only three weeks ago. There's still time to fix things, to get counseling, to—"

My phone beeped, indicating an incoming call—a beautiful sound. "Mom, Bessie's calling," I said without even checking. "I've been wanting to talk to her for a couple of days, so I need to take this. I'll call you when I get home."

Without waiting for her response, I clicked over. "Hello?" I honestly didn't care *who* it was.

"I finally caught you!" It really was Bess. "So, how's Aruba?"

"It's great. I went scuba diving in the ocean for the first time today and found a ring. How was your audition last night?"

"Wow, Mom, you're not letting any grass grow under your feet, are you? Or is there grass in Aruba?"

"Not much. It's mostly desert."

"Cool. I hope you're taking pictures! The audition went great. I got called back for a second one—that'll be tonight."

"And this is for—?"

"Oh, I didn't say? Sorry to be such an airhead. Beef & Boards is doing *Little Shop of Horrors*. But the audition is actually to become part of the company, not just for this show. That would be actual paid acting work. Pretty cool, huh?"

"It certainly beats doing it for free."

I tried not to sound judgmental, but it was hard not to remember all that money spent on a degree in voice and theater, then the expensive year in New York while she aimed for the stars. Lately she'd been waiting tables and working temp jobs between auditions in the Midwest.

"Break a leg tonight, sweetie. They'll love you," I added, belatedly supportive. Who was I, after all, to discourage anyone's dreams? I'd done that to my own, and look where that had led.

"Thanks, Mom. I'll let you know how it goes."

"Oh, and if Grandma calls, try not to let her know where I am and what I'm doing. Don't lie to her, of course, but you don't have to offer, either."

She chuckled, and the sound suddenly made me miss her acutely. "You've got it, Mom. I just won't answer the phone if she calls. That'll be easier. Okay, gotta go. Love you!"

"Love you, too, sweetie."

I hung up smiling. Bessie usually had that effect on me, with her over-the-top enthusiasm for life. When she didn't irritate the heck out of me for having her head in the clouds, anyway.

After a quick shower to get the salt out of my hair, I dressed and took out the ring again. Yes, definitely at *least* a $20,000 ring. Someone, somewhere, had to be missing it. No doubt it was insured, but still...

Before I could change my mind, I tucked it into my front shorts pocket, slipped on my sandals and headed out the door. The least I could do was see if there was a jewelry store in Oranjestad and ask if it had been reported missing.

The first "taxi" that came past the hotel was a rickety van already holding half a dozen passengers.

"Five dollars to town," the driver told me, so I got in. As he pulled away, I realized I could see the road zipping past through a hole between my feet. Forcing myself to relax, I let the Papiamento of the other passengers flow over me, praying that the van wouldn't fall completely to pieces before we reached Oranjestad.

It didn't.

"I stop there, other side of street, to go back to hotel. Every half hour," the driver told me with a wide grin when he let me out in the middle of town, between Royal Plaza and the open-air Seaport Mall.

I smiled back and nodded noncommittally, though I was hoping to find something a little more substantial for the ride back. Turning, I scanned the storefronts and saw with surprise that at least a third of them were jewelry stores.

Jewelry was obviously big business in Aruba. Who knew? Well, I did now—but I'd already lost four shopping days!

Dazzled, I stood there looking back and forth between Pearl Gems and Gandelman Jewelers, Little Switzerland and Kenro Jewelers—then glanced further down the mall and saw Cartier Boutique. I blinked, then started in that direction. If anyone on the island could trace the ring, that place could. And if they couldn't...

I hesitated, trying not to think about what I could do with the price of the ring. The divorce hadn't exactly left me destitute, but Tom had done a good job of tying up our joint assets, and I hated having to ask him for money. Twenty thousand dollars would mean I wouldn't have to for a while.

Tom would say I was stupid to even consider turning in the ring. Was I? After all, Tom was a respected elder of our church, unbelievable as that seemed given everything I now knew about him. Of course, that was the main reason I'd stopped attending that church.

Pressing my lips together, I kept putting one foot in front of the other until I was inside the store.

"May I help you, ma'am?" asked the woman behind the counter in very slightly accented English.

Mentally telling Tom to shut up, I nodded and pulled out the ring. "I found this while diving this morning. It has a Cartier mark, so I thought maybe you could find out who it belongs to."

She sent one surprised glance my way, then gingerly took the ring from my palm to examine it. She turned it this way and that, then said, "Just a moment."

Taking a pad and pencil from near the cash register, she carefully copied the inscription and made a few other notes about the ring itself, then handed it back to me.

"I'll make a few calls. Where can we reach you?"

I gave her my name, the name of my hotel, my room number, and the date I planned to check out, all of which she added to the notes on the pad. Then she looked up at me and smiled.

"I must say, Ms. Seally, I'm impressed by your honesty. If the ring was engraved by Cartier, we may be able to trace it, but if it was engraved later, we probably can't. If you haven't heard back from us by the time you leave Aruba, I'd say you can consider the ring yours."

"Thank you. At least this way, if I get to keep it, I can do it with a clear conscience."

Putting the ring back in my pocket, I left the store with a lovely sense of having done the right thing. And who knew? Maybe I'd be rewarded for my virtue by getting to keep my prize. The saleswoman had implied that was the most likely outcome.

Suddenly, I was in a mood to celebrate.

I headed back toward Royal Plaza and spotted a bar with the whimsical name of Iguana Joe's. Why not? I climbed the open stairs to the second level, went in and took a seat at the bar—something I couldn't remember ever doing before in my life.

"What can I get you, pretty lady?" asked the bartender with a grin, sending my spirits soaring.

"Something fun, with an umbrella." I scanned the menu behind the bar. "How about a Pink Iguana?"

"Coming right up."

While I waited for my drink, I half turned so I could scan the room. The decor was as whimsical as the name of the place, with bright, cartoony murals on the walls featuring a lizard (Iguana Joe, I presumed) in a hammock. Not many people were here yet—it was only about five o'clock—but the ones that were seemed to be having a good time.

"Here you go." The bartender set down a half-liter carafe of a pink, frozen drink, sprouting the obligatory umbrella. Definitely fun. "Would you like to run a tab?"

"Sure," I said, throwing caution to the winds. It wasn't like I'd be driving.

I took a long sip of my Pink Iguana and sighed. It was delicious —tart and fruity and cold. Why hadn't I done this sort of thing before? Besides the fact that Tom had always disapproved of drinking—at least *my* drinking.

"Wynne?"

I turned to see Bebe behind me, flanked by two men and a woman I didn't know, all about Bebe's age.

"Oh, hi," I said, resisting a guilty impulse to hide my drink. What on earth did I have to feel guilty about? Bebe wasn't one of my daughters—or Tom—and I wasn't doing anything wrong.

"Guys, this is Wynne. She's in my diving class. Wynne, this is Jim, Kevin, and Nicole. Do you want to join us, or are you waiting for someone?"

I almost picked option two, uncomfortable with the idea of being the "mom" of the group, but realized in time how easily they'd see through that lie when no one showed up. "I'd love to join you. Thanks."

They found a table and pulled up an extra chair for me, seeming not at all put out at having a fifth wheel present—not that they appeared to be paired off, particularly.

"So, Wynne, what brings you to Aruba besides diving lessons?" Kevin asked me after they'd all ordered drinks.

"Vacation," I replied with a little shrug. This was definitely no time to go into my sordid marital history.

"Great place for it," Nicole commented. "Though I didn't expect all this wind." She giggled, and my estimate of her intelligence went south, though she seemed nice enough.

"Think how hot it would be without it," I said, and they all murmured agreement. "And what brings all of you here? Besides diving lessons, Bebe."

It turned out they all worked for the same pharmaceutical company in Portland, Maine, had come to Aruba for a conference the week before, then stayed on for an extra week's vacation. Since Maine must be even colder than Indiana in February, I didn't blame them.

We drank and chatted until I felt completely comfortable—not "mom" at all. A couple more people from the pharmaceutical conference wandered in—from Minnesota, I think, though I was getting fuzzy by then—and we all ordered dinner. My Caribbean jerk chicken sandwich was wonderful—or maybe it was the company.

At some point we all wandered across the street to check out Pepe & Pete's, which I was told was Aruba's most famous bar. It was surely the loudest and wildest, with college girls dancing on the bar and everyone else dancing on the floor.

My kids would have loved it, but despite my pleasant buzz, I began to feel out of place again. Much as I hated to admit it, I really was getting too old for this sort of thing. I glanced at my watch. Amazing—it was past eleven. Time for this old broad to head back, I decided.

I managed to find Bebe in the crowd to tell her I was leaving. She was dancing and just nodded, not that I'd expected anything more. Kevin offered to walk me to the bus stop but seemed relieved when I declined. Ah, well, he was twenty years too young for me anyway.

Walking back to the main drag to find a bus or cab, I felt distinctly muzzy-headed. I'd probably have a hangover in the morning for our last dives—and serve me right. I was glad now that

I'd resisted when Bebe and Nicole had tried to talk me into a Lethal Lizard with its four shots of liquor. I doubted I'd be walking at all.

As luck—or lack thereof—would have it, the same "cab" I'd taken earlier pulled up just as I reached the street.

"Back to Palm Beach?" the driver asked with a delighted grin.

Too tired to think of an excuse, I nodded and climbed in. This time I barely noticed the holes in the floor or the ominous shaking of the little van as a pleasant lethargy stole over me. It seemed like we were back at my hotel in no time at all.

"Thanks," I said, giving him a ten. A 100 percent tip, I thought. Wasn't I the generous one? I stifled a giggle.

I nodded sleepily to the man at the front desk as I made my way to the elevators, suddenly wanting nothing more than my comfy, king-sized bed. Reaching my room I put my card in the slot...and nothing happened.

Grumbling a bit, I tried again. Still nothing. I looked at the number, wondering if I'd gotten off on the wrong floor in my fog, but no, it was definitely my room. Blasted card keys, I thought. Now I'd have to go all the way back downstairs and get a new one.

I stuck the card in the slot one last time, without much hope, and to my surprise, this time the light turned green. Sighing with relief, I opened the door and flipped on the light—only to stop and stare in disbelief.

The bed linens were rumpled, the desk chair had been pulled out, and one of the dresser drawers was open an inch or two. I looked into the open closet to see the room safe at an odd angle, its little door forced open.

I'd been robbed.

---

# CHAPTER FOUR

---

OR HAD I?

The first thing I did was glance into the safe, only to find my passport, wedding ring, and diamond earrings—my only real valuables—still there. How odd.

I flipped on the bathroom light and saw that while my toiletries on the counter were out of position, nothing appeared to be missing—not that a thief was likely to want used lipstick, foundation, or toothpaste. Feeling increasingly disoriented, I continued into the room. The desk drawer was also open a crack.

For a long moment I just stood there, unsure what I should do. It flashed through my mind that I should call Tom, that he'd know. He'd always been good in a crisis, his judgment reliable. I was actually reaching for my cell phone before that moment of weakness passed.

No. I'd handled plenty of crises myself, especially in recent months. I could handle this one. After one more glance around the room, I went to the nightstand phone and called the front desk.

"Someone has broken into my room," I told the man who answered—probably the same one I'd nodded to less than ten minutes ago. "I don't think they stole anything, but I thought you should know."

"Room 1411?" He sounded alarmed, shaken. I guessed this sort of thing didn't happen often. "I'm sending security up right now. Um, you should probably wait for them out in the hall."

I started to ask why, then realized it must be in case the intruder was still hiding in the room. A cold wash of fear hit my belly, and suddenly I was completely sober.

"Yes. I'll wait," I managed to say before hanging up and scurrying out of the room, terrified someone would lunge out from behind the bathroom door to stop me.

No one did, of course, and by the time two security guards joined me a couple minutes later I was feeling more than a little foolish.

I felt even more foolish when they preceded me into the room and looked around. Really, there wasn't any place for someone to hide. The bed was even on a solid pedestal.

"You told the night clerk nothing was missing?" the taller of the two men asked.

"As far as I can tell. I haven't checked all the drawers yet, but there was nothing valuable in them."

They exchanged glances. "Ma'am, what made you think someone broke in?"

It took a moment for me to realize what he was implying. "I'm not imagining this. Someone was in here. The room isn't how I left it. Look at the bed. Look at the room safe."

"You're sure you didn't leave the safe open?" the shorter man asked. "Sometimes—"

"I'm sure," I snapped. "And I didn't touch the bed after the maid was here, or leave any drawers open. Someone's been in here."

The taller man was examining the safe. "It does look like this was forced open. I'll have maintenance take a look." He made a quick call with his walkie-talkie.

"Have him look at the door to the room, too," I suggested. "It took me several tries with my card before it would open."

Meanwhile, the shorter man was prowling around the room, peering into drawers and behind the dresser and TV. I tried not to wince as he examined my large-ish collection of herbal supplements and vitamins, which probably made me look like a hypochondriac on top of everything else.

Then he pulled aside the drapes to check the balcony door and whistled. "Marco, take a look at this," he said.

The taller man, Marco, clipped his walkie-talkie to his belt and crossed the room. He looked at whatever had caught the other man's interest, then turned to me.

"I assume you didn't leave this door open when you went out?"

"No, of course not. I remember locking it, in fact."

"Well, it's not locked now," the shorter man said. "And the drape was caught in the door, like someone shut it in a hurry. Could be your intruder went out this way when you came into the room."

They both went out onto the balcony for a minute or two, while I tried not to think about what that meant. But when they came back into the room, Marco laid it out bluntly.

"My guess is that he—or she—was still searching your room when you got back. You said it took a few tries before the door would open? That would have given him time to slip out onto the balcony before you came in. He probably waited there while you were in the room, then, when you went back into the hall, he could have climbed down to the next floor, or even to a balcony on either side, if he's agile."

I felt my heart thudding again. So someone *had* been in the room when I'd made that call—or very nearly.

"Do you...do you think they'll let me change rooms tonight?" I asked. "I know it sounds silly, but—" But no way would I be able to sleep a wink here, I was positive.

"I'm sure that won't be a problem," Marco assured me. "Let me call the front desk."

While he was on the phone, the maintenance man arrived to examine the room safe and the electronic lock of my door. He took his time, but finally verified what the security guys had already concluded—I had indeed had an intruder, and one who was apparently no novice at this sort of break-in.

"If you want to pack up your stuff, Ms. Seally, you can move to room 1436 at the end of the hall," Marco told me when the maintenance man finished his explanation. "It's a mini-suite, but there'll be no extra charge."

The hotel clearly hoped that would pacify me enough that I wouldn't make any trouble about the break-in. Not that I'd planned to.

"Thanks. That'll be great. I can be packed in five minutes." I was already hauling my suitcase out of the closet as I spoke.

Much to my relief, Marco and the maintenance man remained in the room, fussing over the door lock, while I packed. I knew it was irrational, but I absolutely didn't want to be alone in this room.

I didn't bother folding or rolling things, but just tossed them into the suitcase any which way—very unlike me, but I guess stress will do that. I was about to empty my underwear drawer when I paused, revolted by an unwelcome image of some unknown person pawing through it. On sudden decision I dumped all of my undies into the trash, instead. I could buy new tomorrow.

After cramming my toiletries into the little case on the bathroom counter and draping my still-damp swimsuit over my arm, I announced that I was ready.

"Here, I'll take that," said Marco, picking up my suitcase. "Room 1436 is this way."

I was oddly comforted by his take-charge attitude. I knew I should fight that feeling, that I shouldn't need some man to make me feel safe, but I was too tired by then to summon more than a vague sense of guilt. And I still felt comforted.

"Here you are, Ms. Seally," he said, opening the door with what I assumed was the kind of universal key the housekeepers had. "I hope you'll be comfortable here. Someone should be up with a new room key in just a few minutes."

"Thank you, Marco—for everything." I almost added an apology for being so much trouble, but I bit it back. None of this was my fault.

"It's what I'm here for, ma'am." He returned my smile with an added warmth that startled me. While he wasn't nearly as attractive as Ronan or Jason, the hint of admiration in his eyes went a long way to restore my confidence.

Still, when he left a moment later, I was relieved to be in a safe room, one that only a small handful of people could know I was in. Not that there was any reason to think I'd been personally targeted, of course. It had to have been a random break-in.

Didn't it?

I turned away from the door and looked around. If I'd thought the other room was opulent, it was nothing to this one. There was a separate living area in addition to the king-sized bedroom, and each had its own balcony. The bathroom was twice the size of the other one, as well.

Exhaustion hit me like a wave, and I decided to save further observations for the morning.

Morning! I was supposed to be at the dive shop by eight-thirty to gear up for our final open water dives, and it was already well past one.

Leaving my unpacking for tomorrow, I draped my swimsuit over the tub and pulled my toothbrush out of the toiletry case. Fifteen minutes later, I was asleep.

I WAS PULLING my shorts on over my swimsuit the next morning, groggy from too much drink and too little sleep the night before, when I felt the ring I'd found yesterday still in the pocket. I dug it out and stared at it, a thought very belatedly occurring to me.

Could this, just possibly, be what someone was after when they broke into my room last night?

Surely not. No one even knew about the ring, except the others in my dive class. And the clerk at the Cartier store. Okay, and whoever the clerk might have contacted, though it seemed unlikely that would be someone here on the island.

As for my dive buddies, I just couldn't believe any of them could have done this. Besides, I hadn't told any of them which room I was in.

Still, even the slight possibility that I'd been specifically targeted instead of the victim of some random break-in gave me the willies.

"Here she is! Wynne, the party animal," Bebe announced as I approached the group already assembled by the door of the dive shop. "I've got to admit, you look perkier than I feel today. I should have left when you did."

I forced a laugh, wondering what she'd been telling the others. It's not like I'd done anything really embarrassing—had I? No, no, I could remember the whole evening.

"I'm pretty out of practice at that kind of thing," I said then. "I was afraid if I stayed out much later, I wouldn't get up at all this morning."

I took a quick inventory of the group: Bebe, Rick, Dobry, Jason —everyone was there except Greg and Linda, who were the very least likely "suspects" anyway.

"You'll never guess what happened when I got back to my room last night," I said, trying to keep an eye on everyone's expressions at once. "I found out someone had broken into my room!"

"Omigosh!" Bebe squealed, and the guys made outraged noises. The surprise on every face looked genuine, much to my relief. After all, I *liked* these people, even the occasionally obnoxious Rick.

"What did you do?" Bebe asked. "I thought Aruba was supposed to be so safe."

"I called security, and they checked things out. Nothing seemed to be missing, which was kind of weird." I decided not to mention the change of rooms, just in case.

"That is weird," Jason agreed. "You're at the Royal Aruban, right?" I nodded. "I've never even heard of a break-in there, and I've been here three years. You think maybe one of the staff was looking for something?"

It occurred to me that Jason was the only one who would have had access to my room number, since I'd put it on the form I'd filled out for the class. He seemed sincerely concerned, however, and he was such a wholesome, good-natured guy, I couldn't bring myself to suspect him of anything.

"The security guys didn't think so. They thought whoever it was escaped off the balcony, a dozen floors up. Not something one of the maids was likely to do."

I glanced at Rick as I spoke and saw him staring at me. "And you weren't scared?" he asked. "That's kind of cool." There was real admiration in his tone which made me acquit him on the spot. Ah, vanity.

Rather than lie, I changed the subject. "I figure whoever it was probably broke into the wrong room, looking for something specific. Oh, here are Greg and Linda."

"Okay, then let's all head to the boat," Jason said, motioning them to hurry. "Your gear is already aboard."

Ronan was already aboard, too, along with another man Jason introduced as Bertie, our missing captain from the day before. He still looked a little bleary, I thought.

"Did you hear what happened to Wynne?" Bebe said to Linda as we took turns stepping from the dock to the boat.

Of course, Linda hadn't, so I told my story again. As I'd expected, there was no sign whatsoever that either Linda or Greg knew anything about my break-in. Ronan seemed mildly interested, though it was hard to tell since he was busy with the ropes.

"Anyway, I had the impression they were going to do more investigating today—maybe check for fingerprints and stuff," I improvised. "They seemed pretty upset that something like that had happened in their hotel."

"They should be upset," Ronan said, setting down the coiled rope. "Just think if you'd surprised the guy and he'd hurt you." He sounded indignant and maybe a little bit worried—which gave me a warm feeling.

Before I could analyze that feeling, or just how foolish it was for me to feel it, Jason launched into the day's pre-dive lesson.

"Today we're going to start with the Arashi Reef. It has a couple of sunken airplanes, which add some extra interest. We'll be diving to about forty feet, somewhere between the depths of yesterday's two dives." He went on to explain the skills we'd be practicing, as well as giving more details about the dive site itself.

Already I was feeling a tingle of anticipation in my belly as I zipped myself into my wetsuit. That process wasn't any easier today than yesterday, though I managed not to pinch myself in the zipper this time. I decided I had to lose at least a little bit of weight before my next dive vacation.

*My next dive vacation?*

I paused, that thought reverberating in my head—then decided I was okay with it. Though I wasn't even certified yet, I felt sure I'd be diving again in the future. Interesting, even weird, but...definitely okay.

"Since Ronan is going to dive with us today, I'll be somebody's buddy, as well as instructing," Jason was saying.

I turned my head sharply and saw that Ronan was, in fact, wearing a wetsuit. Somehow I'd missed him stripping to swim trunks before putting it on, darn it. Still, the navy blue neoprene outlined his chest and thighs impressively. With an effort, I told myself that I barely knew the man, so any lustful thoughts were out of line.

Not that they'd have been *in* line, no matter what. Sheesh.

"So, Jason, will you be my buddy?" Bebe asked before anyone else could.

He grinned at her, but shook his head. "You and Dobry made a great team yesterday. I thought I'd buddy with Rick, and let Ronan pair up with Wynne."

Was that a wink he sent Ronan's way as he spoke? No, my over-active imagination had conjured that, I was sure. Still, I couldn't deny another unsanctioned thrill at the idea of being Ronan's underwater buddy. And this one didn't go away, no matter how I scolded myself.

"—much left of the actual airplanes, but the reef is pretty good," Jason was saying when I managed to focus again. "Once we've done our drills, look around for parrotfish, angelfish, and blue tangs."

Again, the boat ride was short, no longer than it took us novices to get all of our gear ready and onto our bodies. I forced myself to concentrate as I attached my hoses and tightened the various cinches. I was determined not to do anything stupid in front of Ronan, despite the fact I'd probably never see him again after today.

"In you all go," Jason said once the boat was tied to the mooring ball. "Wynne, Ronan, you're both ready, so you go first. Greg, help Linda with her mask—her hair is caught in it. Rick and I will bring up the rear."

Since I'd already discovered being on the boat in full gear was my least favorite part of diving, I was fine with this plan. I stood and shuffled to the back platform. Ronan put a hand on my elbow to steady me, and I forced myself to ignore my reaction to the contact.

"After you, Wynne," Ronan said. What *was* that accent? I'd try to muster the nerve to ask after the dive.

One hand on my weight belt, the other on my mask and regula-tor, I stepped out into air and plunged into the water. I got my bearings a little quicker than yesterday, popping back up, locating the boat, then kicking away from it to give Ronan room to jump in.

Not surprisingly, he made even less splash than Jason had yester-day, slipping into the ocean like a seal. I wondered how many years he'd been diving. In fact, I was wondering way too much about Ronan.

He grinned at me around his regulator—how did he do that?—and moved to my side, bobbing within arm's reach as we waited for the others to join us.

Once everyone was in, Jason motioned us to follow him down. I obediently let the air out of my vest and felt the increasingly familiar sensation of the ocean around and above me as I descended. I was really getting good at this.

I glanced over at Ronan to see if he noticed how smoothly I was performing—then felt a sharp pain in both ears at once. Oops. I'd forgotten to equalize. Quickly, I pinched my nose and blew, but the only thing that happened was an intensification of the pain.

Feeling foolish, I kicked upward until the pressure eased, did the nose-pinch thing again until I heard the welcome squeals in my ears, then started back down, more slowly. Okay, maybe I wasn't so great at this just yet.

Remembering—now—to equalize frequently, I made it down to thirty-five feet without further problems, and then looked around. The visibility wasn't quite as good as it had been for yesterday's dives, and I had to squint to see the reef, some thirty feet away. I didn't see any sign of an airplane.

A dull pinging brought my attention back to Jason, who was motioning us to gather around him for the first lesson of the day. Trying to ignore Ronan, knowing that if I thought about him watching me I'd likely mess up again, I concentrated on following Jason's nonverbal instructions.

First, he had us flood our masks and then clear them. That was always an extra challenge for me, because my contact lenses meant I had to do it blind. I was glad I'd had lots of chances to practice this in the pool. I watched everything Jason did and waited until he was done before I started, since I wouldn't be able to peek at him during the process.

Screwing my eyes shut, I took my mask completely off, remembering to breathe only through my mouth as water surrounded my nose and eyes. Then I carefully repositioned my mask by feel, making sure no stray strands of hair were trapped in the seal.

Tilting the mask up at what I hoped was the right angle, I blew air from my regulator up into it to displace the water. When I felt air instead of water around my nose, I pushed the mask against my face and cautiously opened my eyes.

It had worked, except for a little bit of seawater tickling my upper lip. How did I—? Then I remembered. Barely cracking the seal at the bottom of my mask, I blew out through my nose until I'd forced the rest of the water out. Jason gave me an approving nod, then went back to helping Linda, whose hair was caught in her mask again, making it leak.

Against my better judgment—not that I thought about it enough to *use* judgment—I glanced at Ronan to see if he'd noticed how well I'd done. He was nodding at Dobry and Bebe, who'd just finished their drills, but turned almost as though he felt my eyes on him.

Again, he grinned around his regulator and winked. Definitely winked. I was glad there was no way my confusion could show with my mask and regulator obscuring most of my face. I tried to grin back, but saltwater flooded my mouth so I quickly stopped. How *did* he do that?

Jason pinged for our attention again, and I was just as glad to turn away from Ronan to complete our other drills of maintaining neutral buoyancy and regulator recovery. I noticed that Rick remembered to clear his regulator this time without prompting from Jason.

After that, we were waved off to explore the site. The ledge of the reef was covered with sea fans waving gently in the current, as well as multicolored sponges. And again, me without a camera. Why hadn't I bought one in Oranjestad yesterday? I wished for one even more when two enormous parrotfish swam within five feet of me.

Ronan stayed close, which was flattering—until I remembered that he'd been appointed my buddy, which meant he was obliged to do just that. I was doing my best to ignore his proximity until he tapped me on the shoulder.

I turned to see him pointing at a spotted ray that had to be almost four feet across, hovering just above the ocean floor. Ronan *did* have a camera, of course, a complicated, expensive-looking thing, and he brought it up and smoothly snapped a shot or two of the ray before moving on.

All too soon, the dive was over, Jason collecting us for our ascent to the surface. I made it back onto the boat without incident, trying not to think what my shrink-wrapped bottom must look like to Ronan, who was behind me. Once everyone was aboard, Jason debriefed us, then told us to change out our tanks as Bertie started up the engine to take us to the next site.

Ronan made quick work of his own tank, then sauntered over to where I was still struggling to tighten the strap around my second cylinder. I was sure I'd never be able to saunter on a moving boat no matter how much practice I got.

"Here," he said, giving the strap a yank and flipping the cinch closed. "Don't forget to turn your air on."

"I haven't yet," I replied, miffed that he'd think I might. Just because I'd had a little trouble equalizing last dive didn't mean I was stupid.

"Sorry." He must have heard the snip in my voice. "I didn't mean it that way. You're doing great."

I finished attaching my first stage to the tank and twisted the knob to turn on the air flow before grudgingly saying, "Thanks." I remembered now why I'd decided I never wanted a man in my life again.

"So, did you try to track down the owner of that ring, like you said you might?" he asked then.

I glanced at him, surprised by the change of subject. Wow, his eyes were blue. "Um, actually, I did. I stopped by the Cartier store in Oranjestad last night, and the lady there said she'd look into it."

"So you left the ring there?"

"No, she just took down my contact info." Which included my room number, I realized. If my intruder *had* been after the ring, it was probably someone connected with the store.

"You didn't leave it in your room after someone broke in last night, did you?"

I must have looked as startled as I felt, because he quickly grinned and shrugged. "Just wondering. None of my business, of course."

"That's okay." Another possibility occurred to me—one I didn't like at all. "Anyway, no, I—"

"Okay, everybody, we're coming up on the wreck of the *Antilla*," Jason announced, and I broke off.

As he described our final dive site, I realized it was probably a good thing he'd interrupted me. I'd been just about to tell Ronan that the ring was still in my shorts pocket, here on the boat, and if there was any chance at all that my momentary suspicion was right, that would have been about the dumbest thing I could have done.

## CHAPTER FIVE

"THE *ANTILLA* is probably Aruba's most popular site, as you can see by the other dive boats here," Jason continued, gesturing at the half-dozen vessels anchored within a quarter mile of us. "That makes it important to stick together. Don't lose sight of your buddy."

"No chance of that," Ronan murmured beside me.

Was he flirting, or was it something more nefarious? The tingle I felt wasn't quite as warm as before.

"We're going to start with a few surface drills as soon as everyone's in the water—removing and replacing weights, and navigating with our compasses just a few feet below the surface. Then we'll descend, practice buddy breathing, use our compasses to get to the wreck and do some exploring. Since it's our last dive, go ahead and use up whatever film you've got. This site will be worth it."

As before, I was the first one in, with Ronan right behind. We'd already practiced weights and compasses in the pool, but just like everything else, it was trickier in the ocean. Rick dropped his weights, in fact, but Jason managed to grab the belt before it sank out of reach.

"That would have delayed us a good fifteen minutes," Jason said, handing the weights back to Rick. "We're in sixty feet of water here, so it would have taken me a while to go down and get back with them. Remember, if you drop your weights, someone else has to retrieve them, since you can't get to the bottom without them."

I made sure to cinch my weight belt securely around my waist, thinking how stupid I'd feel if Ronan had to fetch it for me.

The compass navigation went smoothly, though Dobry and Bebe somehow ended up twenty yards from the boat at the end of it.

"Okay, you were right, and I was wrong," I heard Bebe admitting sheepishly. Dobry didn't even look smug; he really was a nice guy. I was going to miss these people.

This time I remembered to equalize early and often on the way down and reached the bottom without incident. We gathered around Jason on a sandy spot of the ocean floor—we'd been well drilled by now not to touch coral or other marine life—and he demonstrated buddy breathing with Rick.

Somehow I'd managed not to think ahead, but now I felt my heart speed up a bit as Ronan removed his regulator and held it out to me. Reminding myself that it was only a drill, that the seawater had already washed away all traces of his mouth, I took out my own regulator and replaced it with his.

After three or four breaths, I handed it back to him, waited a moment, then offered him my regulator, telling myself that this was *nothing* like kissing by proxy.

The grin and wink he gave me before inserting my mouthpiece between his lips undermined that thought somewhat. I counted seconds while holding my breath rather than dwell on that.

When we all had our own regulators back, Jason had us gather closely so that he could show us on his compass which direction we needed to go to reach the wreck. Then he waved us off in pairs.

Since I was the one taking the class, Ronan indicated that I should do the navigating. I nodded and squinted down at my compass, turning it until it pointed precisely the same way Jason's had, just a hair north of true east. It was a lot harder to keep the compass needle steady in the ocean than it had been in a pool with no currents.

Though I had to correct course several times, less than five minutes passed before the bulk of the *Antilla* loomed up before me. Triumphant, I glanced back at Ronan to see him giving me the "okay" signal. I knew he'd have managed it in half the time, but I still felt pretty proud of myself.

Once the rest of the class arrived at the wreck, Jason gathered us together, nodded his approval and indicated we should follow him. We all spent the next twenty minutes or so exploring the *Antilla*, a four-hundred-foot monstrosity.

A German freighter sunk during World War II, many of its enormous compartments now lay open to the sea, creating metal caves and tunnels big enough to swim through—not that I'd have dared to do so, if Jason hadn't been leading the way.

I felt like protesting when Jason indicated that it was time to begin surfacing, but when I checked my air gauge, I saw that I was down to one thousand PSI, which meant I had enough to surface safely, but not much more than that. I half promised myself that I'd make another trip to the Antilla before leaving Aruba—with a camera.

Not until we were back on the boat removing our equipment did I remember the odd questions Ronan had been asking me about the ring between our two dives. My suspicion seemed silly now. But how could I be sure?

Well, I supposed I could always just *ask* him. If I had the guts.

"Congratulations!" Jason said as we struggled out of our wetsuits —some of us (me) struggling more than others. "You've all now completed your training to become certified Open Water Divers. We'll go back to the classroom for one last quiz, fill out some paperwork, and I'll give you your temporary dive cards. You can use those to dive until your permanent ones come in the mail."

It occurred to me that Ronan might disappear before we

finished with all that, never to be seen again. Which meant that if I was going to ask him anything, it had to be *now*. While we were still on the boat. I screwed up my dwindling courage and walked over to him before I could talk myself out of it.

"Ronan, you seemed awfully interested in that ring I found. Why?" I asked all in one breath.

He straightened from his task of detaching tanks from vests and looked me right in the eye. For a moment I thought he intended to lie, probably very convincingly, but then he gave a slight nod.

"Yeah, I guess you should know what I found out. If you want, we can talk after all of your class stuff is done."

"Yes, I definitely want," I said, referring only—okay, mostly—to information about the ring. Certainly I was now burning with curiosity.

My impatience to hear what Ronan had to tell me nearly overshadowed the importance of the next hour or so. Still, I couldn't deny a flush of pride when Jason presented me with my very own (temporary) dive card, knowing I'd earned it. I hadn't felt such a sense of achievement since Debra's birth—something else I'd done on my own, as Tom had been too "busy"—read: squeamish—to be with me.

The moment Jason released us from the classroom, I looked around for Ronan, half expecting that he'd reconsidered and left. But no, there he was in the dive shop, waiting among the t-shirt displays.

"Just a sec," I said to him. On impulse, I grabbed a *NO FEAR* t-shirt off the rack—in pink, to match my fins—and plunked it on the counter by the register. I was going to work at making that my new motto.

"Are you planning to join the others at Pepe & Pete's tonight?" Ronan asked as I paid for the shirt. "You can dance on the bar with Bebe and Linda to celebrate your certification."

I snorted and shook my head. "I was there last night, and once was enough. And no, I did not dance on the bar." The image almost made me laugh—and I didn't even want to think what it would do to my daughters.

"Do you want to get some lunch while we talk?" he asked then.

"Sure. I'm starving." I was glad he'd changed the subject.

"Diving will do that. There's a good steak place across the street and down a block or so. My treat."

Flattered as I was, there was no way I was going to be obligated to him for the price of a meal. Not yet. "Steak sounds good—but we'll go Dutch, if that's okay."

He shrugged and headed to the door. "Sure, if that makes you feel safer. This way."

Safer? I started to protest, then realized he was right. I was still playing it safe. But fearless didn't mean stupid. Right?

"Care to give me an overview on the way there?" I asked, not wanting to examine my motives any more closely.

Ronan hesitated for so long that I thought he might renege altogether, but then he shrugged. "Sure. Why not. In a nutshell, I believe that ring you found could be a clue in a high-profile murder case."

That was so completely not what I'd expected that I stopped walking to stare at him. "A murder case?" I squeaked, then cleared my throat. "How— What makes you think that?"

"The inscription." He touched my shoulder to get me moving again. "As I recall, the names were Stefan and Melanie, and the year was 2008. Right?"

Mechanically moving forward, I nodded. I hadn't realized he'd looked that closely at it yesterday.

"About eight months ago, industrialist Stefan Melampus's wife, Melanie, disappeared at sea, and he was later charged with her murder. It was all over the news for a week or two. You might have seen it."

That was right about the time I'd caught Tom cheating on me, so I hadn't been paying a whole lot of attention to the national news, but the names sounded vaguely familiar. "I think so," I said uncertainly. "And you think that could be her ring?"

"They were married in '98, so it's certainly possible. Besides—" He broke off and shrugged. "Anyway, if it is, it could be important."

"Why? I mean, if she was lost at sea, wouldn't it make sense that her ring would be in the ocean?"

He arched one dark brow, giving him a slightly devilish look. "She disappeared off the coast of Miami, for one thing. For another —How, exactly, did you find the ring?"

We reached the restaurant then, so I waited until we'd been seated and were again alone to answer. "How did I find the ring? Well, you saw it. It's in great shape. But that's kind of the point of platinum, isn't it? It doesn't corrode?"

"That's not exactly what I meant. Was it buried in the sand, or what? You didn't say."

"Oh." I thought back to yesterday—was it only yesterday?—and my triumph. "It was right above that big moray eel under the keel of the *Debbie II*... Oh, that's right, you were on the boat. Well, there's a—"

"I've been down there. I've seen the eel you're talking about. Huge sucker."

I nodded. "The ring was on a little piece of metal sticking out from the side of the wreck, above and a little to the left of the eel. There was sand on the shelf, but the ring wasn't buried in it. It was just sitting on top."

"Which means it can't very well have been there for eight months," he said, "even if it somehow got there from Miami."

"No, I guess not. So what would that mean?"

"Either it's not the same ring, or Melanie Melampus wasn't wearing it when—"

"Um, may I take your order?"

Ronan broke off what he'd been about to say at the waitress's interruption. I wondered how long she'd been standing there.

"A bottle of the Malbec to start," Ronan said as I hesitated, glancing at my menu for the first time. "And an order of the crab-stuffed mushroom appetizers."

She nodded and left, and he looked back at me. "All of the steaks are good, but the tenderloin is my favorite."

"That'll be fine," I said, just as glad not to have to decide for myself. "Now, what were you saying about Mrs. Melampus and her ring?"

One corner of his mouth quirked up, acknowledging with amusement that I wanted to keep things businesslike. Which I did, of course.

"This is all assuming it really is her ring. You never did tell me what you did with it after your room was searched last night."

I hesitated for a long moment, then decided that even if he was a legitimate suspect, he wasn't likely to do anything heinous here in a public restaurant. "I've got it right here," I said, digging it out of my pocket and displaying it on my palm.

He blinked. "It was in your shorts pocket, on the boat, while we were diving?"

"Well, yeah. I have no particular reason to think whoever broke into my room was after this ring. They could have been looking for cash, drugs, anything."

"Good point." I didn't think he sounded convinced, though. "Mind if I take another look at it?"

I only hesitated for a short moment this time, then handed it across to him. "It hasn't changed since yesterday, and you took a pretty good look then. You were the one who pointed out that it's engraved."

He didn't reply, but held the ring just above the table top to examine it. The light in this restaurant wasn't as bright as the pizza place yesterday had been. After a moment, he shot me a glance I couldn't quite decipher, then pulled a pair of glasses out of his breast pocket and put them on. I managed not to snicker out loud, remembering my own reluctance to do just that yesterday.

When he handed it back to me, I glanced nervously around

then pocketed it, wondering what I was afraid of. "Well?" I asked him.

"I think that's Melanie's ring. Assuming she was wearing it the night she disappeared, your finding it here could mean that her killer, or someone associated with the killer, is—or was recently—here in Aruba. Which means someone isn't going to be happy you found it."

I stared at him, dread starting to creep up on me. "And that's why you think whoever broke into my room last night was after the ring?"

"I'd say it's a definite possibility, yes."

"And what makes you so sure this is—was—her ring? Two first names and a year isn't a lot to go on." I was clutching at straws, trying to keep panic at bay.

"Last night I went online to look up the Melampus case, since it had been a while since I'd followed it. This ring was listed among her effects, the things missing along with her body."

"That information is available online?" I couldn't keep the skepticism from my voice. "I know you can find almost anything on the internet these days, but—"

"You have to know where to look," he said with a disarming grin and a shrug. "I've done some work in insurance."

I opened my mouth to say I'd worked in insurance too, but didn't know how to access that kind of info, but the server arrived just then with our wine and appetizer. After she opened the wine, Ronan ordered the tenderloin for both of us. By the time she was gone, something else had occurred to me.

"So that's what you spent your evening doing? Digging into insurance records?" I'd almost said "hacking."

Again, he shrugged. "I was curious. What, did you think I'd spent the evening searching your room, instead?" He said it with a grin, but I still felt myself flushing.

"No, of course not. I just didn't know why you were so interested in the ring, that's all." Suddenly I was the one on the defensive.

"Well, now you know. I guess you could say I'm kind of a news junkie." He took a sip of the ruby-red wine. "Excellent, as always. Anyway, enough about me, Wynne. What brings you to Aruba, all by your lonesome?"

There was more I wanted to know about the ring—about him—but I accepted the change of subject...for now. "My twenty-fifth wedding anniversary," I said, then paused, waiting for his reaction.

He didn't look so much startled as curious. "Not many couples take separate vacations for their anniversaries. Or is your husband already a diver?"

I couldn't help smiling at the thought. "Hardly. And no, it's not a separate vacation thing, exactly. I booked the trip—and the dive lessons—last summer, but we've since divorced."

"Ah." Was it my imagination that he looked relieved? Probably. "And you decided to come anyway? Gutsy. Good for you."

I took a sip of my own wine, then a bite of the crab-stuffed mushroom, to conceal my pleasure at his validation of my choice. "These are both delicious. And thanks. Most people would say I was crazy to come here alone."

"I'm not most people," he said with a twinkle in his very blue eyes. "I think it's important to stretch boundaries, to refuse to live life according to other people's expectations."

That was so exactly what I'd been telling myself that I was both startled and gratified. "It's good to hear someone else say that. But it's easier to say than do, I've found." I took another sip of the excellent Malbec.

The look he gave me was a little too perceptive. "It gets easier with practice."

"That's good to know." I glanced down and realized I'd eaten at least my half of the appetizer, and probably more. "Oops, sorry. The rest is yours."

"No apology necessary. I'm glad you like it."

He popped the last mushroom into his mouth, then drained his wineglass. He refilled it from the bottle, then looked at me questioningly. Mine was nearly empty too, to my surprise. After a slight hesitation, I nodded, and he topped it off.

"I'm also glad that you plan to keep stretching your boundaries," he said after a moment.

I blinked. "Did I say that?" One glass of wine wouldn't have—

"Not in so many words. But you do, don't you?"

I considered before answering. "Yes, I suppose I do. I've, well, I've spent most of my life living for others. It's my turn now."

"Good girl." He reached across the table and patted my hand encouragingly.

For a moment I frowned at his hand on mine, then I pulled away. "Don't."

He looked confused. "Don't what?"

"Don't patronize me. I've had enough of that to last me a lifetime. It's one thing I came here to escape."

His brows rose, and he drew back his hand. "Fair enough. Though for the record, I wasn't patronizing you. In fact, you don't strike me as a woman it would be easy to patronize, Wynne."

I gave a sour little laugh. "Oh, my ex-husband could give you lessons, believe me."

"Any man who'd let you go isn't one I'd want lessons from—on anything."

My new cynicism wasn't proof against that kind of flattery, but the novelty threw me off balance. "You haven't said what brings you to Aruba," I said, deliberately turning the topic away from myself. "Or do you live here?"

"Not full time, though I visit when I can. This time around, I'm house-sitting for a friend."

"February is a good time to do it."

He nodded. "Miami isn't bad in the winter, but Aruba is infinitely better. Especially now." His smile had me feeling disoriented again. Luckily our salads arrived before the silence became awkward.

After a few bites of the excellent spinach, mushroom, and raspberry vinaigrette concoction, I decided the safest thing was to get back to business—and away from the personal stuff. "So what's the next step?" I asked. "Do we call the police and say we have the ring?"

"We?" His look was something between curious and amused.

I felt myself flushing again. "I, well, you seem to know a lot about the case, and I'm the one who found the ring, so I..." *just thought I'd insert myself into your life, if you don't mind.*

His eyes crinkled at the corners, almost as though he'd heard the unfinished part of my sentence.

"So you're willing to let me help you?" he asked.

"It seems to make sense. Especially after what happened last night—assuming it had anything to do with the ring. Which it probably didn't."

He took a bite of his salad and chewed it thoughtfully before answering. "Probably not, but it never hurts to be cautious. I don't like to think of you at risk, Wynne."

This time I couldn't rationalize away his meaning—or his interest, unlikely though it still seemed. I mean, this was a very good-looking man, one who was probably at least two or three years younger than I was. After what seemed like an embarrassed eternity, I managed to find my voice. Sort of.

"Er, thanks. I don't like to think of me at risk either."

His laugh startled me. "There's something very refreshing about you, Wynne. Do you know that?"

That was a lot more startling than the laugh. Refreshing wasn't a word I could recall anyone ever using to describe me. I liked it.

"Thanks. I think." Suddenly uncomfortable with the trend of the conversation, I again shifted back to the less personal matter of the ring. "So what do you recommend I do next?"

"If the hotel has a real safe downstairs, I'd put the ring there before we pursue this any further. Then it might be a good idea to go back to the Cartier store and find out who they contacted."

I'd half expected him to suggest I turn the ring over to him. The fact that he hadn't erased any lingering suspicion that he'd had something to do with my break-in.

"I suppose I can do that. I have to admit I'm feeling more than a little out of my depth here." I paused, belatedly recognizing a pun of sorts. "When I found the ring, I figured it was either a cool trophy or something I should try to return. I certainly never expected it to turn into something sinister."

He grinned. "Sinister? That's a little strong. You have a flair for the dramatic, don't you?"

"No, that's my daughter," I said automatically, then immediately regretted it. I wasn't ready to discuss my family with this man. Also, there was a tiny part of me that wanted to pretend I was too young to have two grown daughters. Silly, of course, but there it was.

"I'd say she comes by it honestly," was all he had time to say in response before our steaks arrived.

I seized on the opportunity to change the subject. "Now I can see if Argentinian beef is all I've heard." I took a bite of the tenderloin, and my eyes nearly rolled back in my head in ecstasy. "*Mmm*. Definitely."

"It was worth bringing you here just for that," he said, snapping me out of my euphoria.

"Sorry. I don't usually—"

"No, please don't apologize, Wynne. I love seeing a woman enjoy her food. So few seem to do so these days."

Though still self-conscious, I managed a smile. Certainly I couldn't refute his statement. I *did* love exceptional food, though I seldom indulged myself. And most women I knew spent more time complaining about calories or carbs than enjoying it when they did order something sumptuous. I resolved on the spot never to do that again.

Not until I was halfway through my meal did my mind really

start working again. When it did, I asked, "So, do we call the police about this or not? You never said."

He looked thoughtful. "We probably should, but there are reasons not to."

"Such as?"

He hesitated for a moment, then shrugged. "Stefan Melampus is more than an industrialist. For years, it's been believed he was connected to organized crime. There are police—and others—from several countries who would like to see him convicted of something, and they may not care exactly what that something is."

"Are you saying that the police might cover up any evidence that could clear him?" This thing was getting more sinister by the minute.

"I won't say it's not possible."

I discovered my appetite was gone—though the impressive amount of food I'd consumed might have had something to do with that.

"If you're willing to wait a day or two, I can make a few calls, maybe find out a little bit more. Then I might be able to give you better advice on what you—we—should do next," he suggested.

I shrugged. "I don't suppose a day or two will make much difference." Not to the fate of the ring, anyway. What it might do to my peace of mind was something else entirely.

## CHAPTER SIX

I WAS FEELING decidedly mellow when I finally got back to my room an hour or so later. The meal and the wine had been excellent —along with the company. Okay, the actual conversation had been unsettling. At least, I was pretty sure I'd feel unsettled once the wine wore off.

Not until after I'd showered did I notice the message light blinking on the phone by the bed. Not my daughters or my mother —they would have called my cell.

Curious, I picked up the receiver and pushed the button, to discover I had not one but three messages waiting. The first was just a hang-up, probably a wrong number. The second was from the hotel staff, checking to see if everything was satisfactory with my new room. I grinned at the solicitous tone. They really, really didn't want me to file a complaint—or sue.

The third message was interesting, though.

"Ms. Seally, this is the Cartier Boutique," said the feminine voice without giving a name. "We may have found the owner of that ring. We'd appreciate it if you could come back to the store at nine o'clock this evening so that we can get more information from you." Then, after a brief pause during which I thought I heard a male voice murmuring in the background, "There may be a reward. Thank you."

I'd deleted the first two messages, but after listening to this one twice more, I saved it before thoughtfully replacing the receiver. Definitely interesting.

The more I considered that message, the more I wondered whether it had actually come from the jewelry store. Certainly it hadn't been the same woman I'd spoken to last night. She'd had the accent common to local Arubans, while the voice in the message sounded purely American. And why would they care what time I came in, if they just needed more information?

Ah, well, I needed to go into town anyway, and Ronan had suggested stopping by the Cartier Boutique again to ask who they'd contacted about the ring. I'd just make sure I did so long before nine o'clock, in case the message was bogus. I should be able to find that out from the jewelry store, too.

I did hope the message would turn out to be legitimate, though. After last night's break-in, I didn't need anything else to make me paranoid. I just wanted to do some shopping—I still had to replace the underwear I'd impulsively trashed—and play tourist. With those simple goals in mind, I headed downstairs to catch another rickety taxi to Oranjestad.

It was only about five o'clock when I reached Royal Plaza and headed for the Cartier store, a full four hours before the message had indicated I should come. I didn't see the clerk I'd talked to last night. Instead, a young man was behind the counter, helping a customer. As soon as the customer left, I came forward.

"Hi, I'm Mrs. Seally. I was in last night, with a ring I'd found, and—"

"Ah, yes. You got our message, then?" he said.

So it *had* been legit. I felt some of the tension between my shoulders ease, only then realizing how keyed up I'd been.

"Yes, but since I was in town, I thought I'd stop by now instead of later."

He looked vaguely confused, but said, "That's fine, though you could have just called."

I'd wondered about that, but since I was already here, I said, "So, what information did you need?"

"Um, as I believe Valerie said in her message, we heard back from the owner of the ring, and he wanted to know how to contact you. Of course we can't give out that information without your permission, which is why we called to ask."

That was nothing like the message I'd received. Then it hit me: I'd given the clerk my original room number last night. If Valerie had just asked for that room, instead of for me by name...

"But who—?" I started to ask, then stopped, the tension between my shoulders creeping back. The message I *had* received hadn't been from this store after all.

He was still looking understandably confused. "So, um, are you okay with us giving him your name and number?"

"Who? Stefan Melampus?" That's what I'd planned to ask them about anyway.

I'd obviously caught him off guard with that question, though he tried to cover it. "I, er, I'm not supposed...that is, I really can't say. But if you'll allow him to contact you, it may be that he's prepared to offer you a reward. Or, if you prefer, you can let us mediate."

I considered for a moment. I really didn't want to give my new room number out to anyone just yet, especially a possible mob boss —or murderer?—like Stefan Melampus. But what if someone connected with the store had made that other call? Could I really trust these people?

"You can give him my cell phone number," I finally said. That wouldn't give away where I was staying, so shouldn't put me at any extra risk.

"That should be fine."

I wrote it down for him, then said, "I don't suppose anyone else has contacted you about this ring, by any chance?"

He looked startled again, but then nodded, eyeing me strangely. "Actually, now that you ask, someone did come in earlier today, claiming to have lost a ring of a similar description."

"Really?"

"Yes. I thought it odd, since we'd already heard back from the man who originally purchased the ring. I asked her to leave her name and number, but she refused."

*She?* More and more interesting. "Did she do anything else... suspicious?"

"Well...I thought she was leaving, but a few minutes later, while I was helping another customer, I caught her behind the counter. I nearly called the police, but nothing had been stolen, and she apologized profusely, so I let it go. Most likely, she was completely unconnected with the ring you found. We're a bit concerned that she might have been planning a robbery, though."

If she'd been behind the counter, it was possible she'd found my name, I realized. "Um, can you tell me what she looked like?" If there was a threat, it would be good to know what form it might take.

"Tall, dark hair, maybe late twenties or early thirties. Pretty. Oh, and well dressed. She didn't *look* like a criminal."

"Maybe she was just confused. I'll wait to hear from the owner of the ring. Thanks."

I left the store, thinking hard.

If everything Ronan had told me was true, one possibility was that Melanie Melampus was still alive and had come looking for her lost ring—and had made that call to my room. But how could she have known it was found in the first place?

Another theory, less dramatic but more likely, was that it had been someone who'd overheard me yesterday, when I was in the store with the ring. Either way, I didn't think it was just chance.

There might be other plausible theories, but my first order of business was to find out whether Ronan had told me the truth. I hadn't brought a laptop to Aruba with me, but I spotted an ice cream parlor that claimed to also be an internet cafe. Venturing inside, I got a hot fudge sundae and asked how to use one of their computers.

It took me a while to find what I was looking for. I wasn't particularly internet savvy but didn't want to ask for more help, given the rather delicate nature of what I was doing. My girls were always "Googling" things on their phones, so I figured that was a good starting place. After a few fruitless searches, I eventually managed to find a few old news stories about the Melampus case.

Everything I read confirmed what Ronan had told me: eight months ago, Melanie Melampus had disappeared from the *Hestia* in the middle of the night and hadn't been seen since. She was presumed dead, and her husband had been charged with her murder.

The absence of a body was an issue, but apparently there had been substantial—and grisly—physical evidence pointing to her death. I shuddered. So much for my first theory.

Since then, the wheels of justice had been turning with their usual agonizing slowness. Stefan Melampus was out on bail but not allowed to leave Miami, under virtual house arrest while awaiting trial. Which at least meant I didn't have to worry about him coming to Aruba and finding me. In fact, now that I understood just how wealthy and powerful Melampus was, I doubted he would contact me himself. Men like that delegated such things to lackeys.

On that exact thought, my cell phone rang.

My hands were shaking as I dug it out of my purse. I was so nervous at the prospect of talking to Stefan Melampus—or even one of his lackeys—after my research, that I didn't even check the caller ID screen before opening the phone.

Bad mistake.

"Wynne? It's Mom. I thought you'd be back by now."

Relief, disappointment, and irritation fought for supremacy. Irritation won.

"I'll be back in a week or so, Mom. I told you I'd call when I got home. I'm on vacation."

"Oh, Honey. I guess I can understand you wanting to get away right now, with your anniversary this week and all, but—"

"Did you want something specific, Mom?" I stopped myself from saying that she was one of the things I'd needed a vacation from.

"I did, actually, and if you're going to be gone that long, I'm glad I didn't wait for you to get back. This is too important to wait a whole week."

I knew from her smug tone that I'd regret asking, but I also knew she'd tell me whether I did or not. "What's too important, Mom?"

"I ran into Tom as I was leaving church today, and we talked for a few minutes. He's definitely not with that blonde anymore, and he actually told me he'd made a mistake. I *think* he meant he'd made a mistake letting you go. Which of course he did, but I saw no point in rubbing his nose in it."

Of course not—though she'd done her best to rub *my* nose in what I was giving up by divorcing the cheating bastard.

"Maybe the sermon did him some good."

"Anyway," she continued, ignoring my dry tone, "I suggested he give you a call, and he said he might. I really think he might be willing to reconcile, Wynne!"

"How nice for him. Fortunately, I'm not. Please don't get in the middle of this, Mom. It's over."

She gave one of her gusty sighs that I knew was supposed to instill guilt. Years ago, it had worked, but once my own daughters were grown, it had lost its power.

"You've always been stubborn, Wynne, but don't cut off your nose to spite your face."

"My face is doing fine without that particular nose, thanks. I'll call you when I get home, Mom."

"But where—?"

I hung up before she could finish the question. I really didn't want her to know I was in Aruba, since I was pretty sure I'd told her that's where Tom and I were going to spend our anniversary, the day I booked the trip. The day I found out Tom was cheating on me. I didn't need her reading anything into that.

With an exasperated shake of my head, I turned back to the computer to continue my research on the Melampus case.

One article about the erstwhile industrialist *cum* crime boss mentioned that over the past year or two, Stefan Melampus had donated large sums of money to various charities, many of them church-related. He claimed to be a recently born-again Christian— a claim that predated his wife's disappearance by less than a year.

While I found that interesting, given my own conflicted relationship with church, of more immediate interest was a photo spread from *People Magazine* dated just over a year ago, with a couple of good shots of Melanie and Stefan.

They'd certainly been a striking couple. He was tall, dark, with distinguished graying at the temples and a commanding presence. She was tall, exotically beautiful, and very blonde. She also appeared to be at least twenty years younger than her husband. I tried to ignore the sour twinge of memory that observation evoked.

I clicked on a few more links, but most turned out to be duplicates of what I'd already seen, so I logged off, dropped off my ice cream dish and headed back out to the square to consider what I should do next.

Maybe some mindless shopping would help me to sort things out. I headed over to Seaport Mall, which wound around under the Aruba Renaissance hotel, its array of shops opening onto covered breezeways. My main mission was to replace the underwear I'd tossed, so I walked into the first women's clothing store I found.

And walked right back out, when I realized two steps in that it was aimed at a much younger crowd.

But then I stopped and reconsidered. Did I really want to buy a six-pack of practical, white Fruit-of-the-Loom briefs like the ones

I'd thrown away? Now that I thought about it, I most emphatically did not. Squaring my shoulders, I turned around and went back into the store, bracing myself against the assault of pop music blaring over the speakers.

Lingerie was at the very back, of course, which meant I had to make my way past microscopic skirts, tops, and shorts that no woman my age could ever wear without looking stupid. I couldn't help feeling like everyone in the store was watching me, wondering what on earth I could possibly be doing in there.

Still, I persevered until I found a display of panties that would have done credit to Victoria's Secret—both in style and price. Forcefully telling myself that I was creating a new me, I plucked half a dozen pairs off the rack: satiny things in hot pink, electric blue, even leopard spots. And I didn't even pretend to the cashier that I was buying them for my daughter.

It was a small triumph, but I still felt empowered as I left with my crinkly fuchsia bag of wildly impractical undies. And with that empowerment came inspiration.

Whoever had left me that bogus message would no doubt be waiting at or near the Cartier store at nine o'clock tonight—perhaps with some nefarious plot to get the ring from me. Suppose I set a trap of my own, staking out the store—from a safe distance, of course!—to see who that person was?

Walking aimlessly through the mall, I considered my plan from every angle, trying to decide whether it was brilliant or incredibly stupid. Maybe both, but the risk to me should be minimal, since there would still be plenty of people in and around Royal Plaza at nine o'clock.

Besides, if I didn't give myself away by going into the Cartier store, no one should have any reason to target me. At least I hoped not, since I was still carrying the ring around in my pocket. I wished now I'd put it in the hotel safe before coming downtown, like Ronan had suggested. But I didn't see how my mystery caller could possibly know what I looked like.

To make sure, though, I went back to the internet cafe and Googled Wynne Seally. Rather to my surprise, there were a few hits that were actually me—but none with pictures. Just a couple of old newspaper articles about a charity ball Tom and I had attended, and one about Tom being named an elder of our church two years ago.

I closed that window quickly, trying not to think about the way certain church members had seemed to blame me rather than Tom for our divorce, despite the fact he was the one who'd cheated. But Tom brought in both members and money. I'd done nothing but teach Sunday school for a few years and sort through donated clothing for the homeless.

Yeah, I definitely had some issues with church.

Back out on the plaza, I glanced down at what I was wearing: capri-length khaki pants, a scoop-necked jungle print tank top, pink flip-flops, and an oversized hot pink purse. (What had I been thinking? Oh, that's right—Debra had given me the purse).

I decided I'd pass as a typical tourist—which was more or less what I was. That was good, since the last thing I wanted to do was stand out in the crowd tonight. With any luck, a cruise ship would be docked, giving me even better odds of blending in with the milling throng of shoppers.

I dug my phone out of my purse and put it in a more accessible side pocket, along with a small notebook and a pen. I was ready for my stakeout.

## CHAPTER SEVEN

IT WAS A quarter past eight and nearly dusk. I considered grabbing some dinner before finding an appropriate lurking spot, but decided my stomach was too jumpy. Besides, I'd had that enormous lunch with Ronan, then ice cream. That would hold me a while yet.

Music poured from the upper level bars on either side; maybe a drink would calm my nerves a bit. I started up the stairs to Iguana Joe's, then changed my mind. If Bebe or her friends were there again, one of them might call me by name—and who knew where my stalker was right now?

I went back down to the pavement and across the square to another bar instead, pausing before entering to make sure I didn't recognize anyone inside. That's what a real undercover agent would do, right?

Twenty minutes later, I was sipping a frozen margarita, pretending to be cool and sophisticated, when a touch on my shoulder made me drop my glass. Luckily it was plastic, so instead of breaking it just bounced noisily, splattering my legs with most of my drink. Now I'd be sticky for my stakeout. Great.

"Oh, man, I'm sorry! I'll buy you another one." It was Rick, looking very young, very earnest and very drunk. So much for me acting like a real undercover agent.

"That's okay. I didn't really need it." A definite understatement.

"No, no, really, let me get you another drink. What was it?" He squinted down at the green plastic glass on the floor.

"Please, Rick, don't worry about it." I glanced at my watch: twenty till nine. "I need to be going anyway."

Rick nodded vigorously. "I was about to leave, too. I'll come with you. Since I owe you a drink, maybe I can buy you one later on."

I wasn't sure if the idea of Rick "helping" me on my stakeout was more hilarious or terrifying. "Thanks, but I'm meeting someone. I'll take a rain check."

"Rain check. Yeah," he said vaguely, following me out of the bar. "So, where are you meeting this person? Is it a guy?"

Since I needed to get rid of him quickly, I wasn't above lying. "Yes, it's a guy, and we're going to want to be *alone*."

Comprehension dawned gradually in his bleared eyes. "Oh. Oh! So it's like a date? I guess that's cool." He took a step back and looked me over. "I guess you are kind of hot for...well..."

"Someone old enough to be your mother?" I suggested, not even trying to hide my amusement. "Thanks, I think."

"Nah, no way you could be my mother. I didn't mean—"

"It's okay, Rick. Really. But I do need to go." It was a quarter to nine, and I still had to find a good lurking spot.

"So, what are you two up to?" came a familiar voice, and I turned to see Ronan approaching us. Perfect. Just perfect.

Rick answered before I could. "I'm off to Pepe & Pete's, but Wynne has a hot date."

Ronan's brows rose as he looked to me for confirmation.

*Thanks, Rick.*

"It's not—That is—Okay, fine, yeah, I have a hot date." What else could I say at this point? I wasn't about to launch into an explanation in front of Rick, and I really needed to get over to the Cartier store.

"Do you, then?" Ronan was smiling, one brow still raised. Somehow his skepticism irritated me much more than Rick's had.

"I do. With a gorgeous, impatient gentleman. Now, if you two will excuse me?"

"C'mon, Ronan," Rick said. "We can meet everyone else at Pepe & Pete's. It'll be fun. Maybe you can join us later, Wynne?"

I had no desire for another uncomfortable hour at that teen/twenties hangout, but to get rid of them I said, "Maybe."

"If you don't get a better offer?" Ronan asked with a wink. I wondered how much he suspected.

"Exactly. Have fun, guys!" With a cheery wave, I headed across the square, in the opposite direction from Pepe & Pete's, resisting the urge to glance over my shoulder.

I didn't go directly to the Cartier store, of course, but I kept my eye on it as I aimed for another shop two doors down. There appeared to be only one customer inside the Cartier Boutique at the moment, a man. I didn't see anyone obviously loitering nearby. Just a lot of tourists wandering and shopping and chatting to each other.

I went into the souvenir shop I'd targeted and pretended to browse the postcards near the front while I watched the area around the jewelry store. After a couple of minutes, though, I started to feel conspicuous—and I couldn't very well whip out my phone here at the postcard rack and start snapping shots of people. I needed a better vantage point.

Leaving the shop, I glanced around. Unfortunately, the clock tower was too far away and in the wrong direction for me to pretend to take pictures of that while focusing on the Cartier store. What else was around? About a dozen other jewelry stores, interspersed with an upscale clothing boutique and this souvenir shop. Hmm.

Lacking any better idea, I dug my phone out of my purse and

took a picture or two of the square, first looking east and then west. There was a big planter full of flowers nearby, so I went over to that and pretended to take close-up shots of individual blooms, as I'd seen photographers do in public gardens. Okay, so I probably looked like an idiot using my phone's flash instead of waiting for daylight, but it was better than nothing as a cover.

I worked my way around the planter until I was facing the Cartier Boutique, then crouched down like I wanted to get a super close shot and peered through the flowers. Still no one who looked like—

Wait!

Leaning casually against the corner of a stairway across from the store, a tall woman in a floppy hat was watching the entrance to the Cartier store. Her hair was pulled back, its color indeterminate at this distance, especially since the only light came from the stores across the square.

A few yards away from her, a dark-haired man in a black shirt was also watching the jewelry store. I didn't have a good view of his face, but from his profile I guessed him to be young and handsome. Were they together? It was impossible to tell for sure.

Still crouched, my heart pounding, I pointed my phone's camera through the flowers and zoomed all the way in. Even in the dim light, I thought that woman looked a lot like Melanie Melampus. I toggled off the flash and snapped half a dozen pictures of her, and a couple of the man, for good measure, before my knees started to seize up.

"Stupid knees," I muttered. Sometimes getting old really sucked.

Turning half away from the woman, just in case she did know what I looked like, I rose painfully to my feet, using the edge of the cement planter for assistance. I took a couple of hobbling steps, then, trying to look casual, snapped a few random shots of the square, not focusing on anything in particular.

After a minute or two, I slipped my phone into my purse and

headed back toward the souvenir shop, nonchalantly glancing in the woman's direction. She was gone. I swallowed, trying not to panic as I furtively scanned the thinning crowd around the square, then checked the Cartier store.

The lights were dimmed, and the man I'd spoken with earlier was just locking the door. The woman who looked like Melanie Melampus was nowhere in sight. According to my watch, it was now a quarter past nine, so I could only assume she'd given up on accosting me, or whatever she'd planned for tonight.

I wondered what her next move might be, half wishing I'd found a way to tell Ronan about my suspicions. Suddenly nervous about being alone here in the square, where no one would have any incentive to help me should I need it, I turned and walked quickly back to Royal Plaza and the main road.

Back at the corner where the cab had dropped me earlier, I briefly debated joining my fellow divers at Pepe & Pete's. At least I'd be with people who knew me. But it would be tantamount to an admission to both Rick and Ronan that I hadn't had a hot date after all. Pride won out over fear, and I stepped to the curb to hail the next taxi.

Before one came, however, I saw Ronan crossing the street toward me. He waved, and I waved back, trying to think up a plausible reason my "date" had been cut so short.

"I'm glad I caught you," he said before I could stammer out an excuse about my escort's ailing mother. "Any chance, now that young Rick is safely partying with his chums, you'll tell me what's really going on?"

I stared at him. "You mean—?"

"You were just a little too eager to get away from us earlier, and it wasn't the eagerness of a woman headed to meet a 'gorgeous, impatient gentleman.' Not that you couldn't snag one if you wanted to, of course," he added quickly.

"Thanks," I said sourly. "My ego feels so much better now."

"So?" he prompted.

Everything he'd told me that afternoon had turned out to be true, so I shrugged and described the odd phone message I'd received and the plan I'd concocted—though I left out the part about taking pictures. Until I had those photos safely printed and/or e-mailed off-island, I wasn't telling anyone about those.

"And sure enough," I concluded, "there was a woman loitering near the store that looked amazingly like the pictures I found online of Melanie Melampus."

"Really? Where is she now?" he demanded, looking back over my shoulder toward the square. "Do you think she saw you?"

I was a little startled by his intensity. "I don't think so," I said. "How would she know what I looked like? Anyway, she disappeared once the store closed. I, um, didn't see which way she went." He didn't need to know about my creaky knees.

For a moment I actually thought he was going to charge after her himself, but then he relaxed and smiled. "The important thing is that you're safe. Of course, if there's any chance Melanie Melampus really is alive, it would be useful to verify it."

"You don't believe me?"

"I definitely believe you believe you saw someone who looked like her. But sometimes we can see what we expect to see. The mind is a tricky thing. If only..."

I opened my mouth to tell him about the pictures, but again I stopped myself. Not yet. Not just yet. "I can tell you what she was wearing, if you want to go look for her," I said instead. "But there was a guy—well, I'm not sure, but he might have been with her. I didn't see them speak to each other, so I can't be positive."

"A guy?" His attention sharpened again. "What did he look like?"

"Young, I think. Tall, dark—the light wasn't great, and he wasn't facing me. Anyway, the woman was wearing an electric blue sundress that looked designer, really cute tan shoes with blue heels, and a big hat. He was in khakis and an open-collar black shirt. Very European."

Ronan nodded, clearly thinking hard. "Do you think you can get back to the hotel safely on your own? Or were you on your way to Pepe & Pete's?"

"Definitely not Pepe & Pete's. I was going to catch a cab back and order something up from room service. I've had enough excitement for one night." It was true. Now that I felt safe again, I also felt drained.

"Sounds like a plan. Here's a cab now."

He flagged it down for me, then helped me inside, even telling the driver which hotel to take me to. Normally I'd have protested, but by now I was feeling fragile enough to appreciate it—not that I'd ever been at any real risk, I reminded myself.

I glanced back as the taxi pulled away from the curb and saw Ronan heading in the direction I'd come from. I wondered if he'd find my stalker—and whether I should hope he did or he didn't. His safety mattered more to me than it should.

When I reached the hotel fifteen minutes later, I went straight to the hotel's business center, but it was closed for the evening. I hoped that wasn't a bad omen.

Nervous again, though I had no real reason to be, I hurried up to my room and did exactly what I'd told Ronan I was going to do —after securing the deadbolt on the door and searching every inch of the suite.

I ordered room service, and then my cell phone rang, making me jump. But it was just Bess, calling to tell me she was now a professional actress—she'd been offered a position in the dinner theater's troupe.

"It's only part-time, of course—most of the others have regular nine-to-five jobs—but what a great resume builder! And it will be fun, too."

Her infectious enthusiasm made me smile. "Congratulations, sweetie! That's wonderful." At some point I'd have to find a diplomatic way to suggest that *she* consider a "nine-to-five job," something with benefits. But not while she was in celebration mode.

"Do you...do you think I should tell Dad?" she asked then.

I nearly told her not to bother, that he wouldn't care, but I stopped myself in time. I'd tried very hard not to bad-mouth Tom to the girls during our separation and divorce, hard as it had been at times. I wasn't going to start now. Besides, if what Mom had said was true, he might eventually be interested in reestablishing his relationship with the girls.

"Sure, why not? I think he'd get a kick out of it. He might even come to see you perform."

She laughed, and I was startled to hear an edge to it. Bess was my idealist, after all. "Right. He's going to pay money to see me when he couldn't find time for any of my free school concerts or plays? But I guess I'll tell him anyway. You have a fabulous time with the rest of your vacation, okay, Mom?"

"Okay." I hoped that didn't count as a promise, since the way things were going, I couldn't exactly guarantee it. "I'll call you when I get back. Meanwhile, get together with Deb and celebrate or something."

"We will. Love you, Mom."

I clicked off still smiling, but almost immediately my earlier worries came crowding back. I couldn't help wishing I'd never found that blasted ring—or at least that I hadn't felt morally bound to try to find its owner. I could have simply enjoyed the last week of my vacation, my biggest worry whether I'd get a sunburn.

Instead, I was frightened for my safety and wondering if I'd stumbled into something way, way over my head.

When my dinner arrived a few minutes later, I made sure to check the peephole and deadbolted the door again the moment I'd tipped the server. Even with those precautions, when I went to bed —almost immediately after eating—I slept with my phone and the ring under the pillow next to me.

. . .

AS IT HAPPENED, no one attempted to molest me in the night, so as soon as I was dressed the next morning, I went back down to the business center, phone in hand and ring in pocket.

It wasn't cheap, but half an hour later I had prints of the pictures I'd taken last night. Because of the low light, they were grainy, but the woman still looked like she could be Melanie Melampus.

After some trial and error—mostly error—I then managed to attach the pictures to an e-mail. I sent it to my personal account, and, for good measure, to each of my daughters, with a note asking them to hang on to them for now and that I'd explain when I got home.

Breathing easier, I bought a package of bright blue 8 x 10 envelopes—the only color they had—and put the prints into one and headed for the elevators. Now, what I should do with them? Show them to Ronan, certainly, assuming he contacted me again, but what then?

Thinking of Ronan reminded me of his suggestion yesterday, the one I'd regretted forgetting last night. I stopped and reversed my course, going back to the hotel's front desk.

"Yes, ma'am?"

"I have something I'd like to put in the hotel safe," I told the girl at the counter.

To my surprise, she looked distressed. "I'm afraid that won't be possible until this afternoon, or possibly tomorrow morning, ma'am."

"It won't? Why?"

Now she looked embarrassed as well. "The safe was, er, damaged overnight. We expect to have it repaired very soon, however."

A tiny little chill ran up my spine. "Damaged? Do you mean someone broke into it?"

She glanced over her shoulder. "I'm not— That is, I don't actually—"

"It's all right. I won't tell the manager you told me. I'll just use my room safe for now. Thanks."

I walked slowly back toward the elevators, wondering if there was any possible way this could be mere coincidence. First my room, and now the hotel safe. A mini-crime wave at the Royal Aruban? Or something more personal?

Had my stalker come here after her ambush failed? Or maybe it was her accomplice, assuming she and that man in the black shirt *had* been together. It seemed like a plausible theory, anyway.

Not until the elevator doors opened at the fourteenth floor did it occur to me that Ronan also had good reason to believe the ring would be in the hotel safe last night.

# CHAPTER EIGHT

I REALLY, REALLY didn't want to believe it. Ronan was the closest thing I had to a friend here in Aruba. Okay, and I was more than a little attracted to him. But much as I wanted to, I couldn't ignore the possibility that he'd broken into the hotel safe.

Ronan was the one who had insisted I put the ring there. And he *had* shown an unusual degree of interest in the ring—and in the woman I'd seen last night. Could he be working with her?

But why tell me so much about the Melampus case—all of which turned out to be true—if he was planning to steal the ring from me anyway? That didn't make sense, either.

Though I almost managed to convince myself of Ronan's innocence with all that rationalization, I retained enough common sense to hang on to a shred of suspicion. Where did that leave me?

Ronan had advised against calling the police, but now I had to question everything he'd told me. Still, I doubted the local authorities would do anything, since I had no evidence of a crime committed here in Aruba.

In fact, all I had at this point were theories and circumstantial evidence, in the form of the ring.

And photos.

I looked down at the envelope in my hand. No one knew about these yet, but maybe I could make use of them somehow. First, though, some safeguards.

I slid the photos out of the envelope and spread them on the bed. I'd made three prints each of the four best shots, which gave me twelve pieces of "evidence" to play with.

Two I put into my room safe, even though I knew that wasn't necessarily secure. Still, it was something. Two more I tucked into the Gideon Bible in my nightstand, leaving me with two complete sets. I put them into two separate envelopes, stuck both envelopes in my purse, and headed back downstairs.

This time I had to wait for a computer in the business center. While I stood there, trying not to be conspicuous, I felt like those blue envelopes in my purse were sending out alert signals. I kept glancing over my shoulder, which probably made me a lot more conspicuous than I'd have been if I weren't so worried about being conspicuous.

Five eternal minutes later, a computer opened up, and I was able to log on. I managed to find again one of the articles I'd read yesterday about the Melampus case. Yes, there it was: "Anyone with information is requested to contact Agent Frank Truman at the Federal Bureau of Investigation," followed by a phone number and an e-mail address.

Opening a new e-mail window, I typed, "Dear Agent Truman, I am vacationing in Aruba and have found something that may be evidence in the Melampus murder case. Please e-mail or call to advise me what my next step should be." I concluded with my name, cell phone number, and e-mail address, then sent it before I could change my mind.

Realizing that it could be hours or even days before I heard anything back, I logged off and went to the hotel's front desk again. The same girl I'd spoken with earlier came over to help me, looking a bit wary.

"I know I can't use the safe right now, but would it be possible to leave an envelope here at the desk that I can pick up later?"

"Oh, of course," she replied, her expression clearing. "Just write your name and room number on the outside, and I can put it in a locked drawer until you call for it."

"Perfect." I pulled one of the blue 8 x 10 envelopes out of my purse, sealed it, jotted the requisite info on the back, and handed it to her. "Thanks."

Feeling more than a little proud of myself for mapping out such a logical plan, I moved on to the next step, which involved visiting the hotel gift shop.

I looked over their selection of chains and realized cheap surgical steel would be stronger than solid gold or silver. Darn it. I bought the sturdiest-looking one they had. As soon as I was out of sight of anyone, I took the ring out of my pocket, slipped it onto the chain, fastened it around my neck, and tucked the ring inside my shirt. No one was likely to look for anything valuable there.

It suddenly occurred to me that I hadn't had breakfast yet. I headed for the hotel dining room to check out the buffet only to discover Ronan loitering near the entrance.

"I didn't know you were staying at the Royal Aruban," I said in greeting, mainly to keep myself from blurting out a question or an accusation that I might regret.

He smiled his slow smile. "I'm not. When you didn't answer your room phone, I thought this might be the best place to wait."

Great. The man had known me two days, and already he associated me with food. I couldn't deny I was hungry, though, so I shrugged—mostly mentally—and continued forward.

"Good guess. Since I did room service for dinner last night, I felt like a real breakfast this morning. Care to join me?"

"I was hoping you'd ask."

He put a hand on my elbow as we approached the hostess, and at the warm tingle of his touch, I sternly reminded myself that I had reason to suspect this man of worse than attempted seduction.

"Two?" asked the hostess.

At Ronan's nod, she led us to a small table near the windows overlooking the beach. A beautiful, romantic setting. No doubt she thought we were vacationing together—anniversary or honeymoon. I stifled the bubble of hysterical laughter that rose unexpectedly to my throat. What was wrong with me?

"So, any luck finding your quarry last night?" I asked once a server had poured coffee and left us to make our own way to the buffet.

Amusement twinkled in his eyes, probably at my discreet phrasing. "Not a sign of either of them. Everything quiet here?"

I nodded, waited a beat, then said, "Except that the hotel safe was robbed in the night. I just found out a few minutes ago."

"Robbed?" His surprise and concern *seemed* genuine. "Then the ring—?"

"I still have it. I, um, forgot to put it in the safe yesterday. Luckily, as it turns out. It was when I remembered to do it this morning that I found out what had happened." I started to touch my new chain, but then changed my mind and dropped my hand back to my lap.

"I guess your room safe will have to do, then, if the hotel safe isn't, er, safe," he said. "No more calls, I take it?"

"Not yet." I wasn't going to tell him about my e-mail to the FBI until I was sure I could trust him. Besides, they might assume I was a crank and never get back to me.

On that thought, my cell phone rang, startling me badly. I tried to think quickly. "This is probably one of my daughters. Why don't you go on to the buffet? This should only take a minute."

"Sure." He rose as I fumbled in my purse for the phone and headed away from me.

Other diners were starting to shoot me dirty looks as it rang a second time, then a third as I finally pulled it out. I didn't recognize the number displayed on the screen, so I jumped up and scurried out of the restaurant as I answered it.

"Hello?" I said the moment I was out in the lobby, my voice as breathless as if I'd been running.

"Ms. Seally?" came an unfamiliar male voice. "This is Boyd Walters with the Federal Bureau of Investigation. I'm calling about an e-mail you sent to Frank Truman, my partner in the Melampus case. We'd like to know what sort of evidence you believe you've discovered."

Wow, these guys sure didn't go in for the small talk, did they? But then I remembered the bogus call that had claimed to be from the jewelry store.

"Um, is Agent Truman not available?" Even as I asked, I realized that an imposter would have claimed to be Frank Truman himself, and I'd never have known the difference.

"He lets me screen out the crackpots. If it sounds like you have something, I'll let him know."

I guessed that made sense. They probably got all kinds of weirdos claiming to have had dreams or sightings or theories that never panned out.

I scanned the area around me to make sure I couldn't be over-heard before saying, "I found a ring while diving that appears to be one Melanie Melampus was wearing when she disappeared." I described it in detail.

"You found this in Aruba?" He sounded frankly skeptical. "You do know that Melanie Melampus's murder—ah, alleged murder—took place less than a mile offshore from Miami, don't you?"

"Yes, I read up on the case after I found the ring," I told him, seeing no reason to mention Ronan—yet. "But that's not all..." I craned my neck and could see Ronan returning from the buffet. "Look, can I call you back? I'm in the middle of breakfast right now and don't have much privacy."

"All right. You can call this number or Frank's cell." He gave me the number, and I jotted it down on a scrap of paper I dug out of my purse. "Meanwhile, I'll look up the ring you mentioned."

He hung up without a word of thanks. Nice. I hurried back to the table just as Ronan reached it.

"So, everything okay at home?" he asked, setting down two plates heaped with eggs, waffles, fruit, and pastries, one in front of me. "I didn't know what you liked," he explained, with a shrug and a grin.

I was touched, in spite of my lingering suspicion about his motives. "Wow, you didn't have to do that—I could have gone myself. But it all looks delicious, thanks. And yes, things are fine at home."

"Glad to hear it. I take it your daughters are staying with their father while you're here?"

"Um, no. These waffles are divine," I said then, mainly to change the subject. I had no business eating waffles, but I wasn't ready to give him more details about my family...or my age.

"Yeah, they're not bad."

He accepted my change of subject, probably thinking I didn't want to discuss my ex. He didn't mention the ring again while we ate, either, instead telling a couple of amusing stories about past dives.

"—then he completely refused to swim through the tunnel," he was saying as the server left the check. "We ended up using the rest of our bottom time going around it, when the swim-through was the whole point of the dive."

He was a good storyteller, and I chuckled despite my preoccupation—and the fact that his story hit a little close to home, since I'd probably be just as cowardly as his friend, in the same situation.

"Isn't it dangerous to swim through something like that?" I asked. "What if you got stuck?"

Ronan smiled at my inexperience. "In an unfamiliar area, that would be true. But this was a well-known site. Dozens of divers a day go through that particular tunnel, and I've never heard of one getting stuck. He was just claustrophobic and wouldn't admit it."

My sympathies were still with his hapless friend, but I didn't say so. I charged the meal to my room, and Ronan handed me a twenty, which more than covered his share plus the tip. I protested, but he waved my argument away, and we headed for the exit.

Before he could disappear, maybe for good, my curiosity overwhelmed my common sense. "Ronan, you didn't have anything to do with breaking into the hotel safe, did you?" I blurted out, then immediately wished I hadn't.

He looked surprised, then thoughtful. "So that's the way your mind's been working, is it? Since I'm the one who suggested you keep the ring there, I can see why you'd think that. But no." He swept the lobby area with a glance, then he turned back to me. "What do you say we take a walk on the beach?"

When I hesitated, he tilted his head to look into my eyes. "It's broad daylight, Wynne. What is it you think I might do?"

Feeling foolish, I nodded. "Sure. A walk on the beach will be fine. Do you mind if I run up to my room for a hat first?"

"Take your time. I'll be here."

It took less than five minutes to ride the elevator up, race to my room, slather sunscreen on my face and arms, grab my beach hat and sunglasses, and ride back down to the lobby.

"Okay," I said breathlessly when I reached him. That was starting to become my theme for the day, being breathless. "Let's go."

He accompanied me silently through the lobby, across the landscaped pool and patio area, and down to the sand. Once we were alone, walking parallel to the gently breaking surf with our backs to the wind, he said, "To answer your earlier question, my guess is that whoever tried to break into the hotel safe is the same one who tried to lure you to the jewelry store last night. Doesn't that make more sense than me doing it?"

It did, of course, but I had other questions. "I suppose so, but I've been thinking over everything you told me yesterday, and it seems like you're way more into this Melampus case than the average news junkie. For example, how *did* you know where to find that information about the ring? I've worked in insurance myself, and I don't have a clue how to do that."

Rather to my surprise, he grinned. "You're sharp, I'll give you that. I know because I was involved in the case a few months ago."

In spite of the hot Aruban sun, I felt like someone had poured cold water down my back.

"Involved?" I squeaked, abruptly remembering that I knew absolutely nothing about this man, except that he was from Miami and I found him attractive. I increased the distance between us as we walked. "In a murder?"

"An alleged murder," he corrected me. "And I said I was involved in the *case*, not the crime."

My heart rate slowed, making me aware only then that it had accelerated. "Then you're a cop? I thought you said you were in insurance."

He was still grinning, which made me feel like I was missing something. "Not a cop, no. I work as an investigator for various insurance companies."

Finally, I thought I understood. "And insurance companies don't like to pay out when there are unanswered questions. So you... answer the questions for them?" I couldn't suppress a surge of relief that there was such a logical explanation for Ronan's interest in the case—and his expertise.

"Usually. I have a good record, but in the Melampus case I drew a blank. I couldn't come up with anything better than a gut feeling that Stefan Melampus was telling the truth when he said he didn't kill his wife. Until you found that ring."

Acutely aware of the ring under my shirt, I had to resist an urge to pull it out. Instead, I said, "And then there's my sighting of Melanie herself last night. That should get the insurance company off the hook completely."

"Definitely—if we had proof. The ring, at least, is something concrete I can show them."

I frowned, but I didn't want to argue about what I had or hadn't seen. "Do you really think the ring alone can prove that Melanie Melampus wasn't murdered?"

"No. Ah, look, have you seen those kite surfers yet?" He nodded toward the water, where several young men on surfboards were harnessed to big, colorful kites, using the wind to "fly" for short distances above the waves.

It was an impressive sight, so we stopped to watch them for a minute or two, but I refused to be distracted completely until I got to the bottom of this. "If it can't prove anything, why is the ring so important?" I asked, turning to head back to the hotel.

He smiled at my persistence. "It can provide reasonable doubt, maybe enough to clear Melampus of a murder charge."

"Okay. But if Stefan Melampus is some kind of mob boss, why are you trying to clear him?"

"Nothing's ever been proven." I thought he sounded defensive. "Anyway, my main objective is to protect the insurance company's interests. I'm hoping that your finding that ring here in Aruba will do just that. If it also happens to clear Melampus, that's purely incidental."

I thought for a moment. "But...if Mr. Melampus was suspected of his wife's murder, the insurance company wouldn't pay out anyway. I assume he's her primary beneficiary?"

Ronan's brows rose with respect, but I wasn't in a mood to preen. "You'd think so, but no. The beneficiary is another relative of Melanie's—a sister. Another thing that made me suspicious from the start."

"That's not suspicious in itself," I argued, remembering some of the clients Tom and I had handled. "Especially if there was a lot of money brought into the marriage on either side. Or did the policy pre-date the wedding? That would also explain it."

"No, that's what makes it odd. Melanie took out the policy herself, apparently without her husband's knowledge—only two months before she disappeared."

"Okay, I admit that *could* be suspicious, if only because of the timing. Have you talked to the sister?"

He shook his head. "I generally come in at the other end of things, recovering whatever was insured or, in a case like this, figuring out what happened. I'm not involved in any eventual payout. I just try to keep that from happening, if it shouldn't."

"Figuring out what happened? Shouldn't that be the police's job?"

"Aye, it should, yeah. But their interests don't always jibe with the insurance company's, which is what I'm paid to protect. Plus, I don't necessarily...um, have the same restrictions the police do in an investigation."

My brows went up. "Oh, I get it. Like in *The Thomas Crown Affair*?"

"I've never had a case quite that, er, interesting, but that's the general idea."

If his guess turned out to be correct, *this* case might become as interesting—if not as romantic. It was that last caveat that kept me from saying so out loud. Instead, I dug into my purse.

"I have something to show you," I said, pulling out the envelope with the pictures and handing it to him.

Ronan shot me one curious glance, then opened the envelope. His eyes widened, and he gave a low whistle. "Why didn't you tell me last night you'd taken pictures?"

"I wanted to take a good look at them first," I hedged. "You seemed pretty skeptical that I could possibly have seen Melanie. I wanted to make sure I really did have proof."

He frowned thoughtfully at the pictures. "The light sucks, but it does look like it could be her. Have you shown these to anyone else?"

"Not yet. But shouldn't I make them public, or at least give them to the authorities? Maybe if I do that, the ring won't matter so much to whoever's been trying to get it." And I wouldn't be at risk anymore.

Ronan shrugged, still staring thoughtfully at the pictures. "That does make some sense, I suppose," he said, almost absently.

I realized I still hadn't told him about the FBI. Now that I knew his interest in the case was legitimate, I might as well, though I suspected he might not be pleased.

Before I could think of a diplomatic way to explain, he asked, "Do you mind if I borrow these for a few hours before you do anything else with them?"

My suspicions, so recently laid to rest, suddenly twitched. "Why?"

He only hesitated for a moment before answering. "I thought I'd scan them and send them to the insurance company. I'm hoping they'll consider them proof enough to cut me a check."

So he was a mercenary after all. My cynicism startled me, though it shouldn't have. My divorce, and all that led up to it, had effectively destroyed my old rose-colored glasses. At least his reason made non-sinister sense.

"Um, sure, I guess that would be fine. I've got several other sets." It seemed important that he know that, more important than telling him about the FBI right this moment.

"Will it matter that you didn't take the pictures yourself?" I asked then, genuinely curious.

He grinned. "Not if they don't know that."

Clearly my cynicism hadn't been misplaced. "I won't tell them. But I may have to tell the authorities...at some point."

"I suppose," he said with a philosophical shrug. "But with any luck, I'll have my money by then. I'll get these back to you by this evening, Wynne."

"That'll be fine. You can call my room or just leave them at the desk."

I didn't want him to think I was overly eager to see him again—though I had to admit I was, now that I knew he wasn't a threat.

Not to my physical safety, anyway.

## CHAPTER NINE

WE PARTED when we reached the hotel, and I went up to my room. The housekeeper hadn't come yet, so rather than risk interruption, I hung the "Do Not Disturb" sign on the door. I more than half regretted contacting the FBI, but since I said I'd call back, I figured I'd better do so.

I decided to try Frank Truman's cell instead of calling Boyd Walters back. I hadn't liked Walters's attitude—or his manners.

"Agent Truman, this is Wynne Seally," I said when he answered.

"Right. My partner said you'd be calling. You found a ring in Aruba that you believe might have relevance to the Melampus case, is that right?"

This guy didn't go in for pleasantries either. Maybe it was part of the FBI training. I liked his voice better than Walters's though: cultured, mellow, and a little bit southern.

"Yes, that's right. I found it while diving two days ago." Was it really only two days? So much had happened since then.

"And what makes you believe this ring belonged to Melanie Melampus?"

"It's inscribed with 'Stefan & Melanie, 2008,' for one thing." I'd already told his partner that. Didn't these guys communicate? Or was this some kind of test?

"So just two first names and a year."

"And a Cartier hallmark." My voice was getting just a teensy bit sharp.

"I see." His held no inflection whatsoever.

"Wouldn't Melanie Melampus's ring be important evidence in this case, especially since I found it so far from where she disappeared?" I prodded.

"It could be." Now it sounded like he was humoring me. "*If* we had proof that it was her ring, and *if* we had proof that she was wearing it when she disappeared."

I exhaled noisily. "Didn't Agent Walters's research turn up anything on the ring? It should have been listed among her missing effects, for insurance purposes if nothing else."

"How would you know that?" Skepticism had abruptly been replaced by suspicion. "What's your connection to this case, Ms. Seally?"

"None at all." I didn't want to bring Ronan's name into this without warning him first. "I found a ring. I'm just trying to do the right thing here—but you guys are making it awfully hard."

"Fine, fine. I'm sorry. You told Agent Walters that it's a platinum and diamond wedding band, correct? And the date on the inscription is the year of the Melampus's wedding. Anything else?"

"Yes. Last night I saw Melanie Melampus herself, here in Aruba, right in downtown Oranjestad."

Smugly, I waited for him to respond. Let him discount *that*.

"You might be interested to know, Ms. Seally, that we've been averaging two or three Melanie sightings a week since this case first appeared in the media."

"Oh." My bubble of triumph popped. "But—" Should I mention the pictures? Or would that be breaking my promise to Ronan?

"But I'd never even heard of Melanie Melampus until I found

this ring," I finished lamely. "Isn't it a pretty big coincidence that a look-alike and the ring would both turn up in Aruba?"

He coughed, then said, "I tell you what, Ms. Seally. Once you get back to the States, give me a call, and I'll send someone to get a statement and the ring. If it checks out, we'll tag it as evidence and get a formal deposition from you."

Suddenly I remembered what Ronan had said about the authorities: that they might have reason to discount—or destroy—any evidence that would damage their case.

"How about this instead? Talk to the folks at the Cartier store here. They have the registry number, which should get you a complete description, original purchaser, everything. If it turns out this *is* Melanie Melampus's ring, get back to me. Thanks for your time, Agent Truman."

I hung up, trembling slightly with a combination of humiliation and righteous indignation. He obviously thought I was some crackpot or publicity-seeker. Seemed it was true that no good deed goes unpunished. Shoot, if I *had* mentioned the photos, or even e-mailed them, they'd probably claim I'd faked them.

Belatedly, I thought to use some of the calming techniques I'd learned during my recent divorce proceedings, when I'd often felt much the same as I did right now: disrespected, patronized, marginalized. Lied to.

Breathing slowly, in through my nose, out through my mouth, I counted to fifty, ending with a quick serenity prayer. That was better.

What I needed now was some real downtime, stretched out by the pool. I changed to my swimsuit and slathered myself with sunscreen. A glance at the bathroom mirror had me regretting those waffles at breakfast. I tugged at the bottom of my suit in a vain effort to achieve a sleek line. No dice. I didn't look bad for my age, but I was never going to look twenty again. Or even thirty.

Tearing my gaze away from my thighs, I noticed the ring, hanging blatantly between my breasts. That wouldn't do. I took it off its chain and tested it on my fingers. It fit almost perfectly on my right ring finger, so I left it there.

Turning resolutely away from the mirror, I stuck a book and my phone into my beach bag and opened the door, remembering to remove the "Do Not Disturb" sign. I passed the housekeeper on my way to the elevator. With any luck she'd be done with my room by the time I needed a break from the sun, and I could get a nap later.

IT WAS NICE to come to the pool with no lessons to face. I found a lounge chair in the shade, picked up my book and settled back, determined to relax until lunchtime. There was a nice breeze ruffling the palm branches overhead, I could hear the surf in the background and children in the pool in the foreground. A server was making her way around the pool, taking drink orders. Nice.

Three paragraphs into my book, my phone rang, shattering my hard-won calm.

"Hello?"

"Ms. Seally? This is Boyd Walters. We spoke earlier."

"Yes. I just got off the phone with your partner, Agent Truman." Honestly, didn't these guys talk to each other?

"I know. He briefed me on your conversation."

Oh.

"I had a few more questions," he continued. "This ring you found—have you shown it to anyone else?"

That seemed like an odd question—as odd as when Ronan had asked me the same thing about the photos. "Why?"

"This has been a rather, ah, sensitive case. If the ring should turn out to be important, we wouldn't want to compromise the investigation by having too much information in the media too soon."

"You mean, information suggesting that Melanie Melampus was never murdered at all?"

There was an exasperated sigh on the other end of the line.

"Listen, Ms. Seally, Frank told me what you thought you saw, but I was at the crime scene myself. Believe me, no one could lose that much blood and still be alive. We have a ton of circumstantial evidence pointing to the fact that Stefan Melampus killed his wife and dumped her overboard less than a mile from Miami."

"But no body."

"But no body. Which is why every other bit of evidence, every witness, is so important to this case. If we miss anything, mishandle anything, or let the press get too wild with the theories, Melampus could walk."

I knew it would sound naive, but I had to ask. "Shouldn't he, if he's innocent?"

"Innocent?" He made a disgusting noise that sounded like he'd spat. I was glad he was a couple thousand miles away from me. "There ain't nothing innocent about Stefan Melampus, Ms. Seally, believe me. The crimes he and his so-called companies have committed over the years would curl your hair."

"Then why wasn't he already in jail before this incident?" I wasn't really that stupid, but I wanted to hear his explanation.

"As you probably know if you've ever followed the news, Stefan Melampus is a very rich man with connections out the wazoo. A guy like that, well, he's like Teflon. Nothing ever seems to stick to him. No matter how dead-to-rights we think we have him, someone somewhere pulls a string and presto! The case unravels. But not this time."

"Because the case is so ironclad, or because no one's pulling strings?"

He hesitated, then said, "Maybe both."

Remembering what I'd read about Melampus, I hazarded a guess. "His former cronies won't help him this time because he's turned over a new leaf, is that it? They see him as a traitor?"

"I really can't get into the details of the case," he replied, suddenly laughably prim. "I'd just like to ask you not to talk to anyone about what you've found, what you think you've seen, or what you may suspect, until I or another agent can question you face to face."

"Someone's coming here? To Aruba?" That was a surprise. I guess they hadn't written me off as a crackpot after all.

"Possibly. Or we may just have you send your evidence to our office, if we determine it's important to the case."

That definitely wasn't going to happen. I didn't trust this guy at all, even if he wasn't quite as dismissive as Agent Truman had been. "So you still haven't checked out the ring?"

"Frank's looking into it now. Just keep a lid on it until you hear from us, Ms. Seally."

He hung up before I could tell him that a whole boatful of people, as well as the clerk at the Cartier Boutique, had already seen the ring. Ah, well. That was water under the bridge now. I couldn't undo it.

And the more I thought about it, I didn't see why I should want to. Whatever else Stefan Melampus might be guilty of, I was pretty sure he was *not* guilty of his wife's murder. Whether I'd really seen what I thought I'd seen, whether the Feds believed me or not, Melanie's ring was definitely here in Aruba.

Plus, there'd been that weird phone call, which had very likely come from either Melanie herself or someone connected with her disappearance. Which might mean that Boyd Walters and Frank Truman weren't the only ones determined to see Stefan Melampus convicted of a crime he hadn't committed.

For the first time, I considered what Melanie Melampus's role in all this might be, if she really was still alive. If there was a "ton of circumstantial evidence," as Walters had claimed, the obvious person to have planted it was Melanie. Which must mean she wanted her husband found guilty as well.

And from what both Ronan and Walters had said, there were plenty of other people out there who'd be happy to see Stefan Melampus convicted—or dead. The man certainly seemed to have no lack of enemies. Maybe I was being naive—or just stubborn—to want justice in a case like this. But if Melampus was convicted of a crime he hadn't committed, that would mean whoever *was* guilty went free.

Shouldn't the FBI care about that? Shouldn't someone? Even Ronan seemed primarily concerned about his own profit. He'd already demonstrated that he was willing to bend the truth, if necessary, to that end. As long as he got his money, I wasn't sure he really cared what happened to Stefan Melampus—who, if the news reports were correct, had now repented of his former lifestyle.

I stared out at the pool, feeling more alone than ever. Wasn't there anyone else, anywhere, who wanted the truth—the real truth —to come to light?

My phone rang again, and I sighed, not really feeling up to another sparring session with the FBI, or even the day-to-day problems of my mother or daughters. But when I glanced at the screen, the number was unfamiliar.

"Hello?"

"Wynne Seally?" The man's voice was unfamiliar as well, but as smooth as port wine and dark chocolate.

"Yes?"

"This is Stefan Melampus. I understand you've found something that might be of great benefit to me."

## CHAPTER TEN

BEYOND FLABBERGASTED that he had called me himself, I tightened my grip on the phone and tried to make my voice work.

"Um, yes, that's right," I managed after an awkward pause. "That is, at least, I seem to have found your wife's, um, Melanie Melampus's ring. While I was learning to scuba dive. The day before yesterday. But I didn't realize...I mean..."

Thankfully, he interrupted before my babbling got completely out of control. "You have the ring there? Can you describe it to me?"

"Of...of course." I described the ring, my nerves calming somewhat as I went through the litany yet again.

"Yes, it was her wedding band," he said. "I had it specially commissioned and inscribed, which is how the Cartier people were able to trace it to me. You found it in Aruba—in the ocean?"

"Yes. And, um, there's more," I began, then hesitated, realizing that it would be cruel to get his hopes up if I were wrong about what I'd seen. Presumably, this man thought his wife was dead—murdered—possibly by someone close to him.

"Ms. Seally?" he prompted.

"I'm sorry. Last night, I think...I believe...I may have seen Melanie here, alive, in Oranjestad," I finished in a rush.

There was a long, perfectly understandable pause before he said, "I see." His voice betrayed no hint of what he might be feeling at my clumsy revelation. "Did the Cartier people give you my name as purchaser of the ring?"

"Er, no. They just asked if they could pass my phone number along to the owner."

"Then may I ask how you recognized the ring, Ms. Seally? Are you a friend of Melanie's or, forgive me, someone I know but can't place at the moment?"

He sounded more curious than suspicious, which was a welcome difference from my other calls today. Maybe that's why I simply told him the truth.

"I didn't recognize it, actually. An acquaintance did. He'd been following the case, on behalf of an insurance company."

"Ah. That would be Ronan Gale?"

"Yes," I replied, startled again. "How did you—?"

"I make it a point to stay informed about anything that might affect my future." Now he sounded amused, which somehow made his voice even more delicious. "How did you come to meet Ronan Gale?"

"He was, um, piloting our dive boat. Filling in for the regular captain, actually. It was a complete coincidence."

He chuckled. "I used to believe in coincidence, Ms. Seally."

Remembering his recent conversion, I almost asked an impertinent question but caught myself in time. Instead, I said, "After I found the ring, of course I showed it to everyone on the boat. It was pretty exciting, that being my very first day diving and all."

"Of course. And Ronan Gale told you about the ring and the case?" Now he did sound skeptical. I wondered how well he knew Ronan, or if he only knew *of* him. Either way, I was dying to ask questions I had no business asking.

"Not right away," I said instead. "But the day after I found it, I thought he seemed, well, unusually interested in the ring, asking questions about it, so finally I made him tell me."

"You made him?" The amusement was back. "I believe I'd like to hear that story sometime, Ms. Seally. But now, can you tell me who else knows about the ring, besides Ronan Gale and your fellow dive students?"

"Well, there are the people at the Cartier store, of course. Oh, and there are two FBI guys, too." The list of those in the know just kept growing. "And, um, I'm pretty sure Melanie, er, Mrs. Melampus knows, though I don't know how."

"Melanie? What makes you think she knows?" His voice held a hard edge that it hadn't before.

I wondered again how this whole thing was affecting Stefan Melampus emotionally. Bad enough to lose his wife at sea, and worse to be charged with her murder.

But to discover she might not be dead at all but was making no effort to return to him or clear his name? That had to hurt, however well he managed to hide it. I worried again that I'd spoken too soon, based on too-flimsy evidence, but now I had to explain.

"I went to the jewelry store the same day I found the ring—the day before yesterday. Yesterday, I had a message on my room phone claiming to be from the store. It was a woman, asking me to be at the store at a certain time. After I went back to the store and found out they hadn't called me, I was suspicious enough to, um, stake out the area. That's when I saw Melanie—or someone who looked like her—watching the store." I paused, breathless, waiting for his reaction.

"I see. Someone from the store did call me about the ring, but I told no one except my attorney, as it seemed that it might be pertinent to my defense."

"Then...do you think someone at the jewelry store might have told her?"

He was silent for a long moment before replying. "I don't like to doubt what you claim to have seen, Ms. Seally, but I'm afraid I'm finding it very difficult to believe that Melanie could be alive. I've prayed for a miracle, of course, but..."

Another pause, during which my heart ached for him, then he continued. "The evidence—and both my attorneys and I have examined it thoroughly, as you may imagine—all points to Melanie having been killed, probably by one of my former business associates. I do have some thoughts, however..." His voice trailed off again.

I waited while he thought things through, feeling pity for a man who was probably as wealthy as Bill Gates. How bizarre was that?

"I wish I could speak with you face to face, Ms. Seally, and do some looking around there in Aruba," he finally said. "Unfortunately, I'm currently prohibited from leaving Miami. That being the case, I'd like to send a representative to talk to you, to check things out on the ground, and perhaps to bring back the ring to serve as evidence. I'll consult with my attorneys on that."

"Um, I should probably tell you—or maybe I shouldn't, but I'm going to anyway—that the FBI may be sending someone as well. And I think they'll probably want the ring, too."

I wondered what my obligations might be, considering I was out of the country and, presumably, the FBI's jurisdiction.

"I see. Certainly I can't ask you to act against your conscience, Ms. Seally, especially after the service you've rendered me already. I should mention, however, that my history with the authorities has not always been precisely amicable. Therefore it's conceivable that certain members of the FBI may not have my, ah, best interests at heart."

"Yes, I already had that impression after speaking with Agent Walters. So...I'm really glad you called me. The truth is what should be important."

To my surprise, he chuckled again. "What a refreshing viewpoint, Ms. Seally. The world would be a better place if more people believed that. I must say, I do look forward to meeting you in person, whenever that can be arranged. God bless you."

As I closed my phone, I realized that I was looking forward to that meeting, too. Stefan Melampus struck me as a very *interesting* man. To say the least.

So interesting, in fact, that after lunch—a small salad to make up for that decadent breakfast—I headed back to the hotel business center for some more research.

This time, instead of googling the murder investigation, I looked up Stefan Melampus himself—and found tens of thousands of hits. Where to start? Several links were for bios, so I checked a few of those and finally settled in to read a lengthy Wikipedia entry, along with links which led to all publicly available information on the case—and on Stefan, the man.

I was interested to learn that he hadn't been born to wealth, as I'd assumed, but had worked his way up from humble beginnings. His parents had been Greek immigrants, but Stefan had been born in the States. Ties to organized crime had been alleged since he was in his mid-twenties, but nothing had ever been proven. His genius for investment and a ferocious work ethic were well documented, however.

As was his wealth. He was even richer than I'd realized. I was amazed all over again that such a man had actually called me.

I kept reading, paying particular attention to what the bios had to say about Stefan's supposed conversion. If that part was true, it gave me that much more incentive to help him now. And everything I found seemed to confirm it. Every case brought against him, except for the current one, dated from three or more years ago, and all of those had been dismissed for lack of evidence.

I didn't doubt that he'd been guilty of shady business practices in the past, but his recent charity work and donations certainly pointed to a man reformed.

Now that I fully understood just how rich and powerful Stefan Melampus was, it seemed absurd to think a nobody like me could be of any real help to him. The man surely had a team of highly paid lawyers at his beck and call, even if his political influence wasn't what it had been.

Still, I was left with an unshakeable conviction that if I *could* help, it was the right thing to do.

THE REST OF the afternoon was blissfully crisis-free, unless I counted a call from my mother.

"Wynne, sweetie, I know what you said yesterday but, well... Are you really in Aruba?"

"Who told you that?" I was going to kill whichever of the girls—

"Tom did. I think Bess told him. It's true, then?"

Just great. Now both Mom and Tom would think I'd come here out of some kind of sentimentality over my anniversary when it was actually just the opposite.

"Yes, Mom, it's true. The trip was booked, everything was prepaid, so I thought I might as well get a nice vacation out of it. I figured I deserved that much."

"Oh, Sweetie. I wish you wouldn't do this to yourself, though you're being very brave, what with tomorrow—"

"What did you want, Mom?" I broke in before she could lavish her backhanded sympathy on me—sympathy I did *not* need.

She gave a little sniff I chose not to decipher. "As I said, I talked with Tom again. He actually called me, to ask if I thought he should call you. But after the way you were yesterday, I told him he might do better to wait until you got home. That's when he mentioned you were in Aruba. He assumed I knew, of course, and I must say—"

"So he's not going to call? Good." That would have been all I needed on top of everything else going on right now.

"No, not just yet, I don't think. But I *do* think he'll be willing to go for counseling with you when you get home, if you ask him nicely. I'm pretty sure he's interested—"

"But I'm not interested," I said, interrupting her again. "Not in getting back together, and not in asking him anything nicely. He cheated on me. He threw it in my face and left me. We're divorced. I've moved on."

"Oh, but if he's sorry, you should at least try to forgive him. I'm sure that's what our pastor would say, that everyone deserves a second chance."

I grimaced. I *had* prayed for help forgiving Tom, but I hadn't managed it yet. I wasn't sure if I ever would.

"A second chance to do what, Mom? Make a fool of me? I'm not quite ready to give him that, I'm afraid."

"Oh, Wynnie, Wynnie, Wynnie."

That was it. "I was just on my way to the beach, Mom. I've got to go."

Luckily for me, she still didn't quite "get" cell phones, so it wouldn't necessarily occur to her that I could talk from the beach as easily as from my room. Still, I left the phone behind, just in case. Besides, it needed some serious recharging after all the time I'd spent on it today.

Out on the sand, I inhaled deeply, letting the stress of the past few hours slowly seep out of my body as the heat of the Aruba sun seeped in. Better. Definitely better. With no destination in mind, I started to walk.

The fierce Aruba breeze whipped my hair about my face and a tingling of sand against my bare legs, but I exulted in such purely physical sensations. My goal right now was to not think—to just *be*. I walked faster and faster, and then, amazingly, I broke into a run.

I'd never been a runner, not even in my high school prime, when I'd been on the swim team. But my body seemed to crave the exertion, maybe to shed the last vestiges of tension over the mess I'd somehow landed right in the middle of.

I estimated that I'd covered most of a mile before a stitch in my side forced me back to a walk. That had been weird. Exhilarating, but weird. And good for me, no doubt. Maybe I'd get up early tomorrow and run on purpose.

Or not. I'd play that by ear.

Suddenly the delicious awareness hit me that I didn't have to answer to anyone, to adapt my plans to anyone else's preferences or expectations. Why it had taken until now I don't know, but a sense of my newfound freedom hit me like one of those enormous drinks at Pepe & Pete's.

I laughed out loud, caring not at all that strangers were giving me funny looks. I'd never see any of them again, so what did it matter? Feeling better than I had in years, maybe decades, I continued down the beach with long, swinging strides for another half hour or more, doing my best to think of nothing at all.

Eventually, though, a thought did intrude. Or, rather, a face. Ronan's. He'd promised to return those pictures, which meant he'd be coming back to the hotel. And I was a sweaty mess.

Turning back, I tried jogging again for a few steps but quickly opted to walk instead, though still with long, confident strides. I liked the way that made me feel—strong, a woman who could handle things.

It was dusk, about seven o'clock, by the time I reached the hotel. I stopped at the front desk to see if Ronan had left the photos there, as I'd suggested, but the only package they had for me was the one I'd left myself that morning. I let them keep that and went upstairs to check my room phone for messages.

The light wasn't blinking, which meant Ronan hadn't come by yet. My cell phone *was* blinking, showing a voice mail from my mother, but I decided to grab a quick shower before listening to it and possibly having my strong, confident mood shattered.

Ten minutes later, wrapped in a towel, I stepped out of the opulent bathroom to hear my room phone ringing. My heart pounding all out of proportion to the cause, I grabbed the receiver before it could roll over to voice mail.

"Hello?"

"Wynne?" It was Ronan. "I'm downstairs with the pix, hoping you haven't had dinner yet."

Again with the food. Before I could think better of it, I heard myself saying, "No. In fact, I'm starving." It was true, after my exercise on the beach, but that didn't mean I had to say it.

"So that breakfast didn't hold you all day after all, huh?" There was no way I was going to admit to having eaten lunch. "Do you want me to come up, or will you come down?"

"I'll come down. I just stepped out of the shower, so give me ten minutes or so."

"Take more time if you need it. I'll be in the casino. Come find me whenever you're ready."

He hung up before I could ask where he had in mind to eat—dressy or casual. I shrugged. Nothing seemed *too* dressy in Aruba. A sundress should work for pretty much anything.

It did take me more than ten minutes to get ready, of course. I had to try on a couple of different dresses, then fuss with my hair and makeup more than was really necessary. No matter how many times I told myself I was being silly, I couldn't seem to help myself. Ronan was the first man who'd shown any kind of interest since… well, since marriage had put an end to Tom's courtship.

Once I was primped to my satisfaction, I picked up my cell phone, then changed my mind and set it down, still plugged into the charger. Mom's voice mail would wait, and I didn't want any other calls, from her or anyone else, while I was at dinner.

I found Ronan at the Texas Hold 'Em table. After letting him see me, I discreetly moved out of his line of sight so he could finish the hand without distraction—but where I could still watch. I wasn't particularly surprised when he won.

"Now I can buy dinner," he said as he cashed out his chips. "I like that dress, by the way. It suits you."

I glanced down at my kicky knee-length green paisley sundress, the one I'd worried was too youthful for a woman my age, and tried hard not to blush. "Thanks. So where are we going, Mr. High-Roller?"

"There's a fish place with outdoor seating practically across the street that's pretty good. I thought we'd try there."

"Sounds fine to me."

As we left the hotel, he casually tucked my hand into the crook of his arm. Determined not to show how that flustered me, I blurted out, "So, did your plan with the insurance company work? What did they say?"

Oh, yeah. Real nonchalant.

"They were glad to have the pictures, but they won't release my commission until the case against Melampus is settled. Not surprising, considering that the only reason they pay me at all is because they don't like to let go of money. Here are the photos, by the way."

He pulled the folded envelope from his pocket and handed it to me. I slipped it into my purse.

We crossed the street and walked the block or so to the restaurant, where we were told there would be a ten-to-fifteen-minute wait. Ronan gave the host his name and led me to the tiki bar at one end of the patio dining area.

After ordering us each a drink, he said, "So, how was your day? Relaxing, I hope."

I laughed. "It seemed like I spent most of it on the phone." As soon as the words were out, I wanted to grab them back. I hadn't decided whether I ought to tell him about the FBI or Stefan Melampus just yet.

"Oh? More calls from your daughters?" His tone was offhand, but he was watching me closely.

"My mother this time," I was able to say truthfully. "Imagine every stereotype of a mother you've heard—Jewish, Italian, Irish, you name it—then square it. That would be my mom."

"Full of advice and warnings, eh? I have a mother like that myself—and she *is* Irish. You didn't tell her about the ring and everything, did you?"

I laughed out loud, just as the bartender set down our drinks, which earned me an odd look. "Are you kidding? I haven't even told her about the diving lessons. In fact, she only found out today that I'm in Aruba. I'd just told her I was on vacation. She doesn't need any extra fuel for her worrying, believe me."

Ronan chuckled, and I took a sip of my strawberry daiquiri, hoping he wouldn't ask anything else about my phone calls just yet.

To my relief, he said, "Back to my conversation with the insurance company, they're very interested in the ring, since they handled that policy as well. They wanted details on where and how it was found. I think I remembered what you told me, but I have a proposition."

I managed to not quite choke on my drink. "A proposition?"

"Well, a favor," he amended. "I was wondering if you'd be willing to go diving with me tomorrow, back to the *Debbie II*, so that I can get a few pictures of the exact spot where you found the ring. The more evidence I can give the company, the more likely they are to pay out eventually."

"You mean there's a question of whether they'll pay you your commission, even if they have proof Melanie is still alive? That doesn't seem fair."

He shrugged. "It's more a matter of demonstrating that I've done enough to earn it. After all, if Melanie just turned up in Miami on her own, I wouldn't expect to be paid. I'm hoping to show I helped to flush her out."

I thought I understood. It wasn't enough for the insurance company to get out of paying. Ronan had to prove he had been responsible for their savings. Not that he was, really, but I could help him make it look that way. Suddenly, his dinner invitation didn't seem nearly as flattering.

I was about to refuse when I realized that photos of the spot where the ring was found might be useful to Stefan Melampus and his lawyers, as well.

"I'd be glad to," I said. "I was hoping to dive again before leaving Aruba anyway, and this is a good excuse."

I was pretty sure he could take much better pictures with his fancy camera than I'd be able to manage with an underwater disposable. If Ronan was willing to use me for his own purposes, I was within my rights to use him for mine. I'd tell him about Stefan Melampus and the FBI later.

Maybe.

# CHAPTER ELEVEN

EVEN WITH MY eyes open to Ronan's motives, that dinner was one I'd remember fondly for a very long time. The food was excellent, and whatever his true agenda, Ronan was a heck of a charmer, one of those men who could make a woman feel like she was the only one in his world. After two daiquiris I stopped reminding myself that it was an act and just let myself enjoy it.

Lucky for me, he was serious about that dive tomorrow and called it a night before that practiced charm—or the daiquiris—led me to do or say anything really stupid.

He said good night to me by the elevators, and though the temptation to invite him up to my room was strong, I resisted, telling myself exactly what I'd stopped telling myself two hours earlier—that being attentive to lonely women like me was part of his stock-in-trade. Riding up in the elevator alone, it felt like a hollow victory.

"At least you'll be able to live with yourself," I murmured aloud, just before the doors opened. *And there's still tomorrow*, I added silently as I traversed a hallway that looked longer than ever.

No surprises awaited me; the room was just as I'd left it, and there were no messages on the room phone. My cell phone showed

I'd missed a call from Deb, but she hadn't left a message, so it couldn't have been too important. Nothing from Stefan Melampus or the FBI, which was a relief. No new developments about the ring or the case to keep me from sleeping.

I did finally listen to my mother's voice mail, but as I'd expected, it was just a continuation of her earlier theme—reporting on Tom's doings and urging me to take action I had no intention of taking.

"I'm afraid he might go back to that Darlene woman if you don't take advantage of this opportunity soon, Wynnie," she concluded.

I didn't call her back.

My alarm woke me at eight the next morning. I rolled over and shut it off with a groan, marveling that I'd remembered to set it at all. My head was pounding, and my body ached, but I'd promised to meet Ronan on the boat dock at nine thirty, so I struggled out of bed. This was twice in one week I'd had too much to drink. Wasn't I old enough to learn from my mistakes by now?

I stumbled into the bathroom and flipped on the light, then made the mistake of glancing into the mirror. Apparently the ring, which I'd put back on its chain, had worked its way onto my pillow sometime toward morning. I sported a distinctive red circle on my right cheek that made me look like I was coming down with some exotic new disease. I hoped it would fade before I went downstairs.

I took a quick shower just to wake myself up while coffee brewed in the in-room coffee maker. After downing two cups as I donned swimsuit, shorts, t-shirt, and sunscreen, I felt much closer to human.

It was nearly nine by now, which meant if I was going to get breakfast before meeting Ronan, I needed to hurry. I picked up my mask, fins, and snorkel and headed downstairs.

I bought a pastry, a banana, and another cup of coffee from the little kiosk in the lobby on my way out of the hotel ten minutes later. Outside, I found a bench facing the ocean and settled there for a few minutes to eat.

When I was done, I wiped the crumbs off my lap and stood, nodding cordially to a handsome young man on the next bench. He looked vaguely familiar, and I decided he resembled one of Deb's numerous friends-who-weren't-boyfriends. Which reminded me, I'd never returned her call.

Ah, well. My phone was still in my room, and I wasn't going back for it now. I didn't want to take it on the boat anyway. I'd call her later.

I reached the dock at nine thirty-two, to find Ronan waiting.

"Good morning!" he called—much too cheerfully, I thought. "I was starting to wonder if you'd overslept. I booked us a couple of spots on *Van's Vandal* and rented you some equipment. You might want to check the BCD and wetsuit for size before we shove off."

I nodded, taking deep breaths of the morning sea air and trying to get into the spirit of the thing. "They're going to the *Debbie II*?"

"It's just us and one other couple, and Van knows me, so he was willing to go wherever we wanted. The others didn't have a preference, so I talked up the site, and they're fine with it."

I had no trouble believing that Ronan had been very convincing. The other couple was my age or older, maybe fiftyish, and I noticed the woman kept glancing over at Ronan and smiling. Yeah, he was an equal opportunity charmer, all right.

Ronan introduced me to Van, a heavyset, dark-skinned man I guessed to be in his early sixties, with the accent typical to the locals.

"Yah, I just do this once or twice a week, for the fun and to meet the pretty ladies," Van told me with a wink.

"So Ronan brings ladies to you on a regular basis, does he?" I asked with a grin. The thought didn't really bother me. Much.

But Van just laughed instead of answering.

"You've got me pegged as a player, don't you?" Ronan asked as we stepped aboard the little boat. It was about half the size of the *Scubaruba*, the boat I'd learned to dive from.

"Does it matter?" I knew it shouldn't. I'd only known Ronan a few days, and I'd be leaving Aruba myself in less than a week.

He shrugged. "It matters to me. I'd like you to think well of me, Wynne—even if I don't particularly deserve it."

I couldn't think of anything appropriate to say, so I busied myself with my equipment. The BCD and wetsuit were the same size I'd worn during the lessons. I was touched that Ronan had remembered, then realized he probably hadn't. They only came in about three sizes, so it wouldn't have been hard for someone with experience to guess which would fit me.

"These will be fine," I said.

I started attaching the regulator to the BCD and air tank, then looked up to see the handsome young man I'd nodded to earlier speaking earnestly with Van on the dock. Van seemed skeptical about something, but then shrugged and nodded. The man stepped aboard, and Van pointed at the extra dive equipment piled near the front of the boat.

"Another passenger?" Ronan asked when Van came over to make sure my equipment fit.

"Yah. Name's Lenny. Says he lost his PADI card, but he really wanted to come—was even willing to pay extra. Hope he knows what he's doing. You have your card with you, Missie?" he asked me then.

I fished my temporary card out of my shorts pocket and presented it proudly.

"Ah, just certified, are you? Well, Ronan'll keep a good eye on you, I'm sure." Another wink, then he went to cast the boat off from the dock.

I decided not to be insulted, since I was undoubtedly the least experienced diver here. The older couple had their own equipment and were setting up their tanks like pros. And the young man...

...was watching them like a hawk and trying to mimic everything they did. I wondered how long it had been since he'd dived, and whether we had another Rick on our hands.

With that possibility in mind, I finished setting up my own equipment, then moved in his direction. While Ronan chatted with Van on the bridge, I tried to unobtrusively see whether young Lenny had attached everything correctly.

He hadn't. The air hose that was supposed to feed into his BCD, to inflate it, hung loose. And when I got a little closer, I could see that he'd apparently tried to attach his regulator to the tank with the dust cap still in place. He wouldn't be able to get any air out of the tank at all like that.

"Um, do you need some help?" I offered, automatically slipping into "mom" mode. He did remind me of one of Deb's friends, after all.

He looked up at me with an almost panicked expression, which he quickly disguised, glancing down, then up, then over my left shoulder, never quite meeting my eye. Poor guy—I should have known he wouldn't want me to see him making a fool of himself.

"You need to take this cap off," I said, pointing, when he didn't reply. "Right. Then retighten it. And this hose should go in here." I showed him how to attach it to the vest properly.

"Um, thanks," he muttered under his breath, looking more embarrassed than ever. At least he didn't bluster like Rick had.

"No problem. I guess it's been a while, huh?"

He nodded, still not making eye contact.

I waited for a few more seconds, then gave it up. "Well, enjoy the dive," I said and retired to the other side of the boat, where Ronan joined me a moment later.

"What was that about?"

"He just needed a little help," I said. "I think he must be pretty rusty."

"Yeah, it's surprising how quickly you can forget the details if you don't dive for a while. But he's not your responsibility, you know." His look told me he'd noticed how I'd tended to mother Rick and Linda during our lessons.

My smile was probably sheepish. "I'll try to remember that. I guess it comes of being a mother for so long."

"And just how long is that?" He seemed genuinely curious.

I'd hedged before when the topic had come up, but I refused to lie outright. With a sort of mental shrug, I said, "Bess, my oldest, is twenty-four, and Deb will be twenty-three next month."

"Wow, I never would have guessed you could have kids that old. You must have married in your teens."

I knew it was just flattery, but I appreciated it anyway. "Not quite, but close. I was twenty-one. And thanks."

"Just the facts, ma'am."

His quip reminded me of the FBI guys, one of whom might conceivably arrive on the island in the next day or two. I really ought to tell Ronan about them.

"Guess we ought to get our wetsuits on," he said before I could figure out how to phrase things. "We'll be there in just a few minutes."

Knowing it would take me a while to struggle into my rubberized sausage casing, I peeled off my t-shirt and shorts and got right to it, trying not to ogle Ronan's extremely fit body as he did the same. I'd tell him about the FBI—and maybe Stefan Melampus—after the dive. It probably wasn't something I should talk about within earshot of the other divers anyway.

"So, do you think I'll be able to talk you into at least one more dive after this one, before you leave Aruba?" Ronan asked as he slipped into his own wetsuit as though it were silk instead of rubber. I tried not to hate him for that—or to think too much about leaving Aruba in only a few more days.

"I'd like to," I said. "I was reading up on some of the dive sites, and I thought the wreck of the *California* sounded especially interesting, what with its history with the *Titanic* and all. I'm kind of a *Titanic* buff, since the movie," I admitted with a grin.

Ronan grinned back, but shook his head. "Sorry to burst your bubble, but that bit you've read—it's all over the Web and some tourbooks—is a myth. Our *California* here isn't the same one that ignored the *Titanic*'s SOS. That was the *Californian*. This one sank several years before the *Titanic* even launched."

"Oh. Well, shoot."

"Yeah, they keep the story alive because it's a good tourist draw, I think. But you wouldn't be able to dive it this trip anyway. It's not deep, but it's on the north side of the island—the windward side—which means currents and high surf. It's a tricky dive even for experienced divers. Definitely not one for a newbie."

"Then I guess it's just as well the *Titanic* thing is a myth. Now I won't mind missing it."

"There's not a lot left of it anyway, hundred-year-old wooden wreck and all." He buckled on his weight belt, and I went back to fighting with my neoprene girdle.

The wetsuit challenge hadn't gotten any easier with practice, except that I knew how to avoid pinching myself with the zipper, but eventually it was on. The boat was stopping as I zipped it up to my throat. I tucked the ring on its chain inside the wetsuit, fastened my weight belt around my waist, then scooted back against my tank to snap myself into my BCD.

There were already a couple of other dive boats moored in the area, I noticed, then I turned to see Lenny watching me intently from across the boat. I gave him a cheerful thumbs-up when I saw he'd managed to get into his own wetsuit and BCD unassisted. He quickly looked away without smiling back. Still embarrassed, I assumed.

"You have enough weight there, buddy?" Van asked him as he made the rounds, checking on each of us. "Oh, wait, here's your weight belt here. You won't get far without this."

He helped Lenny unfasten the bottom of his BCD, slip the weight belt around his middle, and refasten the vest.

"You *have* done this before, right?"

"Yes, yes, of course. It's just been a while. I'll be fine." I noticed he wasn't making eye contact with Van, either.

"Okay, if you say so. Check your mask and fins for fit, since they're rentals. Everyone else has their own. Right?" Van glanced around at the four of us, and we all nodded.

"All right, everyone, be back at the boat in one hour, or when your air gets to one thousand PSI, whichever comes first. If you have any problems, come up and give me the signal for help, and I'll fish you out. Ronan here has done the *Debbie II* several times, so he can be your unofficial guide, right, Ronan?"

"Sure, no problem," Ronan replied with an easy grin. "Just follow the blue fins."

He stood up, and I envied the effortless way he walked to the back of the boat with a full tank on his back. With a wink through his mask and a jaunty salute, he braced his regulator and weight belt and strode off into the water.

I hung back and let the couple go next, just in case Lenny needed any last-minute advice or help. I knew Ronan was right that he wasn't my responsibility, but I couldn't switch off mom-mode that easily.

"Go ahead," I said to him when we were the only divers left on the boat. "Don't forget to keep a hand on your regulator when you step in." He probably didn't need that advice, but I gave it anyway.

Actually, he looked more nervous than I'd expected as he shuffled to the back of the boat, but he did put a hand on his regulator as I'd said—though he neglected to put the other one on his weight belt. The boat was rocking just a little, which probably explained his awkward entry.

With a parting smile for Van, I did my own final shuffle to the back, then took my giant stride into the water. As the ocean closed briefly over my head, I was pleased to have made my smoothest entry to date.

Bobbing back up, I saw Ronan waiting for me a short distance away and kicked over to him so we could begin our descent together. The other couple was already on their way down, and the younger fellow was following them. He'd be okay now, I thought.

"Ready?" Ronan asked.

I nodded, and he let the air out of his vest and began descending at an impressive rate, only pausing to equalize once that I noticed. How did he do that? Practice, I guess. I was a good bit slower, stopping to pinch my nose and blow at least half a dozen times before I made it to the bottom, where he was again waiting for me.

He gave me a questioning "okay" signal, which I returned, then he motioned for me to follow him toward the nearby hulk of the *Debbie II*. Glancing back, I saw the others following about ten yards back and remembered that Ronan was supposedly leading this expedition.

I hoped they'd all find other stuff to interest them before we started snapping shots of the place I'd found the ring. Otherwise they were bound to wonder what in the heck we were doing, and I really didn't want to spread the story any further until I'd spoken with either the FBI or whoever Stefan Melampus was sending.

That didn't turn out to be a problem. There was enough to see on and around the *Debbie II* that our group spread out as soon as we reached it. I could see a couple of other divers, presumably from one of the other boats, exploring the hull as well.

Personally, I found the ship even more fascinating the second time around, with interesting stuff growing all over it as well as the eerie glimpses into the interior. Ronan snapped a few shots as we went, the strobe of his camera revealing an array of colors I hadn't been able to see without that extra lighting.

By the time we made our way down the far side of the ship to the place I'd found the ring, we were alone. The others were still twenty feet above, swimming along the more interesting deck of the ship. The older couple had a camera at least as nice as Ronan's, so they were taking pictures, too.

Ronan and I drifted down to the seabed, and I scanned the

length of the ship's keel, looking for the giant moray, which would be the only way I'd find the spot the ring had been. Without Jason there to direct me, I realized it could take me a while. What if the eel was deep under the ship, not showing itself today?

I turned to Ronan and spread my arms in an exaggerated shrug, hoping he might know where to look. Apparently, he did. He made a squiggling motion with one arm that I assumed represented the eel, then turned left along the hull.

We both swam low, just a couple of feet above the ocean floor, carefully searching along the base of the ship. That blasted eel had to be along here somewhere. I actually spotted it before Ronan did, its enormous head barely visible under the dark ledge of the hull. I touched Ronan on the arm and pointed, backing away slightly as I remembered just how big that eel was.

Ronan brought up his camera and waited for me to point out the little ledge where I'd found the ring. I examined the hull above the eel but didn't immediately find the place. It occurred to me that the moray might well have moved since then. We'd seen lots of crannies where it could lurk along the way.

What if it had half a dozen different hidey holes? We could use up all of our bottom time just looking for the place, and never get any pictures at all. I looked around for any other recognizable land-marks, to the right and left of the area just above the eel.

Then, suddenly, I saw it—the little projection, even smaller than I'd remembered, a few feet above and a little to the left of the eel's artificial cave.

Relieved, I turned back to Ronan to get his attention, only to be distracted by a quickly moving dark shape just behind him. For half an instant, I thought it was a shark and nearly panicked before I realized it was just another diver—Lenny, the young guy from our group.

My relief turned back to alarm when he got close enough for me to see the wicked-looking knife he held, poised for attack. Ronan must have seen my expression through my mask, because he turned to follow my horrified gaze just in time to duck, evading what might have been a serious slice from that knife.

Hampered by his camera, all Ronan could do was kick at his attacker while he tried to reach his own dive knife, attached at his waist, with one hand. However, instead of taking another slash at Ronan, Lenny moved to one side, away from the kick, and came at me, his knife again held high.

I stared uncomprehendingly for a moment, my one inane thought that he was being terribly ungrateful after the help I'd given him earlier. Then, at the last second, I kicked backward so that my fins were in his face and my face was as far from that knife as possible.

He kept coming, and being bigger and stronger, he was also faster than me—especially since I was swimming backward so that I could keep my eyes on him. Ronan had his own knife out now and was catching up, but it was obvious our attacker would reach me before Ronan reached him.

With a spurt of speed, Lenny closed the distance, and I braced for a blow from that knife even as I kicked furiously at him. But instead of stabbing me, he grabbed at my neck with his other hand, his fingers digging into the top of my wetsuit.

I twisted away, managing to land a kick on his chest that slowed him enough for Ronan to reach us. Lenny turned, and then the two of them were fighting, each trying to slice the other with their knives. It was the most terrifying thing I'd ever seen—at least until the giant moray eel came out to investigate.

I'd underestimated its length: it was at least fifteen feet long, tapering along its length from its basketball-sized head. Lenny saw it too, and it must have scared him as much as it scared me, because he gave a scream through his regulator that I could hear from six feet away.

The eel didn't come any closer, but just circled around on the ocean floor a couple of times before heading back into its lair. Maybe it had decided none of us were small enough to swallow.

Ronan took advantage of Lenny's distraction to grab his wrist, forcing him to release his knife. Unfortunately he seemed to recover his nerve the moment the eel was gone and started fighting again, now trying to wrest Ronan's knife away from him.

I floated nearby, feeling useless, rubbing the spot on my neck that he'd hurt with his fingers. My own fingers encountered the chain with the ring on it, and suddenly everything clicked. That's what he was after—it had to be. Nothing else made any sense.

In quick succession, I remembered the way he'd stared when I'd tucked the ring into my wetsuit, his refusal to meet my eyes when I'd offered him advice, his last-minute joining of the dive group. His ineptitude suddenly made sense, too. He'd probably never dived before.

I swam in closer to the struggling pair and saw that Ronan had managed to flood Lenny's mask while Ronan's mask was half off, on top of his head. That wasn't slowing Ronan down at all, but Lenny kept shaking his head, as if that might somehow make the water in his mask disappear.

On sudden inspiration, I kicked hard with my fins, darted in between them and snatched Lenny's regulator from his mouth.

To my immense relief, he immediately panicked. He let go of Ronan and kicked away, flailing wildly with his arms but clearly having no clue how to find his trailing regulator. After a few seconds, he did the only thing possible—he swam as hard as he could for the surface.

# CHAPTER TWELVE

WHILE I HUNG motionless in the water waiting for my heart to slow and my nerves to stop jangling, Ronan replaced his mask and cleared it, then started after our attacker. I wondered if I should follow, but he'd only ascended ten feet when he stopped and came back to me.

Urgently, he gave me the okay sign, and I returned it to let him know I wasn't hurt. The same wasn't true for him—I could see the slice on the shoulder of his wetsuit and the little dark cloud above it that meant he was bleeding. I pointed at it, trying not to teeter over the edge into panic.

Ronan looked down at the cut, then shrugged, which helped me to calm down. His camera had been dangling by its safety cord from his wrist during the fight. Now he grasped it in both hands again and motioned for me to show him the spot we'd been searching for before the attack.

He still wanted to take pictures after all that? But then I realized it would only take a minute now, whereas we'd have to do a whole separate dive to make another try at this later. And we were clearly no longer in any danger from the guy who'd bolted for the surface.

For a moment I worried that he'd escape, but then realized he'd have no choice but to return to the boat—and Van wasn't likely to abandon the rest of us, especially since Lenny no longer had his knife for leverage.

I managed to find the little ledge again and pointed it out to Ronan, who proceeded to snap several shots from a couple of different angles while I fumed and fidgeted about Ronan's injury.

Finally he gave in to my silent urgings to ascend. Not only was I concerned that he'd been badly cut, I was starting to get nervous that his bleeding might attract the eel again—or sharks.

On the way up, I wondered what had happened to Lenny. If he'd been stupid enough to hold his breath, he could have suffered a pulmonary embolism, I remembered from dive class—in other words, his lungs could burst as the air in them rapidly expanded. Surely, though, he'd let the air go when it became uncomfortable? If so, the worst he'd risk was a mild case of the bends.

I shook my head, realizing that I was actually worrying about a guy who'd just tried to maim and possibly kill me. That was definitely taking mom-mode too far.

Even though we were in a hurry, Ronan insisted on a safety stop at fifteen feet before we finally surfaced a dozen or so yards from the boat.

"Van! Yo, Van!" he shouted. From here, it didn't look like anyone was on the boat at all.

A moment later, though, Van emerged from the cockpit and waved to us, then made a circle with his arms over his head to ask if we were okay. Ronan reproduced the gesture, then started swimming toward the boat with me following as quickly as I could. Where the heck was Lenny?

It took us a couple of minutes to reach the boat, but as soon as he got close, Ronan took his regulator out again to yell, "Hey, where's Lenny? Didn't he surface ahead of us?"

Van called something back, but I was still several yards behind and couldn't hear. He helped Ronan out of the water, and the two of them started talking, Ronan pointing at his shoulder and Van pointing across the water. I looked in that direction and saw another dive boat. Was he saying that our attacker was on that boat instead?

Frustrated, I made it the rest of the way to the ladder, ripped my fins off more quickly than I'd ever managed before, and hollered, "Hey! A little help here!"

"Oh, sorry, Wynne," Ronan exclaimed, quickly taking my fins, then helping me up the ladder. "It seems our friend swam to another boat—no, not that one, unfortunately. It was one that already had the rest of its divers back on board, so since he was in distress, they radioed Van here, then headed back to shore in case he needed medical help."

"Then they have no idea—" I started, aghast.

"No. Van's going to radio them now, though. With any luck, they can call ahead and have the cops waiting for him at the dock."

"You don't think he'll try something desperate once he knows they're onto him on the other boat? What if he hurts someone? Someone else," I amended, with a pointed look at Ronan's shoulder. "That doesn't look good."

"You just can't help worrying about people, can you?" he asked, but he was smiling. "I doubt our buddy is in any shape to do more damage at the moment. That was quick thinking, by the way, grabbing his regulator. I should have thought of that myself instead of focusing on the knife.

"And as for this—" he flexed his cut shoulder—"I don't think it's deep. I'm more upset about the slice in my wetsuit. It's almost new."

I rolled my eyes at his macho posturing. "Just get out of the wetsuit so I can take a look at that cut, okay? And I don't mean the one in the wetsuit—I'm no seamstress." Which was true. Sewing had never been among my domestic skills.

"A nurse?" he asked hopefully, unzipping the suit.

"No, just a mom who's had plenty of experience with cuts and scrapes."

"I thought you only had girls." He stripped his wetsuit the rest of the way off.

"Right. And girls never get into any trouble at all, do they?"

There was no missing the irony in my tone. After a moment he started to chuckle—then I joined in. Maybe it was the release of tension after what we'd been through at sixty feet below the surface, but we both ended up laughing until we were nearly helpless.

Not until Van joined us after his stint on the radio did I remember to examine Ronan's cut. It was definitely more than a scratch. Van brought out his first aid kit, and I applied a temporary bandage. I didn't think it would need stitches, but that would have to be up to a doctor.

"Yah, you should have that seen to," Van agreed when Ronan tried to shrug off my suggestion.

"Okay, okay." Ronan threw up his hands in surrender. "Now, Van, what's the deal? Did you let the other boat captain know what Lenny did?"

Van gave a sort of half shrug. "I wasn't sure *exactly* what he did, since all you told me was he attacked you down there. I take it he gave you that?" He pointed to Ronan's shoulder.

"Yeah, but I got the knife away from him, so he shouldn't be much of a threat now."

"From what they told me when he first came on board, probably not. Came up gasping and thrashing around, right in the middle of their divers as they were getting back on the boat. They pulled him aboard, then radioed me, like I said. Since I didn't know nothing yet, I said sure, they could take him back. They were ready to go, and I still had four divers out."

"And what did they say just now?"

"Well, it took me a bit to raise them on the radio. When the captain finally answered, I said the man might be a criminal, but he said he couldn't talk right then. Maybe Lenny was listening, or maybe he was dying. No knowing. So I signed off and radioed the dock and told them to call the police."

"I guess that will have to do." Ronan glanced at his watch. "The Simonses probably won't surface for another ten minutes or so."

"Unless you want me to use the horn to call them in now?" Van asked, with a worried look at Ronan's shoulder.

I was all in favor of that, but Ronan shook his head. "It won't make any difference, so let them finish the dive they paid for. Speaking of which, we sure got our money's worth of excitement, didn't we, Wynne?"

But reaction to all that had happened over the last half hour was setting in, now that I'd released all that tension by laughing. I couldn't even manage a smile. In fact, I didn't know when I'd felt so drained. "Money's worth. Yeah."

"Oh, c'mon, Wynne. Don't let a crazy like that ruin diving for you, your first time out after getting certified."

Van nodded vigorously. "He's right, Missie. I been doing this for near twenty years, and nothing like this ever happened before. It was a fluke, that's what it was."

"Of course," I said weakly, knowing it was no such thing. "Look, isn't that the Simonses?"

"Yah, I'll get them on board in jig time, and then we'll be back at the dock before you know it. Don't neither of you worry."

As soon as Van was out of earshot at the back of the boat, ready to help the others out of the water, I touched Ronan on his uninjured shoulder. "You know that attack wasn't a fluke, right?"

He gave me a penetrating look from under his brows. "You mean you think it had something to do with this case? How could it?"

"I'm not sure about the how, but before you came after him with your knife, that guy was definitely trying to grab the ring." I pointed at the spot on my neck that still felt raw, and Ronan's eyes widened.

"And I saw him staring at it earlier, before we went into the water," I added. "There's no way that attack was a coincidence. In fact..." I stopped, stunned by a sudden realization. How could I not have seen it before?

"What, Wynne? What is it?" Ronan prompted.

"Remember I told you there was a guy with Melanie Melampus the other night, only I wasn't really sure he was with her? I'm almost positive it was Lenny. Except I'll bet that's not really his name."

"Maybe we can check." He crossed to the other side of the boat and rummaged through the clothes our attacker had discarded when he'd changed into his dive gear, but came up empty-handed. "No wallet."

"I'm not surprised. But I really think it was the same guy."

He was looking skeptical again. "Are you sure, Wynne?"

"I'll have to look at the pictures on my phone again. I didn't print any of him—they didn't come out that well, plus I didn't think... That explains why he looked familiar, though. I thought he just reminded me of one of my daughters' friends. How could I have been so stupid? If I'd been more on my guard, he never could have done that to you." I frowned at the slice on his shoulder.

"Hey, you said yourself you didn't get a good look at him that night. And if you'd acted suspicious earlier, he probably would have bailed before getting on the boat, and we wouldn't have any evidence against him. Now, with any luck, he'll be in custody, and we can press charges."

"I hope so."

And I really, really did. It was finally dawning on me that I'd gotten into something truly dangerous, and I was more than a little bit scared. Yesterday, my main fear had been that Melanie Melampus would get away with insurance fraud and Stefan would go down for a murder he hadn't committed. Or that the ring would be stolen from me.

I'd been nervous the other night in Oranjestad, yes, but I hadn't believed I was at risk of actual physical injury. Now Ronan was bleeding, and I was bruised, and it could have been much, much worse. These people were playing for keeps.

True to his word, as soon as the Simonses were on board, Van started up the engine and headed back. I went over everything that had happened during the past hour in my mind, trying to lock in any details that might be important to the police. I didn't want this guy getting off on some technicality.

Once we were underway, I moved to the front of the boat to watch our progress. The wind and salt spray helped to revive me, and that strange wave of tiredness ebbed until I felt much more like my usual self. Ronan came up to stand beside me, and I resisted the urge to lean against him.

The shoreline grew larger, details coming into focus as we approached. I thought I could pick out the dock now, but I didn't see the flashing lights I'd expected—hoped—to see. I glanced at Ronan and saw he was frowning, too.

"Do you think the police have already taken him away, or aren't they there yet?" I asked him.

He shook his head. "From my experience with the Aruban police, they're probably not there yet. It's not a very large force, since this is usually such a peaceful island. You know, it's 'where happiness lives,' not the criminal element."

"Right." And I knew he was, even though it didn't feel that way at the moment.

A few minutes later we pulled into the dock, just behind the dive boat that had carried our attacker back, which Van pointed out to us. A knot of people were gathered next to it, but no one appeared to be on board.

Promising Van I'd be back to rinse off my rental equipment, I followed Ronan onto the dock. An animated discussion seemed to be in progress among the group beside the other boat.

"What's going on? Where's the guy you brought back?" he called out as we joined them.

They all turned—there were five or six of them, still in swim-suits and cover-ups, wet and windblown from diving and the boat ride back. One man, presumably the captain, stepped forward.

"Are you the one who radioed me? I thought it was Van," he said.

"No, I'm the one who was attacked by the guy you rescued," Ronan replied, pointing at his shoulder. "Where is he?"

"Well—" began the captain, when one of the two young women in the group interrupted him.

"It was the weirdest thing! We all thought he was completely passed out when we docked, so we left him on the boat, but next thing we knew, he was, like, totally gone. He had to have been faking it."

"Gone?" I echoed, a sick feeling beginning to form in the pit of my stomach. "Nobody saw which way he went?"

They all shook their heads, and several of them started talking at once, explaining how they'd only left him alone for a second, how everyone thought someone else was watching him, how no one could have known... But the bottom line was, he was gone, and no one had seen him go.

Just then, as if on cue, came a brief wail from a siren, and two police cars pulled up in front of the hotel nearest the dock, lights flashing. A moment later, three uniformed officers hurried across the sand to the dock, all looking very serious.

If it hadn't been for the cold knot in my stomach, I might have laughed at their timing.

TWO HOURS later, any urge to laugh had completely deserted me. Ronan and I had repeatedly described Lenny and everything he'd done, separately and together. The police also called a medic to treat Ronan's shoulder, and even took pictures of his cut as evidence.

Finally, they seemed satisfied that we weren't withholding any vital information—even though neither of us had mentioned Melanie Melampus or the ring. Ronan had insisted we keep that quiet, in a quick whisper to me as the cops arrived, and I'd gone along with it, half against my better judgment.

"I'd say we both deserve a good lunch about now, wouldn't you?" Ronan asked when we were finally alone on a bench near the dock, where the final phase of questioning had taken place.

"And then some," I agreed. "I'm not sure the interrogation wasn't worse than the attack. Though of course I won't have a scar to show for it."

"Nah, the interrogation didn't leave a scar."

I just gave him a look, still not in a frame of mind for humor. All I could seem to think about was what Melanie Melampus and her hit man might try next. Which reminded me of something I still needed to do.

"How about the Japanese restaurant in the Westin, next door? Have you eaten there yet?" Ronan asked when I didn't reply.

But I was eager now to get back to my room and my phone. I wanted to take another look at the pictures I'd taken of the man near Melanie Melampus in Oranjestad two nights ago.

After all that time with the police, I was starting to doubt my recollections and thinking maybe I'd imagined our attacker was the same guy. Before sharing that doubt with Ronan, I wanted to verify —or disprove—my original guess. I was acting like enough of a flake already without changing my story back and forth.

Then there was the fact that whoever was after the ring—and me—indisputably knew what I looked like now. Which made me nervous about wandering far from the hotel.

"We'll eat sooner if we just grab a burger at the pool bar here," I responded. "Besides, I'm a mess, still in my swimsuit, no makeup. I'm not sure they'd let me into a nice place at the moment, and I'm too hungry to shower and change before eating."

It was too long an explanation, and he quirked an eyebrow, making me wonder if he guessed my real motivation.

But he only shrugged and replied, "Sure, that'll be fine."

"So, you really think we did the right thing, not mentioning Melanie to the police?" I asked when we were seated near the pool a few minutes later with our burgers and fries. "It felt kind of iffy to me."

"Hey, you saw how unprepared these guys were to deal with our little assault. You really think they're equipped to do anything about an international murder case involving someone as powerful as Stefan Melampus? It would have scared them spitless."

He was probably right, but I still didn't like it. "You don't think we'll get in trouble for not saying anything? I mean, it's bound to come out later that the attack and the Melampus case are connected, and if you want to get credit for solving that case, it will look odd that you didn't make the connection earlier."

"Let me worry about that, okay? You just enjoy your burger for now."

"Don't patronize me," I said, more sharply than I'd intended. But it reminded me all too vividly of the way Tom had tried to "take care" of me while keeping secrets.

He blinked, clearly startled. "No, I—Okay, I guess you're right. I was. Sorry. I should know better than to underestimate you by now."

I was only partly mollified. "Thanks. But you need to know that I'm not willing to put myself at risk—legally or physically—just so you can get your precious payout. That may be your top priority, but it's not mine."

"All the cards on the table, huh?" he said with a grin. "Fair enough. I admit I've been hoping this business with the ring would flush Melanie out of hiding, if she's still alive. But I never expected you—us—to be at actual risk, and I'm sorry for that. Still, my payout and justice being served should go hand in hand, if we're right. Does that help?"

"In theory, at least." While it might mollify my conscience, it didn't make me any less scared. I rose. "Thanks for the burger. You're welcome to my fries if you want them."

"Leaving so soon?"

I nodded. "I'm expecting a call. From my daughter." I was conflicted all over again about whether I should tell him about the FBI and Stefan Melampus, so I put it off—again. "You'll let me know if the police catch that guy?"

"Of course—and about anything else new to do with the case. Enjoy the rest of your day, Wynne." He sounded like he meant it.

"I'll try." But I was pretty sure I wouldn't get much chance to relax.

As soon as I reached my room, I knew I'd made the right decision to hurry back. My room phone was blinking like a Christmas tree, as was my cell phone. Before I listened to a single voice mail, though, I wanted to examine those pictures again.

I scrolled through my photos and found the two I'd taken of the man in Oranjestad two nights ago, but on the two-inch LCD screen, all I could tell was that he had dark hair and wore a black shirt. Not exactly proof.

With a guilty glance at both flashing phones, I headed back downstairs to the business center so I could see those shots full-sized. It took a few minutes to get a computer, and a few more to remember how to view photos this way, but finally I had the first picture on the nineteen-inch screen in front of me.

Unfortunately, it still wasn't what anyone would call proof, just a shadowy profile, but I was pretty sure I'd been right. It looked like the same guy to me. At least I didn't have to worry that I'd voiced an unfounded suspicion to Ronan.

I printed a copy of the picture to show him later, cringing at the thought of what all those prints were adding to my hotel bill, then headed back upstairs to face my waiting voice mails.

I picked up my cell phone first, since that was the number pretty much everyone had. Four new messages, in addition to the two showing on the room phone, for a total of six in about as many hours. I made sure I had paper and pen handy, then pushed the button to start playing them.

The first message was from Deb, wondering why I hadn't called back yet. At the worry in her voice, I felt guilty, then amused, remembering all the worry she and her sister had caused me during their teen and college years by not returning calls. She was an adult now. She could deal. I continued to the next message.

"Ms. Seally, this is Frank Truman of the Federal Bureau of Investigation. We spoke yesterday. Agent Walters and I are flying down from Miami this afternoon to speak with you. Sometime tonight or early tomorrow would be best. I'll call again once we're in Aruba, probably sometime shortly after six p.m."

*Two* FBI agents were coming to talk to me? Clearly they'd decided my evidence was more important than they had let on earlier. Either that, or they'd managed a sweet boondoggle to Aruba on the American taxpayers' dime. I guessed I'd find out when I met with them.

The message after that was from Stefan Melampus.

"As I intimated to you yesterday, Ms. Seally, I'm sending a representative, Argus Haliakis, to meet with you, as I'm unable to travel to Aruba myself at the moment. You can expect a call from him shortly, giving you his arrival time. I'd just like to add how very sorry I am that I must send a proxy, and that I do hope we can meet in actuality in the near future."

I couldn't help but smile at the elegant way he expressed himself. Stefan Melampus was charismatic, no doubt about it—even in voice mail.

The final message was the one just promised. "Yo, Ms. Seally. Gus Haliakis here, Mr. Melampus's personal assistant. My plane's supposed to land in Aruba at a quarter to six tonight. I'll give you a shout once I'm on the ground. Thanks."

He didn't sound nearly as elegant as his employer—rather the opposite, in fact. And young. I was curious enough to look forward to meeting him.

The first message on my room phone was essentially a duplicate of the one Frank Truman had left on my cell. The second one was a surprise, however.

"Ms. Seally, this is Curt Phelps, with Everard, Jennings & Holt. I'm assisting Mr. Holt with the Stefan Melampus case, and he has asked me to fly to Aruba to speak with you. I expect to arrive at 5:47 this evening and will contact you once I'm on the island."

I jotted down the name and the time, wondering why a personal meeting should be necessary. I remembered the law firm and Mr. Holt's name from my internet research on the case. I'd been struck by it at the time, since Holt was one of those high-profile attorneys who had been in the news on more than one occasion for defending rich and powerful men in big trouble.

I supposed it made sense he'd want a statement from me, but he could have obtained that over the phone—or after I returned to the States. Unless he was hoping to retrieve the ring itself? *Hmm.*

As I hung up the phone, it occurred to me that there couldn't be many daily flights from Miami to Aruba. I glanced at my notes. In fact, it was almost certain that all four of these men were on the same plane—right now!

How bizarre that I, Wynne Seally, could be the focus of that many people on one plane. I wondered how many different agendas they represented.

## CHAPTER THIRTEEN

BY THE TIME the first follow-up call came at twenty past six, I'd showered, dressed in my most conservative outfit, and done all the internet research I knew how to do—which almost certainly wasn't enough.

"Ms. Seally, this is Argus Haliakis, Mr. Melampus's personal assistant, but you can call me Gus. Everyone does. You got my earlier message?"

"I did, and Mr. Melampus's message as well. I hope your flight was uneventful."

"It was, thanks. You enjoying your time in Aruba?"

"I was." I realized he would have no way of knowing about what had happened that morning. In fact, none of these new arrivals would. "Things have recently become a bit more, ah, exciting than I'd bargained for, however."

"Yeah? What's up?"

This was the one man among those I'd be meeting that I'd been unable to find a single bit of information about. Not surprising, perhaps, since he had no reason to be in the public eye, but I'd have felt better if I'd managed to find a picture or description—even a

Facebook page. Especially since he sounded almost like a street thug over the phone.

"Perhaps it would be better to discuss recent events in person rather than over the phone," I suggested. Though since I didn't know what Melampus's assistant looked like, I'd be no more likely to recognize an imposter in person.

"Yeah, yeah. I understand. You think we can meet sometime in the next day or so?"

"Sure. When did you have in mind?" I'd just make sure it was someplace public.

"Mr. Melampus said it should be at your convenience, Ms. Seally, so you name the time and place."

Okay, that was kind of nice. Or was that what someone with a nefarious purpose might say? No, Stefan had told me this man was coming. He was no more likely to be a threat than the lawyer. The FBI guys, on the other hand...

"Tomorrow morning, then? Say, ten o'clock in the lobby of the Royal Aruban Hotel?" He had to be tired. That would let him check into his hotel and get some dinner and a good night's sleep before he had to deal with my problems, or his boss's.

"Sounds good. I'll see you then."

One down. I wondered if I'd have time to grab some dinner myself before the next call came. As if in answer, my cell phone rang again before I could even set it down. With a sigh, I carried it out to the balcony before answering it.

"Hello?"

"Wynne Seally?"

"Yes." Who else was likely to answer my cell phone?

"Frank Truman, FBI. My partner and I have cleared customs and would like to meet with you as soon as possible."

Nothing about "my convenience" from this guy. I wondered if men carrying guns had to jump through special hoops at customs, or if their badges expedited them through. Interesting that Mr. Haliakis had made it through ahead of them, if so.

"When and where did you have in mind?" I asked.

"We can be at your hotel within the hour."

Just great. "Will this be a dinner meeting, then?" I hoped not. But if so, I definitely wasn't paying.

I could hear him conferring with Walters for a moment, then he said, "Let's meet at eight. That way all of us can grab a bite to eat beforehand."

So they weren't willing to pay, either. I wondered what kind of budget they had for this trip. Maybe they'd shot it already on the flight and a room.

"Fine. Eight o'clock in the lobby, then." I didn't ask how I'd recognize them. Something told me that wouldn't be a problem.

Curt Phelps's call didn't come until after seven, while I was enjoying my room service salmon salad. He must have waited until he'd checked into his hotel to worry about business.

"Mr. Holt would like me to meet with you at your earliest convenience," he said once we'd exchanged the required pleasantries. "Are you free for lunch tomorrow?"

"As it happens, I am." I couldn't imagine my meeting with Mr. Haliakis would last more than two hours. "Say, twelve thirty?"

"That will be fine. Is there any particular restaurant you prefer? This is my first visit to Aruba."

"Mine, too. But I've heard the Japanese restaurant in the Westin is good." Everard, Jennings & Holt could certainly afford it, and I was doing them a favor. I pushed thoughts of Ronan firmly from my mind.

"Excellent. I look forward to seeing you at twelve thirty tomorrow, Ms. Seally."

Well! My social calendar certainly was filling up quickly. I closed my phone, hoping it was for the last time this evening. A glance at the clock showed I had half an hour before I needed to be downstairs for my meeting with the FBI. I quickly finished my dinner, then began a thoughtful survey of my room.

I really didn't want to keep the ring on me after what had

happened this morning, and I definitely wasn't ready to hand it over to the FBI—or anyone else—just yet. Which meant I needed to find an exceptionally good hiding place for it.

I considered the undersides of drawers and the bed before realizing I didn't have any tape. Maybe I could attach it to the bottom of one of the balcony chairs with dental floss? I fumbled around for ten minutes, wasting half a container of floss, then decided it would be too easy to find there.

Finally, I settled on the hem of the drapes. With my nail scissors, I was able to snip a couple of threads and create an opening just large enough for the ring. I slipped it into the hem, then shook it along the bottom until it was a foot or more from my tiny hole. I'd sew up the hole before I went to bed, but the ring should be safe enough for the hour or so I expected to be gone.

The bedside phone jangled, bringing me quickly to my feet. Now what? It was still five minutes till eight, so it shouldn't be the FBI guys, unless they were running late.

"Hello?"

"Wynne? Ronan. I was just wondering if you'd had dinner yet."

Well, shoot. "Actually, I have. Sorry."

"Ah, well, that's what I get for waiting so late to ask. Would you like to meet for a drink or something anyway? I thought we could talk."

There was no avoiding it. "I can't right now, I'm afraid. I'm supposed to meet someone in about two minutes. I take it you haven't heard anything more from the police?" I added quickly, hoping to distract him.

It didn't work. "Not yet. So, um, who are you meeting? Should I be jealous?"

I forced a laugh. "Probably. I'm meeting two guys at once." Then, deciding there was no point trying to keep it from him, I added, "They're with the FBI."

"You're kidding." But there was no kidding in his tone now. None at all.

"No, unfortunately, I'm not. They insist on talking with me."

"Why didn't you mention this before? Is this because I didn't want to tell the Aruban police about the Melampus case? You decided to go to the Feds?"

"No, it had nothing to do with that—and I didn't know this morning that they were coming. And once I did, I, ah, had no way to reach you. You've never given me a number or told me where you're staying." Which was perfectly true. Not that I'd have called anyway.

As I'd hoped, it stopped him in mid-rant. "Oh. I guess I hadn't thought of that. But—"

"Look," I interrupted, "I really do have to go now, but we can meet later and I'll tell you all about it, okay?"

"All right. Take down my number and call me as soon as you're free."

He gave it, and I jotted it down, hung up, then looked at the clock. It was two minutes past eight. I was late. Cursing under my breath, I grabbed my purse, stuck my feet into my shoes, and headed to the elevator.

Of course, because I was in a hurry, the elevator stopped at almost every single floor on the way down. Then I had to wait for the elderly couple in front of me to make their way out of the elevator. They took so long the doors actually tried to close twice before we were all out.

I rounded the corner to the main area of the lobby and saw I'd been right about not needing descriptions. Two men waited there, and even though they weren't in suits, they were so stiff and ill-at-ease I could tell at a glance they were the Feds. For their sakes, I hoped these guys never had to go undercover.

The taller one was actually looking at his watch as I hurried over to them. An apology for being late was right on the tip of my tongue, but I swallowed it. I refused to start off on the defensive.

"Agents Truman and Walters?" I said instead. "Wynne Seally. Welcome to Aruba." Island time, I reminded myself when that apology almost slipped out in spite of my decision. They might as well get used to it.

To their credit, neither one mentioned that I was at least five minutes late.

"Thank you for meeting with us, Ms. Seally," the taller man said, extending his hand. "I'm Frank Truman, and this is my partner, Boyd Walters." He discreetly flipped open a wallet showing his badge and ID. "Is there somewhere we can go to talk privately?"

Frank Truman looked exactly like I'd have imagined him, if I'd thought to do that. Square jaw, light brown hair and eyes, attractive in a serious sort of way.

Boyd Walters was blond and looked like he'd been a wrestler in a previous life: shorter, barrel-chested, and muscular, too apple-cheeked to be considered handsome. In fact, if I'd met him under other circumstances, I might have described him as jolly looking.

"We should be able to find a quiet corner outside near the pool this time of night," I suggested. I wasn't about to invite them up to my room.

They nodded and followed me out to the enormous, intricately landscaped area surrounding the meandering pool. A couple of kids were playing down at one end, so I took a path going the other way between the mazelike hedges and found us a table and chairs in a secluded area, with no one remotely within earshot.

"Give me five minutes to scout the area before we start," Walters said. He ducked through the nearest opening in the hedge and disappeared while I did my best not to smile—or laugh out loud—at such exaggerated cloak-and-dagger tactics. Did these guys think they were in a movie or something?

"What exactly are you afraid of?" I couldn't help asking. "Do you think the bushes might be bugged? It's a lot more likely you were seen loitering in the lobby, if you're worried Melanie Melampus will find out you're here."

Agent Truman looked a little sheepish, which made him seem a lot more human—and attractive. "I guess we don't exactly look like typical tourists, do we?"

"Not exactly, no. And I'm afraid someone *has* been tracking my movements, or at least... Well, I'll wait until Agent Walters gets back to tell you that story."

He came back around the hedge right then, so on cue that I wondered if he'd been eavesdropping.

"No one nearby," he said. "We'll just have to assume they haven't managed to acquire or install any high tech surveillance equipment."

"So you *are* afraid they've bugged the bushes?" I asked, only half jokingly. It was hard to treat this business lightly after this morning's attack, though these FBI guys somehow brought out my sense of the ridiculous.

"I doubt anyone's had time, but we can't rule it out," Walters said, betraying not the slightest trace of amusement.

"Obviously you're taking my story a little more seriously than you seemed to during our conversations yesterday. Decided I'm not some publicity-seeking crackpot after all?" I couldn't help myself.

"The ring you described checked out, Ms. Seally," Agent Truman said. "We spoke with the people at the Oranjestad Cartier store and looked at the list of effects that went missing along with Melanie Melampus."

"Speaking of which, can we see it?" Agent Walters asked, then actually held out his hand for the ring.

Alarm bells went off in my head. So that's what this was about—getting their hands on the evidence before I showed it to anyone else? I glanced at Agent Truman, who looked politely expectant, then at Walters, who looked positively avid.

"I don't have it with me," I replied with what I thought was admirable coolness. "After what happened this morning, I felt it was wiser not to carry it around."

"And what was that, Ms. Seally?" Agent Truman asked. "You said something about your movements being tracked?"

"Yes. Someone—I can only assume someone connected to Melanie Melampus—has apparently been following me. He joined a dive I went on this morning, at the last moment, then tried to get the ring away from me while we were underwater."

It sounded so matter-of-fact, stated like that, conveying none of the terror I'd felt during the attack—and which echoed through me even now at the memory.

"You had the ring with you underwater?" Walters sounded skeptical.

"On a chain around my neck, tucked inside my wetsuit. The hotel safe was broken into a couple of days ago, and my own room was searched shortly after I first contacted the Cartier store, so keeping it on me seemed the safest option. Of course, I never expected someone to physically assault me for it."

The two agents exchanged looks, then Walters asked, "So the man who assaulted you is in custody now? Did you find out his name?"

I shook my head. "He swam to another boat and got away. And I doubt the name he gave our captain was his real one."

"And what makes you think he was connected to Melanie Melampus?" Agent Truman asked. "He could have been a common thief, or even someone working for Stefan Melampus."

"I can't imagine a common thief paying for a dive plus rental equipment to steal a ring he couldn't even have known about. And why would Stefan Melampus want the ring stolen? It seems it would be in his best interest for me to publicize where I found it, or turn it over to the authorities. Or his lawyer."

I started to add that one of his lawyers was here in Aruba, then changed my mind. I didn't want to get into a wrangle just now about who had rights to the ring.

"Yeah, we've been talking about that," Walters said. "It would have made sense for Melampus to have arranged to have the ring planted here in Aruba for you to find. He could have kept the ring when he killed his wife, then sent it to someone here."

I almost laughed. "What, and had them fling it in the ocean on the chance some random diver might find it? Not much of a plan. I'm starting to think you guys are making this up as you go along."

"He *could* have arranged in advance for that 'random diver' to find the ring."

I stared at Agent Walters, then looked to Agent Truman for support. He, at least, looked a little uncomfortable with his partner's theory.

"You really think I'm in league with Stefan Melampus?" No way was I going to mention his phone calls or his lawyer to them now. "Do you think I also arranged to have someone attack me underwater this morning? Me, a brand-new diver? You can check that story out with the local police, by the way."

Walters just shrugged, refusing to give anything away.

"But if Melanie Melampus faked her own death and framed her husband," I continued, "she wouldn't want anything out there that would screw up that scenario, would she? Especially given that I saw her, here in Aruba, it makes much more sense that she'd be behind this."

Now Agent Walters was scowling. "Then why didn't you bring the ring with you when you came to meet us? Once you turn it in, you'll be out of danger."

"Only if Melanie knows I've turned it in," I pointed out. "And what, exactly, will you do with the ring if I give it to you?"

"If?" Walters barked.

"Submit it as evidence," Agent Truman said, slanting a glance at his partner. "What else?"

But I was watching Walters, who still looked angry. "Even though that would undermine the case you've been building against Stefan Melampus?"

"Who said we were building a case?" Truman asked sharply. "This isn't the first time you've said something to make me believe you're more closely connected to this case than you're letting on, Ms. Seally."

I raised a brow for effect. "It was Agent Walters who told me that, if you must know." I looked pointedly at Truman's partner.

Walters glared at me, then, with a visible effort, schooled his expression to something approaching neutrality. "I said that there was circumstantial evidence pointing to Melampus's guilt."

He'd said a lot more than that, but I decided not to press it right now. I also decided there was no way Walters was getting his hands on the ring. If anyone was likely to make it "conveniently" disappear, it was him.

"Is there anything else?" I asked, glancing pointedly at my watch. I was anxious to hear Ronan's take on this conversation.

"I'm sorry if you have plans, Ms. Seally." Agent Truman didn't sound sorry at all. "We've come quite a long way to speak with you, however, so we'd appreciate it if you'd answer our questions."

I stifled a sigh. "Fire away. Though I'm not sure why this couldn't have been handled over the phone." Except that they wanted that ring.

Truman took out a flip-pad and a pen, just like the guys in the TV crime shows. "You claim you saw Melanie Melampus in Oranjestad. When would that have been?"

"The night before last—almost exactly forty-eight hours ago, in fact."

"So it was dark at the time?"

"There were lights from the stores around the square, but it was night, yes. About nine o'clock."

"Had you ever seen Melanie Melampus before?"

"Only pictures. When I realized the ring I'd found might be relevant to the Melampus case, I did some research on the internet and found quite a few photos of both Melanie and her husband."

"So you'd been following this case in the news all along?" he asked.

"Well, no. I really didn't know much about it—or the Melampuses—at all until I did that research. But that was just a couple of hours before I saw her, so those pictures were pretty fresh in my mind."

"I see. Then just how did you become aware that the ring might have something to do with the Melampus case?"

*Yikes.* I'd walked right into that one. Out of the corner of my eye, I could see Walters grinning but Truman's face was still stone-serious.

After too long a pause, I said, "Someone on the boat—one of the other divers—recognized the names in the inscription. He'd been following the case, I guess." It was basically the truth, but it still sounded lame.

"So you showed the ring to everyone on the boat?" Agent Walters demanded before Truman could probe my story further. "Why didn't you mention that before?"

"When would I have done that?" My innocence might have been feigned, but my indignation wasn't. Jerk.

"When I talked to you on the phone yesterday," he said. "When I told you not to discuss the ring with anyone else until we got here."

"You never said for sure that anyone *was* coming here. You just issued edicts and then hung up on me, after implying I was some kind of nut case. The next thing I heard from you guys was your phone message today saying you were on your way."

Again, Frank Truman sent his partner a look that told me he'd had to deal with Walters's temper all too often in the past. Then he turned back to me.

"I apologize, Ms. Seally, for the way we've handled things. It's true that I originally suspected that you were another, ah, nut case, as you put it. We've come across more than our share of them in connection with this investigation. It was actually Agent Walters who convinced me you might be telling the truth."

"Then I guess I should be grateful to him." I didn't even try to keep the sarcasm out of my voice.

He ignored it. "Now, can you tell me the name of the person in your diving group who recognized the ring as pertaining to the Melampus case?"

I'd been hoping Truman had been deflected from that line of questioning, but he was like a pit bull. "It was one of the men," I said slowly, stalling for time as I tried to think of a way to satisfy my questioner without giving Ronan away. "Rick, maybe? I'm terrible with names, I'm afraid, and everyone was talking at once."

I thought it sounded plausible, and though he practically drilled through me with his gaze, Agent Truman didn't challenge my story.

"I'd like the name of the dive shop and instructor. If they can give me the names of everyone in your group, maybe you'll remember which one showed such interest in the ring. I'd like to question him, if possible."

"Sure. It was the dive shop here at the Royal Aruban, and our instructor was Jason. I don't remember his last name," I lied, "but he's probably the only instructor there named Jason."

At least now I'd have time to warn Ronan before they came looking for him—if they did. Since he wasn't one of the students, maybe they wouldn't ask for his name. It was time to distract these guys further, so I finally pulled out my big guns.

"I do have something else here you might find helpful," I said, taking the envelope I'd previously given to Ronan out of my purse and handing it to Agent Truman.

He pulled out the photos and examined them in silence before handing them to his partner. "Why didn't you mention these before?" he asked.

"Again, I wasn't given the opportunity. Both of you were pretty abrupt in our earlier conversations." I told them about the phone message purporting to be from the Cartier store, which had given me the idea to stake out the place, and how I'd managed to get the pictures without being seen.

"Of course, the quality isn't great because of the distance and lighting," I said, "but surely you'll admit that looks like Melanie Melampus."

"Or her sister," Agent Walters said, handing the pictures back to Truman with a dismissive gesture. "You do know that Melanie Melampus had a sister, don't you, Ms. Seally? Michelle Alvares. Word is, they looked an awful lot alike—and she was last known to be in Aruba."

I stared at him, my mouth hanging open until I remembered to close it. "Melanie has a sister in Aruba?"

Even as I said it, I remembered Ronan telling me about a sister. She was the beneficiary of Melanie's life insurance policy. But he hadn't said anything about her being in Aruba. Wouldn't the insurance company have known that? In which case...wouldn't Ronan?

"That's right," Agent Truman said. "We're hoping to track her down and speak with her while we're here, since it's possible Melanie spoke with her before she was killed. If Melanie feared for her life and spoke to her sister about it, it will strengthen our case."

"So you think this—" I pointed to the top photo—"is Melanie's sister and not Melanie at all."

"It would make sense, Ms. Seally. A lot more sense than Melanie Melampus suddenly appearing some two thousand miles from where she disappeared off her husband's yacht."

I had to admit it was possible. Maybe even probable. Still, something didn't add up. "But...how could the ring end up in Aruba, then?"

"Maybe she gave the ring to her sister before she was killed—or mailed it to her," Walters said.

"Then why would you come here to get it? And why would Michelle Alvares threaten me over it? Why send a thug after the ring if she'd had it in the first place?"

"As I said before, it's possible that attack had nothing to do with the ring or the Melampus case."

But I wasn't buying that one. "And whoever ransacked my room? And broke into the hotel safe? I suppose those had nothing to do with the ring either. And then there was that bogus message on my phone. That's a lot of coincidences, Agent Truman."

For the first time, I saw a trace of amusement in his expression. It looked even better on him than his earlier embarrassment.

"I'll give you credit for using your head, Ms. Seally. No, I can't claim all of those were coincidental, but that doesn't mean Michelle Alvares was behind any of it. There are plenty of people all over the world who'd like to see Stefan Melampus get what's coming to him. He's made a lot of enemies, particularly over the past year or two. Some of them are very powerful—and wouldn't be above violence or even murder to destroy any evidence that might set Melampus free."

"Oh." I sat back, deflated.

And much more frightened than I'd been before.

## CHAPTER FOURTEEN

AFTER ASKING me a few more questions about where and how I'd found the ring, and about that morning's attack, Agents Truman and Walters finally left. I walked back to the lobby with them and waited until I saw them get into their car before calling Ronan.

"If that offer of a drink still stands, I think I could use one," I said by way of greeting.

"That bad, huh? Poor baby. I'll be waiting in the lobby."

"I'm already here," I told him and shut my phone.

I couldn't remember ever being called "poor baby" by anyone other than my mother. And she hadn't said it in a couple of decades, at least. Even during the divorce, she'd been more interested in talking me out of it than comforting me.

"Hey, there."

I turned to see Ronan coming across the lobby.

"That was quick. Where were you, in the casino again?"

He grinned. "Guilty as charged. So, do you want to go somewhere, or just get drinks in one of the bars here?"

I remembered what Agent Truman had said about the ruthlessness of Stefan Melampus's enemies and said, "I'd just as soon stay here, I think. Maybe the pool bar? It's a beautiful night."

Besides, I didn't want to associate that lovely area with my FBI inquisition.

"Great idea. Come on." He grabbed my hand, which was both startling and pleasant, and headed for the patio with me in tow. Ironically, once out back, he turned toward the same corner where I'd just spent an hour with Agents Truman and Walters.

"Um, how about something a little closer to the bar," I suggested, pointing to a relatively isolated table set well back from the pool.

He changed course without argument. "So, what'll you have? I'll go get us drinks, then you can unburden yourself to me."

I couldn't help returning his smile, though I knew I shouldn't let him pamper me like this. It would be way too easy to get used to, and once I left Aruba, no one was likely to pamper me again for a long time—if ever. Besides, I had a serious bone to pick with him, and I didn't want to get distracted before I'd done so.

"A margarita on the rocks, with salt," I told him.

While he was at the bar, I pulled out my phone and turned it off. If those agents wanted to talk with me again, it wasn't going to be tonight. I also didn't want any demands or worries from my mother or even my daughters. I was going to unjangle my nerves, get some truth out of Ronan, then go to bed.

After a good night's sleep, I'd decide whether to keep those other two appointments or catch the first flight back to Indianapolis. At the moment, I was leaning toward the latter—safer—option.

"Here you are, my lady," said Ronan, setting down my margarita with an exaggerated bow. "On the rocks, with salt. Now, what kind of wringer did those Feds put you through?"

"Just a lot of questions." I didn't meet his eye. "Where I found the ring, what the guy looked like who attacked us, stuff like that."

"Us? You told them about me?" he asked sharply.

I looked up at that. "Actually, no. But would it matter if I had? What haven't you told me, Ronan?"

"I've told you plenty—more than I probably should have." It

wasn't really an answer, and we both knew it. "How did the Feds know to contact you in the first place?"

"I e-mailed them," I said bluntly. "Yesterday morning, before you and I met for breakfast. After seeing that woman who looked like Melanie the night before, I read up on the Melampus case online, and it seemed like the right thing to do."

"And you always try to do the right thing, whatever the cost, don't you?" His tone wasn't as cynical as his words, but it still made me defensive.

"I think most decent people do—don't you?"

He didn't answer that, instead just saying, "I don't want you to get hurt, Wynne. I hope you know that by now."

"Won't I be safer if I know what I'm up against?" I challenged him. "For instance, how long have you known that Melanie Melampus's sister was here in Aruba?"

He hesitated so long I didn't think he was going to reply. "You showed them the pictures, didn't you?"

I nodded. "You suspected from the start it was the sister and not Melanie herself, didn't you? *Did* you know she was here in Aruba?"

"She's the reason I'm here."

Goose bumps flared all over me, despite the fact it was still about eighty degrees. "You mean...you know her?"

"No, of course not," he said so emphatically that I believed him. I relaxed marginally.

"But why didn't you tell me before that she was here on the island? I even asked you directly if you'd talked with her, and you said no."

"And it was true. I haven't spoken with her yet. The only address the insurance company has is a PO box, and there's no phone number listed. We weren't even sure she *was* in Aruba, but it was the only place left to look."

"So where has she been? The FBI guys thought she might have

spoken with Melanie before her disappearance. I assumed from that she'd been in Miami."

He shook his head. "To the best of my knowledge, she hasn't been in the States for years—maybe decades. I haven't even found anyone who's seen her, though she granted a couple of phone interviews after Melanie's disappearance. That's the real reason I wanted to borrow those photos—to make copies."

"But Agent Walters said Melanie and her sister look a lot alike. How would he know that if no one's seen her?"

"Because Melanie said so herself. It was in the news a little over a year ago, how she'd finally found her long-lost sister and flew to Brazil to see her. You didn't follow that story either, I take it?"

I shook my head, trying to remember if I'd seen any mention of it in my various internet searches. If I had, I must have skimmed over it.

"It wasn't that big a story—just a blip, really, mainly on the entertainment-type news shows. The gist of it was, Melanie and her sister were separated when they were very young—like five or six years old—when they went into foster care."

"Foster care?" Obviously, I hadn't done nearly enough research on Melanie. "Why were they in foster care?"

Ronan shrugged. "Mother died, father was abusive—or maybe it was the other way around. I forget. But it was a rough way to grow up, I imagine. Not much in the way of opportunities. No one ever would have heard of either of them again if Stefan Melampus hadn't fallen for Melanie."

Now I was really curious. "And how did that happen? I assumed she was a socialite-type, but it sounds like they didn't exactly move in the same circles."

"No, not at all. It was like something out of a classic romance, actually. He saw her on stage at some community theater in Miami —I think he was there for some fundraiser—and arranged to meet her afterward. A real Cinderella story. I think she was working as a waitress at the time, barely making rent."

"And the sister?"

"She'd apparently been adopted out of the foster system, and her parents moved to Brazil with her. Melanie never had the resources to track her down until after she married Melampus."

I mulled that over for a minute or two. "So did it take her that long to find her, or did she only start looking a year or two ago?"

"I have no idea. Those kinds of details haven't been in the news, at least that I've seen, and I've had no reason to go looking. Why?"

"Just curious," I said with a shrug. I supposed it made sense that the first thing on a new bride's mind—especially one who'd gone from rags to riches as dramatically as Melanie had—wouldn't be a sister she hadn't seen since she was six.

But maybe later, once the first gloss was off her fairy tale? Yeah, I could buy that, having been there.

"Okay, let's assume it was Michelle Alvares I saw in Oranjestad the other night and not Melanie. That would still mean she was the one who tried to lure me to the Cartier store. Agent Truman brushed off her involvement in all this, but—"

"Yeah, I've been thinking about that ever since you saw her downtown that night. It's why I tried so hard to find her then, in fact. She had to know about the ring—maybe even lost it herself and is trying to get it back."

"Then you think Michelle killed her sister for the insurance money?" I felt another chill wash over me. Melanie Melampus wanting the ring back so she wouldn't be found was one thing. But a possible murderer trying to cover her tracks was much, much scarier.

He spread his hands. "I honestly don't know. When I came here to find Michelle, I didn't really think she had anything to do with Melanie's murder. I was just hoping to discover some kind of irregularity about the life insurance policy. But your finding Melanie's ring, plus the stuff that's happened since, make it look like she was involved, one way or another."

"Agent Truman mentioned other people, former associates, who want to see Stefan Melampus go down for this supposed crime," I said, trying not to let fear take over. "He thinks the guy who attacked us this morning might have been one of them."

"Did you tell him you saw the same man with Melanie's sister?"

I tried to remember. "I don't think so. They were firing so many questions at me, I didn't get much of a chance to volunteer anything. Anyway, that doesn't mean they're wrong. Michelle could be working with Melampus's enemies. If she knew about the life insurance policy, she'd have a financial incentive to see her sister dead and Stefan Melampus framed for the murder."

"So you think—what? That Michelle somehow orchestrated whatever really happened on Stefan Melampus's yacht that night?" He actually seemed interested to hear my theory.

"It's not impossible, is it? You said yourself you didn't think Stefan Melampus was guilty." I thought for a moment, a scenario unfolding in my imagination.

"Melanie might even have been in on the scheme herself," I speculated. "Maybe she and her sister planned to split the life insurance money. It would explain her taking out that policy. But then her sister double crossed her and really had her killed. Maybe she had the killer—if it was someone else—send her the ring as proof or something."

"Which would explain that ring turning up in Aruba." He stared at me for a long moment with an odd half-smile playing about his mouth, then said, "In case you're interested, you just came up with the exact theory I've been operating on since I first saw that ring."

"I did?" I couldn't help feeling a bit proud of myself. After all, he'd had years of experience at this kind of thing and I'd had what —three days? "I guess I'm just a natural, huh?"

"So it seems." He clinked his glass against mine. "So, are you going to drink that before all the ice melts?"

I picked up my forgotten margarita and took a sip, marshaling my courage for my next question. "So, why didn't you tell me your theory from the start? Why didn't you trust me?" I didn't quite manage to keep the hurt from my voice.

He hesitated for a long moment, and when he answered, it was with obvious reluctance. "I guess I was afraid if you knew the person after the ring could have been involved with a murder, you might bolt. So I let you go on believing it was Melanie you'd seen."

Anger started to stir, temporarily pushing my fear to the background. "And you didn't want me to bolt—why? So you could use me as bait? To lure Michelle out of hiding? So much for all of your claims that you don't like to think of me at risk."

"I don't, Wynne. I do mean that. And except for that attack this morning, I don't think you really have been. If you want to fly back to the States tomorrow, I won't try to stop you. But this thing may well go far beyond Michelle Alvares and Aruba. And I won't be able to protect you, once you go home."

With a shiver, I remembered again what Agent Truman had said about Stefan Melampus's powerful, ruthless enemies. Which meant there might be some truth in Ronan's words, even though I was pretty sure he was saying these things to keep me here for his own mercenary purposes.

"So, just how much was that insurance policy worth?" I asked, suddenly curious. "You never said."

Again, he hesitated. "Ten million dollars," he finally said, with obvious reluctance.

"Holy sh—! I mean...that's a lot of money." Definitely enough to make a person capable of violence. No wonder Michelle Alvares wanted that ring back. But I needed to know the rest. "And what's your cut, if you get the insurance company out of paying?"

"My usual fee, plus expenses. And...a bonus. Ten percent of whatever I save them." He said it without expression, but my eyes widened.

"A million bucks? I'm surprised you haven't tried to take the ring from me yourself," I said without thinking.

The look he gave me was hard to decipher. "Do you really think I'm that kind of man, Wynne?"

"I've only known you for a few days," I pointed out. "I was married to my husband for almost twenty-five years before I found out what kind of man he was."

"Point taken. And it's not like I've been completely honest with you, even for the short time you've known me. I won't say the thought of taking the ring didn't occur to me, though I never considered doing anything that would put you in danger. I hope you believe that, at least."

"I do." And I pretty much did. But that didn't mean he hadn't been the one to break into the hotel safe. Or my room that first night, for that matter.

But I didn't have it in me to ask him about it right now. Though his motives might be mixed, at the moment he was my only friend in Aruba. I didn't want to think about what would have happened underwater this morning if he hadn't been right there with me.

Of course, I wouldn't have been diving at all, if it weren't for his eagerness to get more evidence for the insurance company, I reminded myself. A million dollars...

"I still wish you'd trusted me all along," I couldn't help saying.

He put a hand on top of mine, where it lay on the table between us. "It wasn't a matter of trust, exactly, Wynne. Over the years, I've got into the habit of playing my cards pretty close to the chest. I once lost out on a very big case because I talked about my theories to another investigator. Because I was too trusting."

"Then it is about trust," I pointed out. "But I'm not an insurance investigator."

"Not yet," he replied with a grin. "Maybe you ought to look into becoming one. As you said, you're a natural."

"I'll think about it," I said with a laugh. "But it sounds like a riskier line of work than I'm looking for."

"It's the risk that makes it fun." He really seemed to mean it.

I shook my head. "Maybe for you. You're young, single, foot-loose. I'm—"

"You're not single?"

"Well, yes, I am—now. But I have two daughters—"

"Who have lives of their own. Face it, Wynne, you're as foot-loose as I am—or at least you could be, if you'd let yourself."

I stared at him as his words sank in, realizing it was true. I was as free as I wanted to be. The concept was as scary as it was liberating.

"Paradigm shift?" he asked sympathetically when I didn't reply.

"Yeah. It's a lot to wrap my mind around." In fact, everything I'd learned tonight was a lot to wrap my mind around. It might take me days to process it all.

"Take your time," he said, just like he'd heard my thought. "Meanwhile, maybe we can come up with a plan to flush out Michelle Alvares."

"Not tonight," I told him firmly. "I'm going to head up to bed. Believe it or not, all this excitement has worn me out, after the boring life I've led till now."

He chuckled with me but stood to help me to my feet. "I keep forgetting you're not used to this kind of thing. Do you want me to walk you up?"

I did, to be honest. The thought of returning to my room alone, maybe to find further threats on the phone—or something worse—gave me the willies. But I was determined to be a grown-up about this.

"No, I'll be fine. But thanks."

"Okay, if you're sure. You have my number now. Don't hesitate to call if you need...anything. Even if it's just a sympathetic ear."

"Thanks. I'll do that."

By the time I reached my room a few minutes later, I'd decided that if my key didn't work, I was going straight back to the front desk. And if my room had been ransacked again, I was changing hotels for the night, then flying back to Indy in the morning. My courage was at low ebb.

Of course, since I'd planned for disaster, my key card worked on the first try, and when I cautiously entered my room, everything looked just as I'd left it. Maybe the bad guys, whoever they were, hadn't figured out which room I was in yet. I could only hope.

Still, the first thing I did was to check the hem of the drapes. Yes, the ring was still there. I left it and started to get ready for bed. I'd told Ronan the truth when I'd said the events of the day had taken their toll; I was exhausted.

Not until I was plugging my cell phone into its charger did I remember I'd had it off for the past hour or more. I powered it up, mainly from a sense of duty, and sure enough, I had a voice mail waiting.

"Hey, Mom, it's me," came Deb's voice, and I relaxed. Just more phone tag.

But then she continued. "I've been trying to get you since last night, and I really need you to call. It's not something I wanted to leave on a voice mail, especially since you're on vacation and all and I don't want to ruin it, but—call me back, okay?"

I glanced at the clock and decided Deb would still be awake, since it was an hour earlier there. What could be going on that she wouldn't want to mention in a voice mail? Luckily for my peace of mind, she picked up on the second ring so I could ask her that question myself.

"Deb? I just got your message. What's going on?"

"Oh, Mom, hi! I'm sorry if that message scared you, but I was starting to worry about you, too. I'm really glad you've called."

That didn't calm me a bit. "What is it? What's happened? Are you and Bess okay?"

"We're fine. It's nothing like that. But Mrs. Henderson called me last night and said that when she came by to feed Milo and bring in the mail, it looked like someone had broken into the house.

"I went over to check. You know how Mrs. Henderson is. But I think she's right. They didn't take anything really valuable that I could tell, but the back door lock was broken. I didn't know whether to call the cops or what, so I figured I'd better talk to you."

"So Mrs. Henderson is okay, too?" My next door neighbor was elderly, and I hated to think of her upset because of some teenage vandal.

"She's fine. She wasn't even positive the house *had* been broken into. That's why she called me."

"But you sound pretty sure that it was."

"Well, yeah, once I looked around some, it was pretty obvious, apart from the broken lock. The stack of mail that's come while you've been gone was spread all over the dining room table, like someone had gone through it. Milo didn't do it, because a few things were even opened."

"That's strange. I wasn't expecting anything valuable." Even as I said it, I thought of the ring. Was it conceivable that someone thought I'd mailed it to myself?

No—that was my paranoia talking. Wasn't it?

"Yeah, I thought it was weird, too. What's even weirder is that the only thing that seems to be missing is that family portrait over the fireplace."

I had that awful cold-water feeling again. "When did you say this happened?"

"Sometime yesterday. Mrs. Henderson noticed the lock and the mail when she went to feed Milo last night. He's fine, too, by the way, though he was acting pretty spooked when I first got there last night."

"And you didn't call the police?" Even at this distance, I'm sure she couldn't mistake the outrage in my voice, but I hoped the fear wasn't as obvious.

She hesitated long enough to make me almost regret my implicit scold. She was, after all, an adult now, and doing me a favor by calling at all. But then she said, "I...I thought maybe, you know, maybe it was Dad. Because of the picture and all."

She sounded so young, so lost, that I forgave her on the spot. The divorce hadn't been easy on the girls, even if they were on their own now. I even gave her theory some consideration—for about three seconds.

"No, that's not his style at all. If he'd wanted something from the house, he'd have involved his lawyer. He'd never stoop to breaking in." Whatever else he might stoop to. Nor could I imagine him wanting that family portrait, after the way he'd turned his back on us. No matter what he'd been saying to my mother recently.

Besides, I had a terrible suspicion about who *had* done this. Well, not who, exactly, but why. The ring. If I was right, it could explain how my attacker this morning had known what I looked like, so he could follow me. That portrait.

"Yeah, I guess you're right," Deb said.

I was startled, thinking for an instant she was talking about my theory involving the ring, then I remembered what my last words had been.

"So call the police, okay, Honey? And ask Mrs. Henderson if she'd be willing to keep Milo at her place for now—or you can take him, if your apartment complex allows cats. I'd rather neither of you go back to the house, just in case whoever broke in comes back. Wait until the police come and then get Milo out."

I loved that fat, old, gray tabby, but not as much as I loved my daughters. And I wouldn't risk old Mrs. Henderson for him, either, irritating as she could be on occasion. Thank God they were all safe. I sent up a quick prayer that they'd stay that way.

"Okay, Mom, if you think it'll do any good." She sounded skeptical, and I couldn't blame her.

"It probably won't, but I'd like a report filed anyway. I've worked in insurance, remember?"

She chuckled at that, and I found myself envying her for her ability to take this lightly. "Got it. Do you want me to do it tonight, or can it wait till tomorrow?"

Mrs. Henderson would have already fed Milo tonight, since she was a go-to-bed-with-the-chickens sort, so there didn't seem much point in dragging Deb across town now.

"Morning will be fine. But early—before Mrs. Henderson goes over, okay? Call her now and let her know to wait for them, even if it means waking her up."

"Oh, come on, Mom, what are the chances of them coming back? Especially first thing tomorrow morning?"

"Just humor me, okay? I know you hate getting up early, but this is important. I'll make it up to you—I'll take you and Bess out to dinner as soon as I get home."

"All right, fine. I'll call Mrs. Henderson now and the cops the first thing in the morning. Early, I promise. Now, shouldn't you be getting to bed, or are you living the wild life there in Aruba?"

I had to laugh at the sudden primness in her voice. "Wild. Yeah, that's me. I was getting ready for bed when I saw your voice mail. Good night, Deb."

Even before I set down my phone, I was wondering how early the first flight back to Indianapolis might leave in the morning. I went to the closet and pulled out my canvas bag with all my travel paperwork to find the 800 number for the airline.

I might have to go standby if I didn't want to pay a fortune, but I couldn't leave Deb and Mrs. Henderson to deal with people who might possibly have links to organized crime. Once I was home, I could...what?

With the airline's phone number in my hand, I sat on the edge of the bed to think. The absolute most important thing was to keep my daughters safe. If those thugs had our family portrait, they had pictures of my daughters as well as of me. There was no knowing how thoroughly they might have searched the house, so I had to assume they also knew where my daughters lived.

Scary, scary thought.

But by flying back to Indy, would I be bringing even more trouble with me? At the moment, at least, I was fairly sure the main villains of the piece were here in Aruba. Would they dare to follow me to Indiana? Did I dare find out?

I considered again the portrait they'd taken: a large one, hanging in an obvious spot. Surely, they could as easily have taken other pictures, ones that would be easier to copy and fax or e-mail —ones that might not even have been missed. Surely, real pros could have broken into my home, searched every inch of it, and left no trace they'd even been there, beyond a badly frightened cat.

Which meant that either these weren't pros, or...they wanted to send me a message.

Either way, my best chance of neutralizing the threat, to myself as well as my daughters, would be right here in Aruba.

## CHAPTER FIFTEEN

IT WAS A good thing my meeting with Argus Haliakis wasn't until ten o'clock the next morning. I was so distracted I forgot to set the alarm, then I didn't fall asleep until the wee hours, so many different scenarios were running through my head.

Thankfully, a noise out in the hallway woke me at half past nine. I jumped out of bed, splashed my face, pulled on capris and a blouse, and did a quickie version of my makeup, which got me out of the room at a quarter till.

Downstairs, I raced to the coffee kiosk to grab a bran muffin and coffee, then sat in the lobby to compose myself while I ate. I couldn't help glancing around, alert for any sign of "Lenny," but of course I didn't see him.

Munching my muffin, I told myself it was better for me than waffles, if not exactly a nutritious breakfast. Ah, well, I'd make up for it at lunch, when Everard, Jennings & Holt would be paying. The sushi was probably pretty good in Aruba, it being an island and all.

"Ms. Seally?" came a voice from behind me.

I jumped up, my mouth still full of muffin since it wasn't quite ten yet. I took a quick sip of coffee to wash it down as I turned.

Too quick—I choked and coughed, needing two more gulps of coffee that was still too hot for gulping, before I could speak.

"Mr. Haliakis?" I finally managed. Through watering eyes, I could see that the man facing me was definitely young, certainly less than thirty, and rather outrageously handsome. In fact, with his dark hair and eyes and European air, he reminded me more than a little bit of my attacker from yesterday.

"Yo, Ms. S, I didn't mean to startle you," he said, looking genuinely concerned—and making me feel like an idiot.

"That's okay. Not your fault." I cleared my throat, trying to make my voice less raspy. "I overslept, which is why I was still eating. Would you like a cup of coffee or something?"

He smiled a movie-star smile and shook his head. "I just ate, but thanks. You want we should talk here, or would someplace else be better?" As on the phone, he sounded almost like a street kid, but with a hint of accent—probably Greek, I reasoned, given his name and his connection to Stefan Melampus.

"There's a little lounge off to the side of the lobby that's usually empty this time of day," I suggested. "Unless you'd rather sit out by the pool?"

"Lounge sounds fine. I know you're on vacation, Ms. S, so I'll try to keep it short," he added as we walked to the area that served as a piano bar in the evenings.

Since the bar wasn't serving now, the lounge was deserted. We sat in a couple of the plush turquoise chairs, facing each other across a small table. Despite his youth and his unrefined speech, he looked serious now.

"You're probably wondering why I came all the way to Aruba when Mr. M can talk to you on the phone."

I assumed it was to get the ring from me, but I didn't say so. I simply waited for him to continue.

"He may not have told you this, but Mr. M has enemies—lots of enemies—and some of them pretend to be friends. Even his private phone conversations might not be all that private sometimes. So he really wanted a face-to-face meeting with you."

"And since he's not allowed to leave the States, he sent you," I said. "He told me that, yes."

Again with that dizzying smile. "Great. He wants me to get all the details about that ring you found and anything that's happened since. I'm also supposed to make sure you're safe, since there are people out there who'd like to get their hands on that ring and see him go down, and they might not play by the rules, if you get my drift."

"I understand." For a moment, I pondered how much to tell him, but then realized that if he was working with the bad guys he knew more than I did already. And if he was exactly what he claimed, he might as well have the whole truth to relay to his employer.

So I started at the beginning, with my finding of the ring, all of my interactions with the Cartier store, my sighting of the woman I'd thought was Melanie in Oranjestad, and the underwater attack yesterday morning. I told him about my interview with the FBI last night, and about my house back in Indiana being violated, even about my fears for my daughters.

The only thing I didn't mention was Ronan. Stefan knew about him, of course, but after all that had happened, I couldn't shake my caution, just in case Haliakis wasn't who he said he was.

He listened attentively, making no comments and asking no questions until I had finished. His very appearance was a little distracting, but I thought I made a decent story out of it. At the end, I asked a question that had been bothering me.

"I imagine I'll have to repeat all of this for Mr. Phelps over lunch today. Why have both you and someone from the law office come down here? Isn't that kind of overkill?"

He shrugged. "No one told me about the lawyer, though it's not like Mr. M tells me everything. But he's been backstabbed before, so maybe he's just playing it safe."

I was still confused. "Are you saying that this lawyer, who presumably represents Mr. Melampus, might not have his best interests in mind? Why not fire him from the case, then?"

"Oh, there's probably no proof, even if Mr. M suspects it—which I don't know that he does. But he's had more than one person he trusted turn on him, especially the past couple of years."

"Since his conversion, you mean?" It was a delicate topic, but I really wanted to know.

Mr. Haliakis hesitated for a long moment before answering. "Mr. M is a very, very good man, Ms. Seally. He'd tell you that he was a very bad man for most of his life, but I don't believe it. Even before he got religion, he was way better to me than I deserved. I wouldn't be exaggerating to say he saved my life."

There was no mistaking the sincerity that shone from those gorgeous eyes. This man idolized Stefan Melampus. Which meant I needed to take anything he said with a grain of salt.

"I understand that some of his former, um, associates were rather upset when Mr. Melampus changed his way of doing business."

He laughed, but grimly. "Yeah, you could say that. Someone's tried to kill him at least three times I know of, and I'm betting there've been others he hasn't told me about."

This was news to me. No wonder Agent Truman had said that Stefan's enemies weren't above murder to get what they wanted.

"But why?" I asked. "For vengeance? How would killing him benefit them?"

"They're afraid he'll finger them to the Feds, trying to make up for the stuff he did in the past."

I supposed that made sense. "Why hasn't he already done just that? If he really has changed—"

"He doesn't want to be the one to send any of 'em to the slammer, no matter what they did. He says his own sins were just as bad, but God forgave him. He wants them all to change like he did, and he doesn't think prison's a good place for that to happen."

"But surely he would be much safer himself if they *were* in prison?"

"Well, sure. I've tried to talk him into that a bunch of times, but he won't do it. He claims it's his fault some of them took a wrong turn in the first place, but I don't believe it."

I didn't doubt it, particularly, but it didn't lower my esteem for the man Stefan Melampus was now. Still—"Surely he has taken some sort of precautions, in case one of them is successful?"

"Yeah, he has, and that's why this case is so important to them. Mr. M wrote out a full confession, complete with names of his former, um, associates—dozens, maybe hundreds of 'em—to be given to the Feds if he's murdered. Since he spread the word on that, nobody else has tried to snuff him."

No, Stefan Melampus was no fool, but I already knew that after all of my research on him. "I assume having him convicted of murder wouldn't fall into that category, even if he believes he was set up. Yes, I can see why his enemies would want this case to go forward—unless they're worried about his testimony in court?"

Haliakis shrugged. "Anything he'd say against them there, he could say against them now."

I supposed that made sense. I glanced at my watch: eleven forty-five. My rendition of events had taken longer than I'd realized. Time to wrap things up.

"So now I assume you want me to give you the ring to take back to Mr. Melampus?" I asked, since he hadn't mentioned it.

Very much to my surprise, he shook his head. "No, that could make it look like he's had the ring all along. He says it's important for the case that the ring was found here in Aruba. Also, that you claim to have seen Melanie Melampus alive."

"Well, I thought it was Melanie, but I've now been told her sister is here in Aruba and that they look a lot alike. So I now realize it was probably her and not Melanie that I saw. I've never met either of them, so I wouldn't be a very good judge of that, I'm afraid."

"Yeah, Mr. M thought of that. He doesn't have a lot of hope his wife's alive, to be honest. He thinks it's more likely she was murdered so he could be framed for it. But if the ring was found here and the sister is here, it could point to her being guilty instead of Mr. M. It's still really important."

That made sense. "I don't understand why the sister hasn't been brought in for questioning yet." I almost mentioned the life insurance policy, but realized I'd be bringing Ronan into it if I did that.

And his answer matched Ronan's, almost word for word.

"No one's been able to find her. She has a PO box here, but that's it. I'm pretty sure you're the only person other than Melanie herself who's seen her. That's another reason Mr. M is worried for your safety."

"Oh. I, um, hadn't realized that." I swallowed the lump that had suddenly formed in my throat. It seemed that I was even at more risk than I'd realized—and that simply turning over the ring might not end that risk after all.

"But—" I was still working things through in my mind "—if she has a post office box here, why should she care if someone proves she *is* here? Wouldn't it make sense that she would be?"

"You'd think so, but she's been slippery as an eel. That's why Mr. M suspected her from the first. You may not know this, but Mrs. M hadn't really known her sister for very long. She might have done some things based on the whole sisterhood idea that weren't all that smart."

I assumed he meant the life insurance policy, but of course I couldn't say so. "I, um, read about that. They were separated when they were very young, and Melanie only found her a year or two ago —in Brazil?"

"Yeah. She flew to Brazil three or four times a while back, first looking for, then meeting with her sister. 'Course, Mr. M invited the sister to visit them in Miami, but she never came."

"And is it true that she and Melanie look alike? That I could have mistaken her for Melanie?"

He shrugged expansively. "I've never seen her, like I said. But Mrs. M herself did say they looked a lot alike, so it's possible. Much as I'd rather believe it was Mrs. M you saw."

I could understand that. While Michelle and the ring both turning up in Aruba might cast considerable doubt on Stefan Melampus's guilt, Melanie herself would completely void the whole case.

But I was afraid it sounded more and more like Michelle might have killed her sister—or had her killed—for the insurance money and arranged for Stefan to take the fall. With a sigh, I rose.

"Is there anything else, Mr. Haliakis? As I said earlier, I'm to meet with the lawyer, Mr. Phelps, in just a little bit, and I'd like to run up to my room first."

He stood as well. "Gus, remember? I'll talk to Mr. M and give you another call if he wants me to find out anything else. Thanks for your time, Ms. S."

"It was my pleasure." And it was—or partly pleasure, anyway, given how easy on the eyes he was. It was undeniably a useful meeting for me, as well, since talking everything through, in order, had helped me to put things in better perspective.

As I headed up to my room, I wondered if there really was any chance that Melanie Melampus was still alive. From everything Ronan and the FBI agents had said, it didn't sound like it. Even if she'd orginally been in on the scheme, planning to fake her death and disappear, her sister could well have double-crossed her and had her killed after all.

Either way, the ring might be the key to whatever had really happened. How had it ended up in Aruba, under sixty feet of seawater? I was beginning to wonder whether I'd ever find out.

Back in my room, I first checked that the ring was still safely hidden, then checked my cell phone. No messages, which I supposed was a good thing, though I'd half expected a call from Debra by now. I only had a couple of minutes to spare, so I brushed my teeth, reapplied my lipstick, and headed back downstairs for my next appointment.

Curt Phelps was waiting in the lobby when I arrived, a tall, impeccably-dressed fair-haired man of about my own age. At a guess, I'd say his suit probably cost more than my entire wardrobe back home.

"Mr. Phelps?" I said as I approached, just in case I was wrong. I wasn't.

"Ah, Ms. Seally? I want to thank you for seeing me. Shall we go next door to the restaurant before we begin?" His manner was cool, but I didn't take it personally. I had the feeling he was that way with everyone.

I nodded, and we headed outside. The hotels along Palm Beach stood shoulder to shoulder, so it only took us a minute to walk to the one next door and another minute or two, once inside, to reach the Lotus Blossom. He had actually made a reservation, so we were seated immediately.

We were conveniently secluded from the other diners, both out of earshot of the nearest table and screened by a cascade of greenery and flowers. An artificial waterfall only a few feet away made it even less likely we could be overheard. I suspected Mr. Phelps had scoped the place out in advance and requested this particular table.

"I assume you're going to want the whole story of how I found the ring and what's happened since?" I said when the hostess left us, since he hadn't really spoken to me since we'd exchanged greetings in the lobby.

"Of course. But I'd prefer we order first." He looked pointedly at his menu.

His very precision made me want to do something outrageous —which was unusual for me. Fortunately, I was able to content myself with ordering the most expensive sushi combo on the menu when the server came by a moment later. Mr. Phelps suggested something from the wine list but I shook my head. Tempting as it was to run the bill even higher, I thought it wisest to stick with iced tea.

When the server was gone, he pulled a tiny digital recorder from his pocket and set it on the table between us. "You don't mind, do you? This will be easier and more accurate than taking notes."

Though I was a little taken aback, I shook my head. "That'll be fine." I'd just try really hard not to say anything stupid.

"Curt Phelps, Esquire, interviewing Wynne Seally," he said, for the benefit of the tape. "Now, if you'd start with when, where, and how you found the ring?"

The formality was disconcerting, but after a second or two to marshal my thoughts, I launched into the same story I'd given Mr. Haliakis a couple of hours ago. Unlike my previous listener, Mr. Phelps interrupted me frequently with questions, to clarify various details.

When our salads arrived, he paused the recorder long enough to allow me a few bites and a sip or two of my tea before punching the button again and resuming the inquisition. At first I was self-conscious about eating with the recorder on, but as he continued relentlessly on, I decided he could just deal with any extraneous sounds on the tape and finished my salad between questions.

He paused the thing again when our sushi came. I noticed he'd ordered only cooked fish and veggie rolls. No, not the adventurous type, Mr. Phelps. Of course, prior to this trip, nigiri had been about the limit of my own adventuresomeness, but I decided not to dwell on that.

"And last night you learned your home had been burgled?" he prompted me after restarting the recorder.

I poured soy sauce and dabbled a bit of wasabi into it with my chopsticks. "Yes, though it actually happened sometime the day before. My daughter didn't want to tell me in voice mail, so I hadn't realized her calls were urgent."

For the first time, his professional demeanor cracked a tiny bit around the edges, and he actually looked startled. "Your daughter was in the house at the time? Was she hurt?"

"Oh. No, no. She has her own apartment elsewhere. But the neighbor feeding my cat noticed some things amiss, so she called my daughter, who called me."

"You didn't leave your number with your neighbor?" He seemed to think that strange—as it would seem to anyone who didn't know Mrs. Henderson.

"She's a chatterer. I didn't dare leave my cell number with her, for fear she'd rack me up a five-hundred-dollar phone bill with inconsequentials. Since I knew I wouldn't be able to handle any emergencies from here, it made more sense to leave her my daughter's number."

He nodded and popped a piece of California roll into his mouth, *sans* wasabi.

"And that's pretty much it, so far," I said, picking up a piece of tuna nigiri. "I'm really hoping, now that you and Mr. Haliakis and the FBI are here, there won't be anything else of interest to report."

I bit my nigiri neatly in half—something I'd hardly ever managed to do before without making a mess. It seemed a shame to waste such an elegant moment on ultra-conservative Mr. Phelps. Too bad Ronan wasn't here.

The attorney picked up the recorder and put it back in his pocket. "Mr. Holt will appreciate your taking the time to tell us all of this, Ms. Seally. We're aware that you weren't obligated to say anything to us at all, but your testimony and evidence could potentially keep Mr. Melampus out of prison."

"I do try to do the right thing when I can," I said. Why did so many people seem to have trouble with that concept?

"An admirable attitude." He set down his chopsticks, even though he'd only eaten a couple of his rolls. "May I see the ring?"

I shook my head, suddenly wary. "As I told the two FBI agents last night, after yesterday's attack, I'm not comfortable keeping it with me. It's safely locked away." Well, my room was locked, so that wasn't exactly a lie.

"Understandable. But Mr. Holt has asked that I bring it back as evidence. Once the ring is out of your hands, you should be at no further risk."

"That's just what the FBI guys said last night." I was pretty sure my smile wasn't very convincing. "As I pointed out to them, that's only true if whoever is after the ring knows I no longer have it. And Mr. Haliakis said—"

"I should probably caution you against putting too much faith in Mr. Haliakis," he interrupted. "Mr. Melampus may trust him, but his background is chequered, to say the least. As Mr. Melampus has had more than one close associate turn on him in recent years, his judgment may not be what it once was."

I ate another piece of my sushi, more to give myself time to think than because I was still hungry—though it was excellent sushi. I found it more than a little bit interesting that Mr. Phelps and Mr. Haliakis had said almost exactly the same thing about each other.

Which meant that until I knew more about them both, I couldn't trust either one of them.

## CHAPTER SIXTEEN

"THANK YOU for a lovely meal, Mr. Phelps," I said, standing. "Is there a number where I can contact you?"

He rose quickly but not awkwardly, as I'd secretly hoped he might. I really wanted to see this guy lose his cool.

"My cell number is on my card," he replied, whipping one from his breast pocket. "Or you can reach me at room 1519 of the Royal Aruban—your hotel." He pulled out a pen and jotted the number on the back of his card, then handed it to me.

I dropped it into my purse without comment.

"You'll let me know when you've retrieved the ring?" he said then. It was more statement than question, and I found his assurance more than a bit irritating. "Everard, Jennings & Holt can make certain you'll be safe once it leaves your possession."

"Thank you," I said again. Then, without committing to a thing, I turned and left the restaurant.

Walking back to my hotel, I felt a rush of relief that all of my ordeals were over—at least until the next phone call. I almost hated to go back to my room with its two waiting phones, but I did need to talk to Debra to see what the police had said about the break-in.

The housekeeper was just finishing up when I reached my room

—and sure enough, both phones were blinking. I was anxious to check the ring's hiding place but forced myself to putter around at the bathroom counter for an interminable two or three minutes until the maid left.

As soon as the door closed, I hurried to the drapes and knelt, feeling along the hem. For one heart-stopping moment, I thought the ring was gone, but then my fingers found the small, hard circle, just a few inches from where I'd started. Still, that scare was enough to make me prise it back out of the tiny hole I'd made, just to reassure myself that it was the same ring. It was.

I laughed shakily at my foolishness and put the ring back, then went into the bathroom for my sewing kit and stitched up the hole, as I'd meant to do last night before bed. That done, I finally turned my attention to the blinking message lights and picked up my cell. One message, from Debra.

"Hi, Mom, it's me. The cops just left, so I figured you'd want me to call. Nothing much to tell, though—they looked at the back door, asked a few questions, told me I should replace the lock, and said they'd file a report. Woohoo. Anyway, call me if you want."

And that would probably be the end of it. Since no one was hurt and nothing valuable was taken, the Indianapolis police weren't likely to expend any resources on this.

When my friend Jean's car was stolen last year, all the cops had done was "file a report." She'd been lucky—her car had been found a week later, abandoned, stinking of cigarettes, and out of gas. But not by the police. The guy whose yard it had been left in had looked up Jean's number after finding the registration in the glove compartment.

Ah, well, at least I'd played by the rules. I picked up my room phone next and found two voice mails waiting.

"Ms. Seally, this is Boyd Walters, FBI. Since you didn't have it with you last night, we're going to need to get that ring from you today so we can tag it as evidence. Call the Days Inn, Room 224, when you get in."

I jotted down the number but had no intention of calling it—at least not yet. I wondered if Agent Truman even knew Walters had made that call, since I was pretty sure they didn't have any authority to make me do anything here in Aruba. I did smile at the idea of them staying at the Days Inn. At least the American taxpayers weren't shelling out for a penthouse somewhere.

I continued to the next message, which had been left only a minute or two before I'd returned to my room, half expecting it to be Frank Truman. But it wasn't.

"Mrs. Seally," said a woman's voice, "I'm calling because I am concerned for your safety. An item has come into your possession that puts you at great risk, as you must realize by now. If you wish to get rid of the item and secure your safety, leave it at the front desk of your hotel in an envelope addressed to Chris Smith before midnight tonight."

The receiver still in my fist, I sat down abruptly on the bed, swallowing hard and trying to force my brain to work. The electronic voice of the hotel message system came on, saying, "That was your last new message. To save, press seven. To delete, press three."

I punched seven, then pressed the voice mail button again. "You have two saved messages," I was informed, then it proceeded to play them, in order received.

"Ms. Seally, this is the Cartier Boutique. We may have found the owner of that ring."

I hung up the receiver before it finished. Yes, it was definitely the same voice—Michelle Alvares's voice, I'd be willing to bet.

Just in case yesterday's attack hadn't scared me enough, she was now leaving threats on the phone. I wondered how many flunkies she had working for her, and where they might be.

Again my instinct was to run home, leaving all of this intrigue behind. But the same reasons I'd thought of last night after talking to Deb still applied today. Maybe even more so.

And if the FBI was any part of the threat at all, I'd just be giving them jurisdiction to demand the ring and whatever testimony I could give. I might be at even more risk there than here, since there was no knowing what measures Stefan Melampus's enemies might take to keep me from doing just that.

If I *was* going to give Truman and Walters the ring, I might as well do it here and now. Ditto if I was going to hand it over to "Chris Smith," aka Michelle Alvares.

I contemplated the hem of the drapes, agonizing over what I should do. One thing for sure—I was feeling less safe with every passing hour. I was very, very tempted to just comply with this latest demand. Otherwise, there was no knowing what Michelle Alvares might try next.

Of course, that would undermine Ronan's chance of getting his commission and, more importantly, Stefan Melampus's chance of getting justice.

"Why me?" I asked aloud of the empty room. All I'd done was find a souvenir, and then try to do the right thing with it. How had I ended up with such an awful ethical dilemma?

The very best thing that could happen was for Michelle Alvares to be caught and proof found that she had either murdered her sister or helped her to disappear. That would both end the threat and serve justice.

Maybe I should call the FBI guys back after all. No matter how much they wanted to see Stefan Melampus convicted, they wouldn't let a murderer walk free—would they? I was fairly sure they wouldn't physically threaten me, at least. But if they didn't have jurisdiction here to make me give them the ring, would they have any authority to arrest Michelle, assuming we could somehow find her?

She could be anywhere in Aruba.

The room phone rang, making me jump. Heart pounding, I debated whether or not to answer it, since every phone call only seemed to make things worse. But knowing was better than not knowing—I hoped. I picked up the receiver.

"Hello?" In my effort not to sound scared, my voice was almost belligerent.

"Um, Wynne? Did I catch you at a bad time or something?" It was Ronan.

I gave a shaky laugh. "No, no, sorry. I was just...well, it's kind of a long story, actually."

"Do you want to get together, so you can tell it to me?"

"Well..." I hesitated, gripped by a sudden, unreasoning fear of leaving my room and also a reluctance to explain things yet again, after doing so twice already today. But then I reconsidered.

"Yes, actually, I would. I think I could use your help figuring some stuff out."

Ronan was an experienced investigator. Surely he'd have some ideas on what I could do. I knew his main motivation was profit, but since helping me was likely to work in his favor, I could live with that. And I still trusted him more than any of the other men I'd spoken to over the past twenty-four hours.

"I'm yours to command." The playfulness in his voice calmed me, making everything seem somehow less dire. "When and where?"

I glanced at the clock—just past three. "How about the lobby in half an hour?"

He didn't ask what I needed the half hour for. "I'll see you then."

Though it was tempting to feel flattered by his willingness, I knew it wasn't personal. Besides, I had other things to worry about. I picked up my cell phone and called Debra.

"Hi, you've reached Debra Seally. Leave me a message and—"

I hung up, feeling stupid for forgetting she'd be at work right now. She'd probably had to go in late, in fact, after meeting the police at the house this morning. And she hadn't even complained, though I was sure she felt she was humoring me.

After that call from "Chris Smith," though, I didn't regret my caution a bit.

I started to call Bess to warn her to be careful, too, but stopped myself before hitting the "call" button. Would anything be gained by scaring my girls? Even if my worst assumptions were true, Michelle Alvares would surely wait to see if I complied with her demand before ordering any kind of attack on my family. Which meant I had the rest of the day to make some decisions.

And I had Ronan to help me do that.

I went into the bathroom to put on sunscreen and freshen up my hair and makeup, then headed downstairs to meet him.

He was already in the lobby when I got there—and so was Curt Phelps, over near the reception desk. He wasn't looking my way, so I deliberately turned my back to him, circling around until I could catch Ronan's eye.

Without saying anything, I motioned toward the beach exit. Ronan nodded slightly, and we both headed that way, not noticeably together—or so I hoped.

Nonchalantly, staying a few yards apart, we headed away from the reception desk and out the archway leading to the beach. I resisted the temptation to look over my shoulder. It really didn't matter if Phelps saw me, but if I made eye contact with him, I'd have to say something. And I definitely didn't want to introduce him to Ronan. Not yet, anyway.

"Okay, what was that about?" Ronan asked when we were halfway to the breakers.

"Stefan Melampus's lawyer. I just spent close to two hours being grilled by him and didn't want to give him the chance to ask any more questions he might have thought of since."

"So, you want to walk on the beach again while we talk? It's probably as safe a place as any."

I definitely didn't want to be anywhere we might be overheard, but—"You're not worried we'll be seen together? By the FBI or someone else? It seems like Aruba—and my hotel in particular—is crawling with interested parties."

"Oh? Anyone I should know about besides the FBI and this lawyer we just escaped from?"

"Well, there's Stefan Melampus's assistant. And that guy that attacked us yesterday, along with anyone else Michelle Alvares might have working with her."

"Assistant? When did he—and that lawyer—get here?"

We fell into step, walking briskly away from the hotel, toward the less populated end of the beach.

"Last night. I was so rattled by the FBI interrogation that I forgot to mention the others—though I didn't actually meet with either of them until today."

He gave me a long, considering look, but then shrugged. "Fair enough. I can't expect you to give me every detail of every phone call you've had since you arrived on the island. Not when I wasn't always completely upfront with you."

I was relieved he wasn't angry about it, since I needed his advice. At least, that was the main reason I was relieved.

"Everything has been happening so fast, I've had a hard time keeping up with it myself," I said by way of a partial explanation. "And I'm still not sure who the good guys and bad guys are in this whole scenario—who I can really trust."

He reached over and brushed a strand of windblown hair out of my eyes, an intimate gesture that softened me in spite of myself. "I hope you trust me, Wynne—though as I said, I can't really blame you if you don't."

"I really, really want to," I said with perfect honesty, "because I'm in serious need of some advice right now."

"Why? What's happened since we talked last night?" If his concern wasn't genuine, he was an excellent actor.

"Several things, two of them scary. Remember what you said about this thing not being limited to Aruba? I found out late last night that someone broke into my house back in Indiana, and I'm afraid it might have had something to do with what's going on here."

"I hope no one was hurt."

"No, no one was home except my cat, and he's fine. But they went through my mail and stole a big family portrait from over the fireplace... I think they must have been trying to scare me as much as anything."

He nodded. "Entirely possible. Whoever they are, they won't want you leaving Aruba with that ring, or saying anything to the authorities that might help clear Melampus. Though it would make more sense for them to go after him directly."

"They've tried. His assistant told me so this morning. There've been several attempts on his life, but he's really well protected. And now he's set it up so if they kill him, whole lists of names and specifics will come out, implicating most of his former cronies."

"Thus the motive to frame him for murder. Apart from the insurance money, that is. But I really don't like them targeting you, Wynne, here or back in the States. There has to be a way to flush out Michelle Alvares and collapse their whole plan once and for all."

"Chris Smith!"

Not surprisingly, Ronan looked at me like I'd lost my mind. "Excuse me?"

"That was the other scary thing. I got another phone message today from the same woman who tried to lure me to the Cartier store the other night. Michelle Alvares, I assume."

"What did she say this time? Was she still pretending to be from the jewelry store?"

"No. It was pretty much a straight threat, telling me to leave the ring at the hotel desk addressed to a 'Chris Smith' if I wanted to stay safe."

"Which means we can set a trap. I can't imagine she won't have thought of that, though."

"Maybe she's getting desperate after yesterday's attempt to get the ring failed. She may even know about the FBI being here, and figure if she doesn't get it right away, she may not get another chance. This could be a last-ditch effort."

"Maybe." He still looked doubtful. "Have you told anyone else about this?"

I shook my head. "I only got the message a few minutes before you called, after I got back from my meeting with the lawyer. He wants the ring, too, by the way. Oh, and so does the FBI. What do you think, Ronan? Should I just leave the ring at the desk, like she said, or should I let the FBI guys handle it?"

Since either option would pretty much torpedo Ronan's shot at that million dollar bonus, I wasn't surprised when he hesitated. "You can call in the FBI, of course, if you trust them. Or you could let me do it. I'm pretty good at surveillance, if I say so myself."

"You mean, do what she says, then stake out the reception desk to see who picks up the envelope? You don't think she'd actually come herself, do you?"

"Probably not. Notice she used an androgynous name—Chris. That way either a man or a woman can ask for it without arousing suspicion."

I hadn't noticed, but of course he was right. "What if I leave an envelope for Chris Smith, but instead of the ring, I enclose instructions on where to find it? Then we could stake out that spot instead of watching every single person who goes up to the desk at the hotel. Or would that be too obvious?"

He grinned. "You're really starting to get into this cloak-and-dagger stuff, aren't you? But yeah, even if Michelle's not the sharpest tack in the box, I doubt she'd fall for that—unless she's really, really desperate. Plus, there's whoever she's working with. We can't count on all of them being stupid, unfortunately."

"Then you don't think it's just her and Lenny?" I suppressed another shiver. "Here in Aruba, I mean."

"Could be. And either one would be fairly easy to spot at the hotel, since we know what they both look like."

I grimaced. "Which they probably realize. And Lenny—or

whatever his name really is—won't dare to show his face again anytime soon."

"No, I don't think he will. But even if it is just the two of them, they could pay someone, anyone, to pick up the envelope. Someone we'd never suspect, like a kid."

"I hadn't even thought of that. But it's making my note idea sound better and better."

For a moment I was silent. Ronan was silent too, as we walked along the beautiful white beach, a yard or two from the breakers, both thinking. Then I had an inspiration.

"I know," I said. "How about when I give the envelope to the person at the desk, I tell her—or him—to give us a signal when someone comes to claim it? Something subtle, like scratching their head or coughing?"

Ronan shrugged. "That will only work if the same person is on duty when they come to get the ring. And if they don't anticipate anything like that and use a bribe—or a threat—to keep the reception clerk from doing whatever we asked."

"Two pretty big ifs," I admitted, deflated. "Plus, now that I think of it, there are always at least two people on the desk."

I lapsed back into silence, out of ideas.

"Of course, these plans aren't mutually exclusive," Ronan said after a moment. "We can leave a note for Chris Smith setting up a rendezvous, and then stake out the reception desk to see who comes to pick it up. Even if it's not Michelle, whoever it is might lead us to her."

"*Hmm*. And maybe I can come up with a plausible-sounding reason for not leaving the ring. I could write something about being afraid the FBI will get it if I leave it at the hotel desk, that they've been watching me."

Ronan nodded. "Not bad. And if they buy it, the second stakeout might work if the first one doesn't. Two bites at the apple. You're pretty good at this, Wynne."

"Thanks." I tried not to preen. "It's kind of like a puzzle. I've always liked puzzles—crossword, jigsaw, sudoku. This one just has a lot more riding on the solution."

"It does," he agreed. "Which means once you leave the note, you need to lock yourself in your room and let me take it from there. Things could turn dangerous. I'm trained to handle that and you're not, even if you are a natural puzzle-solver."

Though that was exactly what I'd hoped he'd offer to do, I surprised myself by shaking my head. "I'm already in this deep. I want to see it through."

He put his hands on my shoulders, forcing me to look directly at him. "Wynne, listen to me. These people play for keeps. There's already been one murder. You can't put yourself at that kind of risk. Think of your daughters."

"Who have lives of their own, as you pointed out to me last night. I'm finally at a point in my life where I *can* take risks, Ronan. And I need to do this."

"No. I won't let you, Wynne."

I instinctively bristled at that. "You can't stop me. I'll...I'll go to the FBI with everything if you won't let me help." It was probably what I ought to do anyway, but I knew how much Ronan had riding on this.

"I'd rather you do that than put yourself at risk," he surprised me by saying. "I could never enjoy the money if you got hurt because of me."

He turned and started walking back toward the hotel, and I walked beside him, trying to figure out what my next step should be now that he'd called my bluff. Because no matter how I told myself I *should* call Agents Truman and Walters with this new info, I really didn't want to.

Ronan must have been thinking too, because after a moment, he said, "How about this? If you'll let me handle things—alone—I'll cut you in on twenty percent of that bonus, if I get it."

Twenty thousand—no, two *hundred* thousand dollars? Tempting, but I was already shaking my head again. "No deal. I'm helping.

Then, if you get your bonus, you can cut me in for part of it if you want to, your choice. But I'm not letting you pay me *not* to help."

"You are one stubborn woman, Wynne. Have I told you that?"

"I think so," I said, grinning in my relief. "I promise to try not to do anything stupid, if that helps."

"It does. But I also want you to promise to let me call the shots. And if I tell you to stay put, or to run, you do exactly that. Otherwise, you can go ahead and bring in the Feds and neither of us gets rich."

"Deal. It's not like I *want* to get hurt, you know. I just...well, it's hard to explain. But I feel like if I back off now, I'll never have the nerve to do anything adventurous again."

Now he was grinning, too. "Wasn't it just yesterday you told me you weren't willing to put yourself at risk for what I believe you called 'my precious payout'?"

"And I'm not. That's not why I'm doing it. But wasn't it just last night that you told me that it's the risk that makes your job fun? I've decided it's time I started taking some risks. Not stupid ones," I added quickly. "The kind that will make me braver. The fun ones."

"I think I may have created a monster," he murmured, shaking his head.

I laughed, but Ronan turned serious again.

"Okay, back to the plan," he said. "If we only put a note in the envelope, whoever picks it up will know right away there's no ring inside. Since we don't know who'll be picking it up or what kind of instructions they'll have been given, we should probably get a cheap ring somewhere to use as a decoy and put it in with the note."

"That makes sense. In fact, I've got one we can use." My wedding ring was still sitting in my room safe. Since I hadn't yet carried out my plan of tossing it into the ocean, I might as well put it to good use.

Luckily, Ronan didn't ask for details. "Okay, that'll save us some time. Meanwhile, I need to think of a good place for a rendezvous —not too public, but not so remote it will be dangerous."

"Maybe somewhere in Oranjestad, but off the beaten path?" I suggested.

"Maybe, though if the first half of the plan works, it won't matter. I'll be doing any actual tailing, by the way. Agreed?"

I started to argue, but then realized I'd probably botch the operation, as inexperienced as I was. "Agreed," I said. "I'll just be your...your backup."

Ronan grinned. "I can't think of anyone I'd rather have. But keep the phone number of the FBI guys handy just in case, okay?"

"Okay." I certainly wouldn't be much use by myself if Ronan ran into an ambush or something. It's not like I had a gun—or knew how to use one.

We drew level with the hotel. "Why don't you run up to your room and get that ring you mentioned, then we'll work on the wording of the note," he said. "Meet back in the lobby in fifteen minutes?"

"Sounds good," I said. "Then maybe we can grab some dinner or something before we drop the envelope at the desk. What does one eat before a stakeout?"

He only laughed and shook his head, but I entered the hotel feeling more cheerful than I'd have thought possible an hour earlier. Still, I did think to glance around the lobby for any suspicious—or familiar—characters before crossing it to get to the elevators. No one rang any alarms.

Padding down the hall of the fourteenth floor toward my suite at the end, I wondered if I had time for a quick shower, since it would only take a minute to grab my wedding ring out of the safe. I put my card in the key slot, contemplating potential stakeout outfits, knowing Ronan would laugh if he knew.

Smiling to myself, I opened the door—then froze as a shape rose from the chair by the window.

A man's shape, coming toward me.

A familiar shape.

"Happy Anniversary, Wynne."

## CHAPTER SEVENTEEN

"TOM?" I felt like I'd suddenly stepped into an alternate dimension —or a nightmare. "What are you doing here?"

"I thought I'd surprise you."

"No, seriously. What are you *doing* here? In my room? In Aruba?" My heart rate was starting to slow now, but there was no denying he'd surprised me. And not in a good way.

He closed the distance between us and kissed my cheek. I flinched away, but he didn't seem to notice.

"Your mother told me you didn't seem quite as eager to work things out as I am, so I thought I'd come convince you in person. After all, today is our twenty-fifth anniversary. Besides, it seemed a shame to let all this—" he waved an arm to indicate the suite and the view—"go to waste, after it was already paid for."

I glared at him. "It wasn't going to waste. I've been enjoying it just fine, thanks. By myself."

The look he gave me was the patronizing one I'd always hated— the one I'd tried so hard to forget.

"Come on, Wynne, I know you. What fun can you possibly be having all alone? You can only take so many solitary walks on the beach. And you've probably had room service every meal, since you hate going to restaurants alone."

"Actually, I've learned to enjoy it over the past eight months," I informed him. "I'm learning to enjoy a lot of things I never tried before."

He just shook his head and smiled. "You mother told me how hard it's been for you, all alone. That's why I thought I should come, once Bess told me you were here."

Why, oh why, hadn't I told the girls not to tell Tom when I'd told them not to tell my mother? Because it hadn't occurred to me that he'd ask. Or even that he might call either of them. Which he probably hadn't.

"I assume she let it slip when she called to tell you about getting into the dinner theater troupe?"

"Let it slip? Like it was a secret or something? I asked where you were, since your mother didn't know, and Bess told me. End of story."

"I hope you at least congratulated her first."

He shrugged. "I'm sure I did. But I also told her I hoped this wouldn't keep her from looking for a real job. All those years of college going to waste—"

"Again with the waste. She loves what she's doing, even if she's not making much money at it yet."

But I felt a twinge of guilt as I spoke, knowing I'd thought the same thing. No more, though. If Bess wanted to sing and act, that's what she should do, even if it meant working temp jobs to make ends meet.

"Fine. Fine. I didn't come here to fight, Wynne."

"Then exactly why did you come? And what does Darlene think of your impromptu trip?"

For the first time he looked vaguely uncomfortable. "I don't think she...I didn't...I mean, that's over, Wynne. It was never going to work long term. Not like us. I, well, I've missed you."

"How sad for you." Sarcasm dripped from my voice.

"Oh, like you haven't missed me, too? I mean, it's sweet that you came here in honor of our anniversary, but that's kind of sad, too." He put an arm around my shoulders, which made me acutely uncomfortable.

I moved out from under his arm and took a step away from him. "I didn't come here in honor of our anniversary. I came because the trip was paid for—and to celebrate my independence."

He smiled—an obnoxious, indulgent smile. "Of course. Anyway, I thought we should talk. As I know your mom told you, I've been thinking we should try to work things out. It's only been eight months... Why are you shaking your head?"

"Because it's over, Tom. I told my mother that in no uncertain terms when she called, and now I'm telling you. We're divorced. I've moved on. If you want to vacation in Aruba, I can't stop you. But you're not sharing my room."

"Moved on?" He looked startled. "What do—? You don't mean you're seeing someone else?"

It wasn't what I'd meant, but I wasn't about to admit it. "Why so surprised? Not that it's remotely any of your business now. *You* cheated on *me*, remember? And even when I gave you a chance, you were never willing to explain that to me, back when we were still married. I'm not about to explain myself to you, now that we're divorced."

"Fine. Fine." That was the way he always dropped a subject rather than admit he was wrong. "Tell you what. I'll take you out to dinner—a nice dinner, in honor of what *would* have been our anniversary—and we'll talk things through like rational adults."

I was about to tell him that if anyone was being irrational it was him, when the phone rang. To my outrage, Tom answered it before I could reach it.

"Hello? ... Yes, she's here. Who is this?"

"Tom! Give me that." I reached for the receiver, but he turned his back to me.

"This is Tom Seally, her husband."

"*Ex*-husband!" I shouted, but he'd cupped his hand around the mouthpiece.

"You're with what? The Federal— Why would the FBI be calling here? What's going on?" He swung around to stare at me.

I held my hand out for the receiver, glaring at him, but apparently Agent Truman or Walters was giving him some kind of explanation. Great. That was all I needed.

"I see. Yes, I'll tell her. Thanks." He hung up the phone.

"What is *wrong* with you?" I demanded. "That call wasn't for you. You can't just waltz in here and—"

"Wrong with me? You're on your own for just a few months, and you're in trouble with the FBI. What have you gotten yourself into, Wynne?" He looked both angry and alarmed—probably worried about his precious reputation.

"You mean he didn't tell you?"

Tom narrowed his eyes, and I got the impression he was actually seeing me for the first time since I'd come into the room.

"Agent Truman said that you haven't returned his call and that it's important that you cooperate. So just what exactly have you done that requires cooperating with the FBI? Did you witness a crime or something?"

"Not exactly," I began, then stopped myself. "You know, this isn't any of your business, either. Nothing to do with me is any of your business. Not any more."

Again with the patronizing look. "Wynne, Wynne. If you're in some kind of trouble, you have to let me help you. But to do that, I have to know what's going on."

"I'm not in any kind of trouble," I lied with a perfectly straight face. "They think I may have witnessed something, but I've already told them I didn't see anything. They probably just want me to sign a statement or something, but I've been out all day. If you'd just handed me the phone, I could have cleared everything up."

He looked at me for another long moment, and I wondered if he'd call my bluff, but he didn't. "Okay. He said he'd call back in a couple of hours, so let's go get some dinner, and you can tell me all about it."

"I don't want dinner, and I don't want to tell you about anything. And you're not staying in this room tonight." I sounded shrewish but didn't care. Tom definitely brought out the worst in me. Maybe he always had.

"Okay, fine. We'll go down to the front desk, and I'll book another room. But then we'll go get something to eat. You always get cranky when you're hungry, remember?"

As if I didn't have plenty of cause for crankiness right now, dinner or no dinner. "I already have plans. You'll just have to get a meal on your own."

"Look, Wynne, I really think we need to talk. There's...something I need to tell you about Debra and some decisions we need to make."

"What about Debra?" I asked suspiciously.

"Over dinner. It's too long a story to launch into on an empty stomach."

I started to insist that tell me now, but then I remembered what I'd originally come up to my room for—and that Ronan was waiting downstairs. I'd endure Tom for the space of a meal if I had to, to find out what was going on with Deb and to finally convince him, once and for all, that I had zero interest in reconciling. But I hoped I could convince him to hash everything out without that. I needed to be free this evening, to help Ronan with his plan.

"You go down and book a room, and I'll join you in a few minutes," I said without committing to dinner. "I need to go to the bathroom."

For a moment I thought he was going to insist on waiting in the room, but then he shrugged and left. The moment the door closed behind him, I punched in the room safe combination and removed my old wedding ring.

I didn't have a pocket in the sundress I was wearing, so I stuck it in change-purse section of my wallet. I also grabbed one of the big blue envelopes and a sheet of stationery out of the desk drawer and tucked those in my purse, too.

Then, just in case Tom was outside the door listening, I went into the bathroom, checked my face in the mirror, and flushed the toilet. Good thing, too, because Tom actually was loitering in the hallway when I opened the door a few seconds later.

"Ready?" he said.

I nodded, biting back a comment about his need to escort me downstairs after leaving me to sink or swim for the past eight months. I'd thought I'd worked past most of my anger over his infidelity and the divorce, but obviously not. Still, I wouldn't give him the satisfaction of knowing he could still needle me.

When we reached the ground floor, I said, "You go book your room, and I'll see if I can find a dining guide or something." I really needed to get away from him for a moment so I could find Ronan and give him a heads-up about this new complication to our plan.

"I saw a stack of those guides on the front desk," Tom said, putting a hand on my back to steer me in that direction. Once upon a time, I'd thought that gesture was protective and even romantic. Now I realized it was possessive and controlling—not at all the same thing.

Though I didn't dare create a scene in the lobby, where one of Michelle's cronies might be lurking, I was cursing up a storm inside my head. I surreptitiously glanced around for Ronan—and saw him heading straight toward us. I raised my eyebrows and gave a quick shake of my head to warn him off, but he didn't seem to notice.

"Excuse me," he said, speaking to Tom instead of to me. "But haven't we met?"

Tom stopped, clearly as surprised as I was. "I, uh, I don't recall—"

Ronan put his hand on Tom's shoulder, subtly detaching him from me. "Oh, sure you do. It was last fall, at that big get-together. Here, let me buy you a drink so we can catch up."

He started to steer Tom, who was clearly confused but unwilling to admit it, in the direction of the piano bar. The moment Tom's back was to me, Ronan turned to look at me and mouthed the word, "Run."

Suddenly, I realized what was going on. I was trying so hard not to laugh out loud that I couldn't immediately correct Ronan's mistake. But at the little snorty noise I made, Tom turned and reached for my arm to bring me alongside him.

"Don't touch her," Ronan said, his voice suddenly dangerous. "I think maybe you and I had better go outside and have a talk."

"What the—? Who do you—?" Tom started to bluster.

Ronan gripped his upper arm like a vise and started steering him toward the front of the hotel. "Wynne, go back to the lobby and wait there. Remember what you promised."

I finally found my voice, though it quivered a bit with amusement. "Um, Ronan, I think you have the wrong idea."

Tom quickly turned back to me while Ronan glared, clearly thinking I was refusing his order after he'd arranged my escape from my "captor."

"Wait," Tom said, still looking confused and a little bit angry. "Just wait a minute. You know this guy, Wynne?"

"Ronan, this is Tom Seally—my ex-husband. Tom, this is Ronan. We met during my dive lessons." He didn't need any more information than that.

Ronan immediately released Tom's arm, looking thunderstruck. The words "paradigm shift" popped into my head as he struggled to come up with something appropriate to say.

"Tom showed up *unexpectedly*," I explained, in an attempt to try to smooth over the awkwardness. "He was just about to book a room for himself, weren't you, Tom?"

But Tom didn't budge. "What, so you can... You're friends with this...this thug?"

"Ronan isn't a thug. I'm sure he thought you were some stranger trying to manhandle me. He was just being chivalrous."

Ronan was the one who nearly laughed this time, but he skillfully turned it into a cough and extended a hand to Tom. "My apologies. Wynne is right. I completely misread the situation and assumed she needed assistance. My mistake."

After another long, awkward moment, Tom shook his hand. "Understandable, I suppose, if you knew she was in Aruba alone. I guess I should thank you for looking out for her. She hasn't had much experience fending for herself and tends to be a little too trusting."

His meaning was clear but Ronan didn't rise to the bait. "I've only known Wynne a few days, but I'd say she has a pretty good head on her shoulders. I don't think you need to worry."

"That's good to hear."

The subtext between these two was thick enough to cut with a knife. Maybe I should have been flattered, but I was getting impatient with all the posturing.

"Now, where was it you met, again?" Tom asked, still looking more than a little suspicious.

I decided it was time I reentered the conversation. "During my scuba diving lessons. Ronan was—"

"Scuba diving? You?" Tom was insultingly incredulous. "You're kidding, right? Why on earth would you take scuba diving lessons?"

"Because I wanted to learn to dive, of course." It was one thing to take this from Debra, but I wasn't about to take it from Tom. "I did fine. And I enjoyed it."

"Uh-huh. So do they do special lessons for, well, people like you?"

I couldn't help bristling. "What do you mean, 'people like me'?"

"You know. People who aren't necessarily in the best shape. Older people trying stuff like that for the first time. I mean, it has to be kind of risky, and—"

Ronan cut him off, which was probably lucky for Tom since I was just about to punch him. "Wynne did extremely well, Mr. Seally. In fact, I'd say she was the best student in the class, even if the others were much younger. There's something to be said for the wisdom that comes with age." His tone implied that Tom had somehow missed out on that perk.

"That doesn't mean a whole lot coming from another beginner, but I guess it's nice of you to say."

Ronan smiled a not particularly pleasant smile. "I've been diving for more than twenty years, Mr. Seally, and I've taught dozens of people to dive. Wynne is a quicker study than most. Braver, too."

"Oh, so you were her teacher? A little fraternizing with the students, is that what's going on? Wynne, you can be so gullible—"

"He wasn't my instructor. He was piloting the boat our first day out on the ocean. Since we were the only ones on board close to the same age, we struck up a friendship." I caught myself, realizing I was falling back into my old pattern of defensiveness. No more. "Not that it's any of your business," I reminded Tom—and myself.

"Fine, fine. Whatever. So, are we going to go get some dinner or not?"

"Go book yourself a room first. I'll wait here."

He looked startled at my tone, and for a moment I thought he was going to argue, but then he shrugged and headed to the reception desk. I tried to remember whether I'd ever spoken that firmly to him while we were married. Maybe not.

"I can see why he's your ex," Ronan said as soon as Tom was out of earshot. "Though I guess it's not my place to say so."

I'd been glaring at Tom's retreating back, but now I turned to face Ronan. "You can say anything you want about him. It can't be worse than what I'm thinking. You're probably wondering what's wrong with me that I married a guy like that in the first place."

Ronan shrugged. "People can change a lot over the years. Some for the better, some for the worse. But what's he doing in Aruba all of a sudden?"

"From stuff my mom has been telling me, I think his girlfriend dumped him. I guess she was smarter than I gave her credit for. Now he says he wants to work things out. I pretty much told him to take a hike."

"Good for you. But even if you try to avoid him, his being here is going to complicate our plan. It looks like you'd better let me handle it alone after all. I assume he doesn't know anything about what's going on?"

I glanced over at the reception desk. Tom was waiting behind a couple of other people. Good.

"He knows *something* is going on. One of the FBI agents called my room, and he answered the phone—even though I was right there." I was still steamed about that. "He didn't give Tom any specifics, but now he wants to know why the FBI are calling. I made up a story about them thinking I'd witnessed something, but I'm not sure he bought it. He's going to want more details, especially if I can't talk him out of taking me to dinner."

"What do you plan to tell him?" Ronan was doing an admirable job of pretending it didn't matter to him.

"As little as possible. If he had any inkling of what's really going on, he'd insist on 'handling' things—which would mean putting me on the first plane back to Indy."

"Maybe that wouldn't be such a bad idea. You might be safer if—"

"And then you could handle everything alone, like you just said? Uh-uh. The deal still stands. That reminds me. Here's the ring we can use as a decoy." I dug my wedding ring out of my change purse and handed it to him without the slightest qualm. "Did you come up with the wording for the note?"

Ronan gave me an odd look as he took the ring, but then he nodded and pulled a piece of paper out of his pocket. "See what you think."

It read: "I was afraid to leave the ring here because the FBI have been watching the hotel. It will be safer if I leave the ring for you under the 'No Entry' sign at the side of the red windmill across from the Bubali Bird Sanctuary. I will have it there by noon tomorrow."

"Do you have something to copy it onto?" he asked.

I pulled the stationery and envelope from my purse in answer. Another glance showed that Tom was now talking to the woman at the desk. We didn't have much time.

"I'd better do it later. Or you can do it—it's not like they know what my handwriting looks like."

"You'd be surprised what they can find out—at least, if Michelle is working with Stefan Melampus's old cronies. Do you have something with a sample of your writing with you? I can probably copy it fairly closely."

I decided not to ask where he'd acquired that particular skill. Instead, I dug through my purse and found an old shopping list. "Will this do?"

"Perfect. I'll just say a friend asked me to leave it at the desk, in case anyone asks—or is watching."

"But I thought I would—"

"Your, ah, visitor may make this operation awkward if you try to help. Why don't you go ahead to dinner with him, get him out of the way so I can set things up. Maybe you can convince him to back off."

After a moment's thought, I reluctantly nodded. "I guess you're right. We need to leave the note well before midnight, and this will give you a chance to do that." It rankled, though, making me even more upset at Tom for showing up unannounced. "I'll ditch him as soon after dinner as I can, so I can help after."

"And I promise to give you a full report the moment you get back," Ronan said. Then, glancing behind me, he switched to a louder, more casual tone of voice. "I'd recommend the Argentine steakhouse, if there's not too long a wait."

Tom rejoined us, not looking particularly happy. "All they had available was a standard double-double room."

"Which you took?" I asked. Already I could feel my blood pressure inching up again.

"Yeah, I took it." He sounded positively disgusted. "Are you sure—?"

"Yes, I'm sure." I hoped my tone didn't leave him any room for hope that I'd change my mind.

"A standard room here should be very nice," Ronan offered. "The Royal Aruban is an excellent hotel. Celebrities stay here."

Tom grunted and made a sorry attempt at a smile. "Whatever. We should probably get going, Wynne."

"Ronan was suggesting an Argentine steakhouse nearby." I assumed he'd meant the one he and I had gone to for our first private meal together—the one where he'd first told me the significance of the ring I'd found. With any luck, I could be done with dinner and back here in an hour.

But Tom shook his head. "I'm not in the mood for steak. I asked the woman at the desk what she recommended, and she mentioned a restaurant up by the lighthouse at the north end of the island. I had her call and make us a reservation."

I'd never known Tom not to be in the mood for steak. I opened my mouth to argue, since this plan would add at least an hour to my absence, but Tom was looking stubborn, clearly not wanting to take any advice from Ronan.

"How will we get there?" I asked instead. Somehow, I couldn't imagine Tom getting into one of those rickety five dollar cabs, and I knew the shuttles only went back and forth between the hotels and Oranjestad.

"I rented a car, of course."

"Oh. Of course." I should have known Tom would refuse to be dependent on taxis or shuttles.

"Take a camera," Ronan suggested. "The view from the California Lighthouse is spectacular, especially at sunset. Trattoria el Faro Blanco is supposed to be the most romantic restaurant on the island. But maybe the desk clerk mentioned that?"

I glared at him but he didn't meet my eye, instead smiling placidly at Tom—but I thought I detected a sparkle of amusement in Ronan's eyes.

Tom mumbled something I thought was an embarrassed

acknowledgement, which had me redirecting my glare. There wasn't going to be anything the slightest bit romantic about this dinner, no matter what Tom had in mind.

"Fine," I said, disgusted with both of them and their matching cases of testosterone poisoning. "Why don't you bring the car around, and I'll meet you out front."

Tom gave us both a slightly suspicious look, but then turned and went out.

The moment he was gone, I held out my hand. "Okay, give me back the ring—and your note. I'll copy it myself."

Ronan handed everything to me, and I went to a small table near the reception desk to write his words on the sheet of hotel stationery. Then I dropped it into the big blue envelope along with my wedding ring, sealed it, and addressed it to Chris Smith.

"I'd like to leave this for a friend," I told the woman at the desk, handing her the envelope.

She read the name on the outside, glanced at me, then nodded. "That's fine," she said, and tucked it somewhere under the desk.

I stood there for a second, trying to decide whether that glance meant she recognized the name—which might mean someone had already spoken to her about picking it up. But I couldn't be sure, and Tom would be out front any minute.

As I headed for the entrance, I could see Ronan moving off to a corner where he just happened to have a good view of anyone coming up to the reception desk. He leaned against the wall and pulled out his cell phone, flipped it open and started talking. I was willing to bet there was no one on the other end, but he made it look very convincing.

I felt another pang at not being able to help with the stakeout after my brave words earlier, but there wasn't anything I could do about it now. I could only hope I'd be back at the hotel before anything interesting happened.

"Not bad, eh?" Tom said when I joined him out front, opening the passenger door of his red Porsche convertible with a flourish.

"Aruba is the perfect place for a car like this—they only get twenty inches of rain a year here, and now they're into their dry season."

"Very nice, as long as you don't mind sand in the car," I said, sliding into the passenger seat. "I assume you've noticed the wind."

"You mean it's always like this?"

"Yep. Your hair is already a mess." I just couldn't seem to stop myself from getting little digs in.

He went back around the car and slid behind the wheel. "Look, Wynne, I'm trying. I mean, I came here to try. Can't you give me a little credit?"

I thought for a moment, then shook my head. "Nope, I don't think so. I tried for years—for most of our marriage, in fact—and I don't recall you ever gave me any credit. So, no. No credit. It's too late for that."

"Look, if I'm going to spring for a fancy dinner, the least you can do is—"

"Mrs. Seally?" a voice to my right interrupted him. It was Agent Walters. "May I speak with you for a moment?"

I was almost relieved to see him, since it gave me an excuse to get out of the car. But when I noticed he was alone, I decided to stay where I was.

"Where's Agent Truman?" I asked.

"He's busy, working on another aspect of the case. Now, if your friend will excuse you for a moment—"

Tom got out of the car and stood up, facing Walters. "I'm not her friend, I'm her husband. Are you another FBI agent? What is this about?"

Agent Walters looked directly at Tom for the first time, then smiled. "Ah. Mr. Seally? Perhaps you can help us to convince your wife that she's playing a very dangerous game, and that it would be best for all concerned if she just hands over that ring before it lands her in more trouble than she's bargained for."

## CHAPTER EIGHTEEN

"ARE YOU OUT of your mind?" I demanded of Agent Walters. "Is this the FBI's idea of discretion? You just took this man's word that he's my husband. And he's not."

It gave me some satisfaction to see Walters taken aback. "He's not? But—"

"Okay, okay, I'm her ex-husband," Tom said. "But we've only been divorced a few weeks."

Walters relaxed slightly, though he still looked shaken. He obviously knew he'd screwed up. "So not a real security risk, then."

"But you didn't know that," I pointed out, not cutting him any slack. Walters had set me on edge from my very first phone conversation with him. "And he didn't need to know about this. You're the one who told *me* to keep it quiet, after all."

He shrugged, then resorted to bluster. "It was a calculated risk. If he can make you see sense, it's worth it. You have it with you?"

I was glad I could honestly shake my head. "Of course not. As I told you last night, I'm not taking any chances after what happened yesterday morning. It's safe."

"Safe where?" Frustration showed in his voice.

"I don't think I'll say just now," I replied with a glance at Tom. I was more worried about Walters, to tell the truth, but Walters didn't need to know that.

"Well...okay. You have my number. I expect to hear from you tonight."

"Good night, Agent Walters," I said with all the insincere sweetness I could muster.

With a parting glare, he stalked off. Before I could breathe even one sigh of relief, Tom got back in the car and turned on me.

"Okay, tell me *exactly* what's going on, Wynne. What's this about a ring? And what happened yesterday morning? This isn't about witnessing anything. You're obviously involved in something way over your head."

I didn't owe him any kind of explanation, but I decided I'd rather give him a few details than have him keep badgering me or start speculating—and possibly tell my mother. So I gave him a one-sentence synopsis.

"I found a ring during one of my diving classes that turned out to be a possible clue in a high-profile case the FBI is following."

"Then why haven't you given the ring to the FBI? No matter how valuable it is, it's not worth going to jail over."

I'm sure my disgust showed in my expression. "Valuable has nothing to do with it. In fact, if I hadn't tried to find the ring's owner, the FBI never would have known about it." That explanation left out a few steps, but it was close enough.

"And what happened yesterday morning? Why are you afraid to keep the ring with you?"

Oops. Stupid to have said that in front of Tom. "Someone tried to take the ring from me," I said, trying to keep all emotion from my voice. "It scared me a little."

Tom stared at me. "I should hope so! You mean, someone tried to take it by force? Why didn't you call the police?"

"I did. They took down all of the details. And I told the FBI about it, too, when they arrived last night."

"Okay," he said, starting the car. "You can tell me the whole story, every detail, on the way to the restaurant. And then, as soon as we get back, I'm calling my travel agent and booking us both flights back to Indy tomorrow morning. This is obviously more than you can handle alone."

I opened the door and got out of the car. "I've been handling it alone just fine, thanks—along with everything else, since you left me. Why don't you go have that romantic dinner all by yourself, Tom." It would give him an idea of what my life had been like the past eight months—until just recently.

The stress of the past few days, and particularly the past couple of hours, suddenly overwhelmed me. I could feel tears of mingled anger, fear, and humiliation threatening, and there was no way I was going to let Tom see me cry. Chin up, I turned on my heel and headed back to the hotel.

Unfortunately, I'd only gone a few steps when I heard Tom's heavier footsteps behind me. "Wynne, wait. Of course I'm not going to the restaurant alone. We have reservations. You'll feel better after you eat."

"I can order room service, just like I've obviously done every single night for the last week," I said without turning around.

"I never said—"

"Yes, you did. But it doesn't matter. I'm not going to dinner with you, Tom. Especially not at the most romantic restaurant in Aruba."

He put a hand on my arm, just as we entered the lobby. "Look, it wasn't anything like that. I wanted to talk about the girls. Let's just—"

I moved out from under his hand. "Don't. I'd rather—"

"Good evening, Ms. Seally," called Curt Phelps from just behind me. Oops. Too late to avoid him this time.

"Mr. Phelps," I said coolly, turning and inclining my head, hoping that would be the end of it.

Unfortunately, it wasn't.

"Is this another member of your diving class?" Phelps asked.

Like the FBI guys, he'd been interested in knowing who'd first recognized the ring, and I'd been just as evasive.

"No, this is—"

"Tom Seally," said Tom, extending his hand. "Wynne's husband. Recently ex-husband," he corrected himself when I opened my mouth to do it for him. "Definitely not a diver."

"Curt Phelps, Everard, Jennings & Holt." I saw Tom's eyes widen with respect at the name of the famous law firm. "It's good of you to come and lend your support to Ms. Seally at a time like this. I'm sure she appreciates it."

"Er, yes." Tom glanced at me, then back at Phelps, clearly unwilling to admit he still didn't know exactly what was going on.

Deciding that Tom was the lesser of two evils at the moment, I summoned up a smile and said, "We have dinner reservations, I'm afraid, Mr. Phelps. We were just on our way out."

"Well, I won't keep you. Perhaps we can all talk later on."

"That would be nice," I lied. I accompanied Tom back out of the hotel—and away from Curt Phelps. At least he hadn't volunteered anything more about the case.

His very involvement in it was enough to pique Tom's curiosity, though. "Wow, you said the ring was part of a high-profile case, but I didn't realize how high-profile. Everard, Jennings & Holt doesn't handle everyday stuff. Is some celebrity involved?"

I waited until we were seated in the car again to answer. "I guess you could say that. It's the Melampus case."

Unlike me, he recognized the name immediately. "The Stefan Melampus murder case? Seriously?" I couldn't tell if he was impressed or unnerved.

"Seriously. But the FBI doesn't want me discussing it. With anyone. So the less said, the better, especially in public."

I glanced around, but didn't see Agent Walters loitering in the parking lot—though other people were walking past.

Tom started the car and pulled out of the lot to head north. "I still think you should come home with me tomorrow," he said. "Just give the ring—and a statement—to the FBI and let them take it from there. I can't think why you haven't done that already."

I really, really didn't want to tell Tom about Michelle Alvares, or the break-in back home, or my threatening phone call. That would only increase his determination to "handle" things for me and get me on the next plane out of Aruba.

"The FBI guys only got here last night, and I did talk with them, for over an hour. I didn't have the ring on me at the time, and they had some disagreement over whether or not they should take possession of it just yet, anyway. It's not like I've been refusing to cooperate."

"But that guy in the parking lot earlier said—"

"Agent Walters. I know. But that's not what Agent Truman said on the phone an hour ago, is it? That's what I mean about a disagreement. I think Walters may want the ring for his own purposes and not to see justice served."

Tom was frowning again. "But does it really matter? Once you give him—either one of them—the ring, it's not your problem any more. It's theirs."

Why was I not surprised he'd feel this way? "But it does matter. If that ring can prove Stefan Melampus didn't murder his wife, I shouldn't let Walters, or anyone else, just make it disappear."

He started shaking his head, wearing one of those expressions I'd been so glad to escape. "Wynne, Wynne, Wynne," he said, sounding way too much like my mother, except that she usually called me "Wynnie" when she did that. "Always willing to go out on a limb for the underdog. But Stefan Melampus doesn't need the help of a nobody like you, and you know it."

"Then why did he send one of his high-powered lawyers to talk to me?" I ignored the fact that I'd thought the same thing two days ago. Until Stefan Melampus himself had called me.

I could see Tom was stumped, but he tried to cover it by commenting on the scenery we were passing. I had to admit it was worth looking at.

While I'd seen desert conditions—complete with cactus—on my way in from the airport a week ago, the northern end of Aruba resembled a lunar landscape. Where I could see the shoreline, sand had given way to jagged black rocks, which also dotted the landscape on both sides of the road. The rocks became bigger and more numerous as we approached the lighthouse at the northwestern tip of the island.

"It's like a different part of the world from the Palm Beach area," I marveled.

"Yeah, they obviously put a lot of money into making the tourist areas attractive," Tom said. "Take that away, and Aruba's kind of an ugly island."

I didn't agree, but it wasn't worth another argument. To me, this stark, almost brutal landscape had its own brand of beauty, especially as we started to round the point and I could see the higher surf of the north shore pounding the black rocks and sending spray a dozen or more feet into the air. I'd read that the north side was the "wild side" of Aruba. Now I knew what that meant.

We turned into the parking lot at the base of the lighthouse, by La Trattoria el Faro Blanco, and I could no longer see the shore. Turning south, though, I saw that we had a fabulous view of most of the island. I paused to admire it for a moment before following Tom into the restaurant.

"I have reservations for Seally, on the terrace." Even in a simple statement like that, there was something pompous in Tom's tone that grated on me. It wasn't new. Just newly irritating.

The host led us out to the terrace, which had an even more breathtaking view of the island and western coastline than the parking lot. The sun was already sinking toward the horizon, turning the sky pink. No wonder this was considered the most romantic spot to dine in Aruba. I only wished I were here with... someone other than Tom.

Sheesh, I'd only been legally divorced for a month, and here I was, practically lusting over another man. It would probably be best if I kept Ronan's name out of my head for the next hour or so. I'd try, anyway.

"It's a beautiful setting," I said, by way of a temporary truce. It would be a shame to fight in a place like this.

"I'm glad you like it. I was hoping we'd be closer to a beach, but we may get a good sunset, at least. But now, about this stuff with the FBI and the Melampus case, I've been thinking—"

Luckily the server came before he could finish a thought I was pretty sure I didn't want to hear. Though I knew it was only a brief reprieve, I took my time, asking questions about the specials before settling on the salmon. Tom ordered the largest steak on the menu.

No wine, since Tom didn't drink—with me, anyway. I knew he drank for "business reasons" with clients, but he'd never approved of me doing so.

I ordered a margarita just to irritate him, even though I didn't plan to drink it, since I might still have a stakeout to help with later. He frowned, but didn't quite dare to countermand my order.

"Okay, listen," Tom said once the server was gone. "What I was thinking is, it really would be best if we got this ring business taken care of before going back home. It's a good thing I came here. That means I can—"

I put up a hand to stop him. "You don't even know the details of what's been going on, Tom. And no, I'm not going to tell you," I added when he started to interrupt. "It's complicated and confusing, and I promised not to talk about it."

More importantly, the details would only upset him more, and add to his determination to take charge, which was the last thing I needed right now.

"What did you need to tell me about Deb?" I asked, firmly changing the subject.

He shifted uncomfortably in his seat. "Well, she... That is, I... Okay, I admit it, I just said that to get you to come to dinner.

Because I really do need to talk to you, Wynne. I've…I've been thinking a lot lately. Thinking maybe we should reconcile."

I was more irked than surprised. "And you thought lying would convince me to trust you again?" I didn't care how acid I sounded. "So what brought this on? Why now?"

He shrugged, ignoring my tone. "It's…well…a few clients have asked about you. And some people at church. And it got me thinking. That…that maybe I made a mistake."

A glimmer of understanding broke through. "You mean your sterling reputation is losing some of its polish now that word of our divorce—and the reason for it—is making the rounds? Worried the church elders might ask you to step down?"

"How did—? I mean…" Obviously caught off-guard, he stopped to choose his words. "I want to make it up to you, Wynne. To make things right. I shouldn't have left you to fend for yourself like I did."

"Make things right. So you think—what? That if I come back to you, if we remarry, you won't risk losing any clients? Or have you already lost some?"

He looked even more uncomfortable now. "A few. Not necessarily for that reason. But I can't deny that us getting back together would help me…help to, um—"

"Put the rumors to rest? No thanks, Tom. Not my job. You made your bed with Darlene. Now you can lie in it. Alone, if she's left you."

"Left? Who said…I mean…that's been over for a while. It…never really meant anything, Wynne."

"Gee, that's not what you told me when I first caught you together, or when I begged you to consider counseling. And the last time I ran into her, she was talking wedding plans." Smugly, I recalled.

Tom's salad arrived then, saving him from having to answer. I wasn't particularly surprised when he reverted to the previous topic once the server was gone again.

"Wynne, about this business you've gotten yourself involved with here, finding that ring and all. I think you should let me do the talking to these FBI agents and maybe that lawyer. I know how guys like that can be with a woman. They'll talk legal jargon, get you all confused, maybe make you end up saying or doing something you'll regret later."

My exasperation escaped in an audible sigh. It was hard to believe that just a few nights ago—the night my room had been searched—I'd actually considered calling Tom for advice.

"Is this why things didn't work out with Darlene?" I asked. "She wouldn't let you control her life? I guess she was a lot quicker on the uptake than I was. I'm sorry you don't have her to boss around anymore—well, no, I'm not—but you're definitely not going to start back in on me. You'll have to settle for just running your own life now."

He stared at me. "It's not...I don't... Don't be ridiculous, Wynne. I only want what's best for you." But his voice lacked conviction. It was pretty obvious that what he wanted was what would be best for *him*. And he knew that I knew it.

Our meals came a few minutes later, and we both ate quickly and in near silence. Tom had apparently run out of arguments for the moment. In fact, I had the feeling he was now almost as eager to get away from me as I was to get away from him. He didn't ask any more questions or offer any more advice, for which I was grateful.

When the check came, I reached for it, unwilling to be indebted to Tom for so much as a meal, but he was quicker.

"I can afford it better than you can," he said, handing the server his credit card.

I looked away, biting back a sarcastic reply. Instead, I said, "Look. The sun set, and we didn't even see it."

He glanced at the horizon in evident surprise to see the fading crimson line that showed where the sun had gone. "Oh. I'm sorry, Wynne. I really did want this to be a nice dinner. Special."

The regret in his voice almost made me feel sorry for him. Almost.

"I'm sorry, too," I said. "I appreciate the effort, but it's...too late."

The server brought back the credit card and slip. Tom signed it, and we left. The silence between us lasted until we were getting out of the car at the Royal Aruban, fifteen minutes later. It was weak of me, but I couldn't quite leave things like this.

"Look," I said as we entered the lobby. "Maybe we can talk again before you leave Aruba. Or when I get back to Indiana. It would be nice if we both got together with the girls occasionally. I think it would mean a lot to them."

"Yeah. Yeah, we should do that." He had all the sincerity of a socialite saying, "Let's do lunch sometime."

In other words, if I couldn't be useful to him, if I didn't want to play by his rules, he wasn't interested in putting forth any effort.

But even as I thought that, he stopped and turned to me. "Listen, Wynne, what about that counseling you wanted before?"

"That counseling you completely refused, you mean?"

"Well, yeah, but that was before. Your mother said—"

"Yes, I know Mom wants us to get back together, but it's not her life. It's mine. I can't say I was happy about what happened, but now that it has, I think I'm better off—even if it doesn't seem that way to you or to Mom."

"If you say so. But what about the short term? This business with the FBI. Hey, there's that lawyer—Phillips?—coming this way. I think I'll have a talk with him."

I had no desire for a three way conversation with Tom and Curt Phelps right now, when I was anxious to find Ronan for an update. On that very thought, I spotted him at the reception desk, talking to one of the clerks.

"Phelps is a busy man, Tom. He probably won't have time—"

But Tom was already moving across the big open area of the lobby to greet Phelps, who looked delighted to see Tom again. I watched as they greeted each other, then, without a glance at me, turned and left the lobby together, headed in the direction of the piano bar.

Though I couldn't help but be nervous about those two cozying up together, I wasn't sure what harm it could really do. And it did free me to talk to Ronan.

He was just leaving the reception desk, a distinctly dissatisfied look on his face. I intercepted him before he had taken a dozen steps. "Well?" I asked quietly.

"Oh. You're back. I figured you'd be gone for another hour, at least." Was it my imagination, or was he being evasive?

"Neither of us were enjoying each other's company much, so we didn't exactly linger. So what did I miss?"

He hesitated, and now I was sure he was being evasive. In fact, he looked positively uncomfortable. "The note is gone," he finally said. "And I don't know who has it."

## CHAPTER NINETEEN

"GONE?" I repeated. "But how——?"

"Not here," he cautioned, glancing around. "Let's go around the corner. There are a couple of chairs there, where we won't be overheard. By the way, did I just see your ex and Melampus's lawyer leaving the lobby together?"

I followed him away from the reception desk, in the opposite direction from the way Tom and Phelps had gone.

"Yes, they met as we were leaving for dinner, and Tom's been gung-ho to talk to him ever since. Phelps is probably planning to discreetly pump Tom for info."

We turned a corner and found the pair of plush chairs in an out-of-the-way nook, partially screened by a potted palm, well away from the main part of the lobby or any wandering guests.

"So, will Phelps get the info he wants?" Ronan asked, once we were seated.

"No. Tom doesn't know much—even though Walters, that FBI agent I don't trust, told him more than he should have."

"What did Walters tell him?"

"He just said that I'd found a ring that the FBI wants. He thought Tom might be able to make me see sense." I grimaced.

"Tom pestered me into giving him a few more details—but not as much as Phelps already knows. I'm more worried about what Phelps might tell Tom."

"And Walters? Why don't you trust him?"

"I haven't liked his attitude from the start, but tonight it was pretty obvious he was acting on his own, without his partner's knowledge. I've had the feeling all along that he'd be willing to do almost anything to see Stefan put away for good."

Ronan raised his brows. "So it's 'Stefan' now, is it?"

I felt color creeping into my face. "I didn't... That is..." I shrugged. "It's not like I've ever actually met the man. Anyway, I can tell you're stalling, Ronan. What happened with the note? Why didn't you see who came to get it?"

"Because no one did. Someone staying in the hotel called down to the desk and asked to have it delivered to their room. I can't believe I didn't consider that possibility," he said with evident disgust. "I must be losing my touch."

"I would never have thought of it either," I said, trying to hold panic at bay.

He gave me a twisted smile. "Yeah, but you're not a trained investigator. I am."

"But Michelle can't possibly be staying in the Royal Aruban, can she? Isn't there any way to find out whose room it went to?"

"I was just trying to do that—and I will, believe me. If I'd seen that blue envelope in the desk clerk's hand in time to get into the elevator with her, I'd know already, but I wasn't quick enough. I did watch the numbers, so I'm pretty sure it went to a room on the fifteenth floor."

Just one floor above mine—though that could be complete coincidence, I supposed. "Do you think it *could* be Michelle herself?"

"I doubt it. I've spent a lot of time in and around this hotel the past couple of days, and I haven't seen anyone who looks like her— or Lenny. And I can't imagine they'd take that risk."

"Which would mean someone else is working with them. I

know the FBI guys aren't staying here. They're at the Days Inn. But Phelps is here, and Mr. Haliakis might be—I didn't think to ask him where he was staying."

"Haliakis? What does he look like?"

"Young guy, dark. He actually looks a lot like Lenny." I didn't add *but even more handsome*.

"I don't think I've seen him, then. *Hmm*. Who have you told about my involvement so far?"

I blinked. "No one. Tom just knows you were on the dive boat during my lessons. And I haven't mentioned you at all to the FBI, Phelps, or Argus Haliakis."

"Good. Then none of them will know to avoid me. In fact, it's probably best if we're not seen together, assuming we haven't been already. If any of them are working with Michelle, their not knowing about me gives us an element of surprise when they make their next move."

It made sense, even if the idea of keeping my distance from Ronan was a little scary right now. "And what do you think that next move will be?"

"Hard to say. I'd like to think that it will be to follow the instructions in our note, but we're clearly not dealing with idiots here. They may contact you again with some kind of counter proposal. Or they may try something more direct. You need to be alert and very careful, Wynne. Especially since I won't be right there with you."

"Oh, thanks. I feel so much better now."

He shrugged. "Sorry. But I'd rather have you scared than careless. I don't think you're at any real risk at the moment, if that helps. But we don't dare get cocky."

With a nod, I stood. "I guess I should go upstairs, then, and see if I've been left any more messages."

"Good idea. And I'll go check out the fifteenth floor. I might get lucky."

"I guess we communicate by phone if there are any further developments?"

He frowned, thinking. "I'll have my phone off while I'm lurking around on the fifteenth floor, and then I plan to contact a buddy of mine on the local police force. He may be able to convince the desk clerk to tell him whose room that note went to. How about I give you a call in a couple of hours? And if anything comes up on your end, you can text or leave me a voice mail."

"All right. Assuming I don't hear anything, I guess we go through with the rendezvous tomorrow that we set up in the note?"

"Right." His eyes made another quick sweep of the lobby, then came back to me, concern lurking in their blue depths. He reached over and gave my shoulder a squeeze. "Talk to you soon, Wynne."

His manner made me even more nervous. If Ronan was acting that spooked, I should be terrified. I hoped he was right that I wasn't at real risk just yet. Even if we screwed up tomorrow and didn't manage to nab Michelle or a co-conspirator when they came for the ring, surely the person most likely to suffer was Stefan Melampus.

I waited until Ronan had gone to the elevators, then got up and strolled toward the piano bar, trying very hard to look casual. In fact, I was trying so hard, I'm sure I'd have looked suspicious if anyone had been watching me. Luckily, no one appeared to be doing so.

The bar was in a fairly open area, which made it tricky to approach it without being seen, but I walked behind another couple until I reached one of the big pillars lining the open-air walkway. I leaned against the side away from the bar, then cautiously peered around it.

There were Tom and Phelps, in profile, fortunately, so neither was looking directly my way. They appeared to be deep in conversation over a pair of martinis. Tom apparently considered this one of those occasions that merited an exception to his no-drinking rule.

Reassured that those two were safely out of the way for a while, I retraced my steps back to the lobby, keeping a watchful eye out for anyone who looked the least bit like Michelle Melampus or Lenny—or the least bit suspicious. No one qualified, unless I counted the woman railing at the reception clerk about her feather pillows.

I considered staking out the lobby just in case anyone important to the case did show up, but finally I had to admit that I was stalling. The truth was, I was afraid to go up to my room alone—again. Which was silly, of course. Shaking my head at my fears, I headed for the elevators.

There was no particular reason to think Michelle and company even knew which room I was in. Surely, if they did, they'd have searched it by now, just as they'd searched my original room? Which meant that my room was probably the single safest place I could be right now.

At least that's what I thought until I keyed open the lock and saw the folded sheet of paper lying on the floor, just inside the door.

I stared at it for a long moment, steeling myself, before picking it up and unfolding it. It was typed, or, more likely, printed off a computer.

"Mrs. Seally," it read, "you were unwise to ignore my request. If you don't want to be responsible for harm befalling your daughters, you will follow these instructions carefully. Bring the ring and take the road past the California Lighthouse at midnight tonight. Say nothing to the police or the FBI. If you doubt my resolve, I recommend you speak with your daughters."

My heart pounding, I hurried to my cell phone, which I'd stupidly left in the room when I'd gone to dinner earlier. I had a voice mail from Bess, but rather than listen to it, I immediately called her.

"Mom?" Her voice was higher than usual, and a little shaky. "You got my message. Good."

"I haven't listened to it yet. What's going on?"

"Deb told you about the house being broken into and all, right? And the picture that was stolen?"

"Yes, I had her call the police about it."

"Well, the picture was returned about an hour ago—to me."

I tensed. "To you? You mean, at your apartment?"

"Yes. And...and it was...it was slashed, Mom. Like someone took a knife to it, over and over. It's ruined. And I'm scared."

Cold, clammy terror washed through me. I fought to keep my voice calm and matter-of-fact when I spoke again.

"Bess, I want you and Deb to go to Grandma's house, and then call the police and tell them about this. Then I want all three of you to go somewhere for the night—a hotel, out of town. It doesn't have to be far. But let the police know where you'll be and see if they'll have someone keep an eye on you. I'll call you in the morning."

"Mom, what's going on? It sounds like you know who's doing this."

I hesitated, choosing my words, then said, "I don't know who, exactly, but I do think it has to do with something that's going on here in Aruba. And I think I can take care of it."

"What do you mean? What's been happening in Aruba?"

"It's a long story. I found something, and some bad people want it. I think that picture was slashed to scare me into giving it to them—which is exactly what I'm going to do."

"But—"

"I'll tell you all about it when I get home, Bess. But right now, I want you to call Deb, get to Grandma's, and do exactly what I said. Okay? Promise me?"

"I promise. But Mom? Please don't get hurt, okay?"

At her plaintive tone, the years rolled back, and I was reassuring a four-year-old instead of a twenty-four-year-old Bess. "I won't, sweetie. Don't worry. Everything will be fine. I'll call you in the morning, I promise."

I hung up and looked at the clock. Ten forty-five. Because of all my foolish skulking and dithering downstairs, I had barely an hour to get to the lighthouse.

I found Ronan's number in my cell phone, but when I called it, his phone went straight to voice mail, which must mean he still had it off.

"Ronan, it's Wynne," I said. "The bastards are directly threatening my kids now, so I'm going to give them the ring. I'm supposed to meet them up past the lighthouse at midnight. Don't try anything heroic that could get my girls hurt, okay? But I wanted you to know, just in case anything...goes wrong."

I shut my phone and stared at it, willing back the tears of frustration and fear that were threatening. If only Ronan had answered. I was sure he'd have a plan, or at least a few words of encouragement.

Then I thought of someone else I could tell. I had to scroll through a bunch of incoming calls, but finally I found the one from Argus Haliakis. I still wasn't sure just how far I could trust him, but Stefan deserved to know what I was going to do.

"Yo," he answered.

"Mr. Haliakis? It's Wynne Seally."

"Oh, hey, Ms. S. You sound kinda upset. Something wrong?"

"Yes, I'm afraid something is very wrong. I need you to give a message to Mr. Melampus for me—and an apology." I quickly told him about the slashed portrait and the note, concluding with my intention to comply with Michelle's demand.

"I know Mr. Melampus needs this ring as evidence to clear him, but my daughters' safety comes first. I hope he'll understand."

"He will, Ms. Seally, I know it. He'd tell you to do whatever you have to, to keep them safe. He'd want you to stay safe, too, so be careful, okay? Let me come with?"

"No, but thank you. And please let Mr. Melampus know how sorry I am."

I figured if Gus was working with Michelle, I hadn't told him anything he didn't already know. And if he wasn't, it couldn't hurt to have someone else aware of what was going on. In case I didn't come back.

Swallowing hard, I hurried to get my sewing scissors from my toiletry case, then knelt by the drapes to retrieve the ring. I snipped a few threads and prised it out through the hole.

Next, I quickly changed out of my sundress and into shorts, t-shirt, and sneakers—something I could move easily in. Just in case. Finally, I pulled my hair back into a ponytail and used the bathroom, since I didn't know when I'd get another chance.

I glanced at the clock. Almost eleven thirty. Where had the time gone? I stuck the ring in my pocket and my cell phone in my purse and headed to the elevator.

On the way down, alone in the elevator, I pulled out the ring and held it in my palm for a moment, heartily wishing I'd never found the cursed thing.

But...

But if I hadn't, I'd have missed out on the adventure of a lifetime: underwater thrills, getting to know Ronan, discovering I had a knack for cloak-and-dagger tactics. My part in that adventure would be over in an hour, and I was ready to be done with it, but I was glad I'd experienced it. If nothing else, it had given me stories to tell my future grandkids—and memories that would last the rest of my life.

In fact, my normal life was going to seem pretty boring after the past week. But as long as my girls were safe, I could handle boring. I'd lived with it for forty-six years.

The elevator doors opened, cutting off my musings and catapulting me back into the adventure that wasn't over yet. I hoped the concierge would be able to get me a cab at this hour—a real one, not one of the rickety five dollar ones.

Even more, I hoped I'd see Ronan, or at least get a call back from him, before I left the hotel. Most of all, I hoped that I wasn't doing something completely stupid by complying with the demand in that note. What if it was a trap? But even if it was, with my girls at risk, what choice did I have?

Once in the lobby, I anxiously scanned the area, which was nearly deserted at this hour. No sign of Ronan. I walked partway down the open-air corridors in either direction, hoping to get lucky. I even peeked into the piano bar, which still had several people in it. No Ronan. No Tom or Curt Phelps either, but that was just as well, since I wasn't planning to tell either of them about this.

Disappointed and more than a little panicky, I went back to the main area of the lobby. No one was at the concierge desk this late, so I went to the woman at the reception desk and asked if she could call me a cab.

"Of course," she replied, picking up the phone.

"Wynne?" came Tom's voice at my shoulder.

Crap. "Oh. Hi," I said. "I was just—"

"I heard you asking for a cab. Never mind," he said to the desk clerk. "I'll drive her."

The woman nodded, smiled, and hung up the phone, then turned to help the same woman from earlier that evening, who now seemed to have some kind of issue with the size of her blanket.

"But—" I began, but Tom put a hand on my arm and turned me away from the desk.

"Wherever you're going at this hour, Wynne, I'll take you. I don't mind. Really."

I glanced back at the reception clerk, but the cranky guest was still in full tirade. "I appreciate the offer, Tom, but I really think it would be better if I took a cab. In fact, I insist."

"Oh, going to visit a boyfriend?" He looked more amused than jealous.

"Of course not. It's just...a personal errand. Something I need to do alone."

"Hey, I'll just play cab driver, okay? Once we get wherever you're going, you can do whatever you need to do alone. I won't interfere."

The clock behind the reception desk showed eleven forty. I was running out of time.

"Okay, fine. But when I ask you to let me out of the car, you stop and let me out. No questions asked. Okay?"

"Deal," he said. "Come on."

I was as surprised as I was relieved that he didn't demand an explanation on the spot, but I wasn't going to look a gift horse in the mouth right then, with time so tight. I followed him out to the parking lot and climbed back into the ostentatious red convertible. Not exactly an inconspicuous car. But if he kept his promise to let me out when I asked him to, it shouldn't matter.

"I need to go back to the lighthouse—the same one we were at earlier tonight," I told him as he started the car. "I, um, think I may have left something there."

"Oh. Okay." He pulled out and headed north without further comment or question.

Which struck me as really strange, gift horse or no. I couldn't exactly ask him why he wasn't suspicious—not without making him suspicious. Still, I felt increasingly uncomfortable as we drove in silence up the coast.

We were about five minutes from the lighthouse when Tom said, "So, you have the ring with you?"

I turned to stare at him. "What?"

"The ring. Phelps told me you'd probably be bringing it up here and suggested I drive you. It's okay. He told me the whole story. You're doing the right thing, turning it over to him."

"Turning it over. To Curt Phelps?"

"Well...yeah. That's the real reason you're going to the lighthouse, right?"

I was becoming more confused—and worried—by the moment. "Tom, what *exactly* did Phelps tell you?"

He glanced at me in evident surprise. "About what's been going on here—with you. He asked me what I already knew, and I had to tell him it wasn't much." His mouth twisted down with annoyance.

"That was embarrassing, Wynne. Made it seem like you don't trust me."

"You did cheat on me and then walk out, remember?" I couldn't resist saying, despite my growing fear.

"That's different. This is important stuff. Life and death stuff."

I refrained from pointing out that his infidelity and abandonment had certainly been important life stuff for me. We were nearly to the lighthouse by now.

"So what did Phelps say had been going on?"

"Well, he told me about the murder case—the stuff that wasn't in the press, that is—and about how the ring you found can prove Melampus was framed. You were right about those FBI agents, by the way. Sorry if I seemed skeptical earlier. When I told Phelps I tried to get you to give them the ring, he told me about their real agenda."

"Which is?"

"He said they've been staking out the hotel, trying to get the ring to make sure it can't be used as evidence. In fact, they were the ones behind that guy trying to steal it yesterday. And they've intimidated you to the point that you were afraid to give the ring to Phelps."

We rounded the last curve mounting the hill up to the lighthouse.

"The FBI didn't have anything to do with that, Tom. They weren't even in Aruba yet when that happened. Didn't Phelps tell you about Michelle Alvares?"

"Who? I don't think so."

The lighthouse loomed up, ghostly in the moonlight. Tom slowed, then stopped. The parking area around it and the nearby restaurant appeared empty, but our headlights illuminated a dirt road continuing on past the lighthouse—a road I hadn't even noticed when we'd been up here earlier.

"This was where I was going to ask you to let me out," I said, "but I've changed my mind. Since you bought into Phelps's song and dance, you can help me now. He apparently knows you're coming anyway."

"Song and dance?" Tom repeated. "What do you mean? Phelps is an attorney with a highly respected—"

"I mean that the FBI aren't the bad guys here, but it sounds like Phelps may be. The person who's been intimidating me is Michelle Alvares, Melanie Melampus's sister. I think she's the one who framed Stefan Melampus for his wife's murder, may even have murdered her herself. And now she's threatening our daughters, if I don't give her the ring."

Tom just shook his head back and forth, apparently unable to process this new information. "Bess and Debra? But they're back home in Indiana. Besides, that doesn't make sense. Phelps told me that Stefan Melampus would be grateful if you brought him the ring. Grateful to both of us. That he'd give my business a boost."

I closed my eyes, realizing the futility of trying to work through Phelps's clever interweaving of truth and lies right now, when time was so very tight. He'd obviously read Tom well, playing to his biggest weakness—desire for money and prestige.

"I'll explain it all later. Right now, we need to follow that dirt road." I pointed. "For the girls' sake."

Tom put the car in gear and slowly drove forward, onto the rutted, uneven surface. "I'm pretty sure the rental agreement said not to take this car off of paved roads."

I stared at him in disbelief. "Even you can't really think that's more important than our daughters' lives."

"Of course not! If I really thought—But I'm sure you've misunderstood. A man like Phelps certainly wouldn't threaten our girls, and if anyone else has, Phelps will be able to deal with it. Everything will be fine, Wynne. You'll see. Just let me handle it."

We continued along the dirt and gravel road for maybe a quarter of a mile. I peered forward, expecting at any moment to see something—a car, or someone standing by the road. But so far all I saw in the swath of the headlights was more sand and jagged black rocks.

"Someone's coming up behind us," Tom said. "That'll be Phelps, I imagine. Once he explains, you'll understand—"

"Stop the car," I told him, turning around to watch the headlights of the other vehicle approach, bouncing along the road at twice the speed we'd been going. It appeared to be a large SUV, much better suited to this terrain than Tom's Porsche.

It stopped just behind us. The driver got out, leaving the headlights on, and walked toward us.

"Mr. Phelps!" Tom exclaimed, getting out of the car. "I told Wynne it would be you. She has everything mixed up, but now you can tell her—"

"Get back in the car," Phelps said, cutting him off. "Keep driving until you reach the end of the road. Then we'll talk."

"But—"

"Now."

Tom took a quick step back, and in the light of the SUV's headlights I saw why.

Phelps was holding a gun.

## CHAPTER TWENTY

"I...I GUESS we'd better do what he says." Tom's voice was shaky as he climbed back into the car beside me. "Maybe...maybe the FBI is following him or something, and he wants to be prepared."

"We should be so lucky," I muttered. I couldn't understand why Phelps hadn't just demanded the ring. I pulled it out of my pocket and looked back at him, but he was already getting into the SUV.

Tom started forward again, faster this time, even though the ruts were getting worse as we went on. Meanwhile, I was getting more and more scared as I realized just how badly I'd screwed up by not considering that Phelps might be involved with Michelle and her cronies.

Not only had I told him about seeing Michelle Alvares in Oranjestad, I'd made it clear I'd be willing to testify on Stefan's behalf. Which meant just getting the ring from me wasn't enough. They needed to get rid of me, as well.

On that thought, I dug my cell phone out of my purse.

"What are you doing?" Tom demanded. "He's right behind us, with a gun."

"Which is why we need backup," I said, waking up my phone. "Blast. No signal." I started turning the phone this way and that with no result, and then the road abruptly ended in a pile of black rocks. Silently praying for a miracle, I stuck the phone back in my purse.

"Should we get out?" Tom's voice was shaky again.

"Let's wait and see what he tells us to do."

I preferred not to walk in this terrain in the dark unless we had to. One of us would probably sprain an ankle. And the spray from the ocean, probably no more than a dozen yards away, was misting us where we sat.

"Just give him the ring. Then he'll let us go. You should have done that when we stopped before." His voice got stronger as he tried to exert control again.

"I didn't exactly get a chance," I pointed out. "Anyway—" I broke off as Phelps approached, the gun still in his hand.

"You have the ring?" he asked me.

I pulled it out of my pocket again. "Right here. I could have given it to you back at the lighthouse and saved us all some time."

He looked almost as surprised as I felt at my confident, almost flippant tone. I was feeling anything but confident on the inside. I didn't look at Tom, so I don't know how he reacted.

Phelps walked to my side of the car, took the ring, and pocketed it. "Sorry. Things have become a little bit more complicated than that."

That's what I'd figured, but I wasn't volunteering anything. "Oh?"

Tom wasn't so reticent. "Here, what's going on, Curt? I got her up here like you asked. You have the ring. What's with the gun? Surely that's not necessary."

"I'm afraid it is," he replied. "Ms. Seally here knows more than is safe. We can't afford to let her testify."

Even though I'd guessed exactly that, hearing him say it so matter-of-factly made my blood run cold. I tried to think, to come up with a plan to get away or appease Phelps, to convince him I was no threat, but my brain wouldn't work.

Next to me, Tom made a little choking noise. "You...you're going to kill her? Us? I didn't know anything. I still don't. Only what you told me yourself."

Phelps smiled grimly—it looked weird and frighteningly evil in the harsh light of the SUV's high beams. "Come on, Tom. Do you think I can let you go once I get rid of your ex-wife? If I'd realized from the start just how little you knew, I might have left you out of this. But it's too late now."

"No! No, it's not," Tom pleaded. "I swear I won't say anything. I'll forget I was ever here."

If I'd had any remaining trace of affection for Tom, that would have killed it. Clearly, even if I could force my frozen brain to come up with any kind of plan, I couldn't expect Tom's cooperation.

"My hero." I let sarcasm drip from my voice.

At least he had the grace to wince. Phelps actually laughed.

"She's right, you know, Tom. Is this really how you want to be remembered? Ah, here they are, finally."

I turned and saw another set of headlights bumping along the dirt track toward us. Another SUV or truck of some kind. I had a sinking feeling I knew who was in it.

The truck stopped behind Phelps's SUV, and two people got out, a man and a woman who indeed proved to be Michelle and "Lenny" when they stepped into the headlight beams. So much for two against one, even if Tom weren't worse than useless.

"Did you get it?" Phelps asked them.

"Yeah," the man answered. "Two sets, like you said."

"Well, bring it," Phelps said. "We don't want to spend all night at this."

Lenny and Michelle went back to the truck, and Phelps turned to us. "Okay, out of the car. You can help us carry everything to the shore."

"You're...you're not going to shoot us?" Tom asked hopefully.

I wasn't nearly so hopeful. Not even when Phelps replied, "Not unless we have to."

The other two were returning now, both of them loaded down with something obviously heavy as well as bulky. Not until they reached us could I tell what it was: two sets of dive gear—tanks, vests, wetsuits, the works. It took them two trips to bring everything from the truck to the side of the Porsche.

As Lenny set down his second load of fins, weights, and wetsuit, he grinned at me. "Maybe you won't be so cocky about this dive, lady."

"Dive?" Now there was definitely panic in Tom's voice. "But I don't even know how to scuba dive."

Lenny looked at Tom, then me. "Different boy toy tonight, huh? What happened to the other one?"

I glared at him, not about to mention Ronan in front of Phelps. I wondered what Lenny had told him about the unsuccessful underwater attack.

Lenny didn't pursue the question, but turned back to Tom. "Don't worry, dude, Mom here will show you what to do, won't you? Maybe he won't mind as much as I did."

"You ungrateful bastard," I said to him. "If I hadn't helped you—"

"Helped me? You almost killed me down there. That's what gave me this idea, when we was thinking up a good accident for you. That and what you said about wanting to dive the *California* wreck. Now you'll get your chance."

I remembered my conversation with Ronan on Van's dive boat —within Lenny's hearing. Ronan had said it was a dangerous dive, and he'd meant during the day. I also remembered the map I'd seen of Aruba's dive sites. Until now, I'd forgotten that the *California* wreck was just off this coast—that the lighthouse had been named for that ship, in fact.

"Who's going to believe that a novice diver and a non-diver would attempt a dive like that at midnight?" I tried to sound logical instead of desperate. "Not a very believable accident, if you ask me."

"Oh, I don't know," Phelps said. "Jealous ex-husband trying to prove something to win back his wife. And you were seen arguing in the hotel lobby earlier, which lends credibility. Besides, with luck, your bodies won't be found for a day or two, so no one will know you went out at midnight."

Their luck, not ours. Ours wasn't looking good.

"Anyway, enough talk," he said then. "Get all this stuff down to the edge so they can put it on. You two can help, too. Men carry the tanks and weights, women carry the other stuff."

The vests and regulators were already attached to the tanks, which probably meant they'd stolen the equipment from a dive shop or boat, already set up for tomorrow morning's diving. I doubted Lenny could have put the things together himself, though I had no idea if Michelle was a diver.

Tom picked up one of the tanks with a grunt while Lenny carried the other. I picked up one shortie wetsuit, mask with attached snorkel, and a pair of fins and saw Michelle doing the same. Phelps pulled a flashlight from somewhere and led the way through the jagged rocks and down a short slope to the water.

Every wave that crashed against the rocks was caught by the fierce wind, flinging the water twenty feet in the air and spraying us all liberally. It was awe-inspiring, and from a safe distance would have been beautiful. Up close, it was terrifying.

And chilly. Even though it was probably still eighty degrees, between the wind and the spray, I was shivering. Maybe not only from the chill.

"Now, get the gear on," Phelps shouted over the wind, playing the flashlight beam over the piled equipment with one hand, the gun steady in the other. "Help your husband with whatever he doesn't understand, Ms. Seally."

"You're crazy!" Tom exclaimed, a hysterical edge to his voice. "We can't possibly go out into that."

I agreed, but didn't say so—I didn't want to hear that same hysteria in my own voice.

"It's that or a bullet, Tom, which I admit was my preference. Less margin for error. Unfortunately—" he slanted a glance at the woman— "I was overruled. But the result should be the same." Phelps spoke with the same inflection he might have used to discuss some legal case. "The equipment, Ms. Seally," he prompted me, motioning slightly with the gun.

Then Michelle spoke for the first time—a voice I recognized, though her words surprised me. "Do we really have to do this, Curt? Now that we have the ring back, can't I just disappear again?"

It was Lenny who answered her. "You're the one who insisted it should look like an accident, Mel. I was willing to just..." he made a slashing motion across his throat. "Gotta be one or the other. She's seen you. She testifies, he gets off."

I didn't have to ask who "he" was. But—"Mel?" I repeated. "Melanie?"

"Does that answer your question?" Phelps said to her.

"Still—" she started to argue.

Lenny cut her off. "It's too late for cold feet now, Mel. If you hadn't pitched that ring off the boat during that dinner cruise—"

"Which I wouldn't have done if you hadn't kept needling me about Stefan," she retorted. "I was only trying to prove to you—"

"Enough!" Phelps barked at them. Then, to us, "Get that stuff on, both of you."

I considered telling him to just shoot us and get it over with, and to hell with Melanie's conscience. It would be an easier death. But a certain one—and I wasn't ready to die.

Maybe, just maybe, we could survive out there long enough to get below the waves. Make our way around the island to calmer water, stay on the surface until morning, get rescued. It was a long shot—a very long shot—but a better gamble than that gun.

I thought of Deb and Bess, of some stranger giving them dreadful news. No. It was unthinkable. *Somehow*, we were going to survive this.

"Come on, Tom. I'll show you how to put on the wetsuit." I

handed him the larger one, looking over his shirt and slacks. "You'll never get it on over those pants." My voice shook, but I tried to ignore it. "You'd better strip to your shorts."

He opened his mouth to protest, but then glanced at Phelps's gun and unzipped his slacks without a word.

"Okay, put your right leg through here, then zip up from the left."

"I can't do it. I can't see." It would be unkind to say Tom was whining, given the circumstances.

"We need more light here," I said over my shoulder to Phelps, who obliged without comment. "There, look. It's just like starting a jacket zipper. Be careful not to pinch yourself. Arms through the sleeves, then zip the rest of the way up."

It took him some time and some flailing around, but Tom got his wetsuit on at last. As he was zipping it to his neck, I slipped out of my own shorts and into my wetsuit. In spite of the dark and the unremitting spray, I got it on in record time. Too bad there was no one here who'd be impressed by that.

Warmer now, I had Tom sit on a rock while I checked his equipment. Irrelevantly, or maybe vindictively, I hoped Phelps and the others were shivering the way I'd been a moment ago.

"Here, you'll need a weight belt." Without those, we'd never be able to get below the surface, and I was very much hoping that it would be calmer down there. Assuming we survived the rocks on the way out. Big assumption.

Rather than take the time to explain any of this to Tom, I picked up the heavier weight belt and fastened it around his middle myself. I hoped it would be enough weight to compensate for his middle-aged spread.

Leaving him sitting, I dragged one set of equipment over to him, put the tank against his back and buckled him into the vest. Then I checked the connections—no easy task in the fitful flashlight beam and spray—and turned on his air. To my relief, the gauge read a full three thousand PSI. They'd definitely snatched these sets dive-ready.

"You...you really do know how to do this, don't you?" Tom said almost wonderingly as I turned to go get my own equipment.

"I do. But in conditions like this—" I gestured toward the crashing surf and rocks—"I can't promise that will be enough. Not by a long shot. I'm still a beginner." But my voice wasn't shaking now. That was something.

Before weighing myself down with my own tank, I helped Tom on with his mask and handed him his fins.

"No, don't take your shoes off yet," I said when he bent down. "We won't be able to walk in the fins, and those rocks will tear bare feet to shreds. We'll have to kick off our shoes once we're out there."

He looked down. "But these are... Never mind. They're pretty much ruined already."

I didn't point out that with his life on the line, the price of his shoes shouldn't matter. He was scared enough without an extra reality check. Instead, I sat down and buckled myself into my own gear, then checked my gauges.

"I guess we're as ready for this suicide mission as we'll ever be," I told Phelps, willing my heart to stop pounding. It was like telling the waves to stop pounding on the rocks.

"Not quite," he said. Then, to Lenny, "Let the air out of their tanks."

Lenny came forward, then hesitated, obviously unsure of just how to do that—and I wasn't about to tell him. Instead, I turned to Phelps.

"If you do, we're not going in at all," I told him, my voice surprisingly steady. "Just shoot us instead. It won't look like an accident, but hey, that's on you. It'll be less painful for us than drowning while we're being battered against the rocks."

I started to take off my mask to prove my resolve. My heart was hammering in my throat. I wondered what it felt like, being shot. Behind me, Tom made a faint whimpering noise.

Phelps hesitated, then Melanie said something I couldn't hear, and he shrugged. "Whatever. I don't see you lasting long out there anyway, air or no air. Go on in. But I'll be here with the gun if you try anything." He switched off the flashlight.

He was probably right about our chances, but since I'd won my point, I didn't argue. Maybe we did have a very slight fighting chance this way. Maybe. I struggled to my feet, hampered by the heavy tank on my back.

"Come on, Tom," I said, taking him by the hand. "Stand up. Watch your balance—the tank will throw you off. No, hang onto those fins. You're going to need them if we get past the rocks."

He obeyed me without a word. Through his mask, I could see his eyes wide with fear in the moonlight. Together, bent forward against the wind and under the weight of our tanks, we slowly picked our way through the rocks and into the water.

The next wave knocked me off my feet. I clutched at the nearest rock as I went down, lost my grip on Tom's hand, and skinned my knees. He was still on his feet, but listing sideways against another rock. At least we both still had our fins.

"Hands and knees," I gasped. "Oh, and here." I reached over and grabbed his regulator and stuck it in his mouth. "Breathe through this, so you don't have to worry about inhaling water." I did the same, and watched as he took his first tentative breaths.

Since I couldn't talk now, I waved my fins at him to indicate he needed to hang onto his own. Then I started crawling toward the ocean, trusting him to follow me. My hands and legs were going to be a mass of cuts and bruises, but that was the least of my worries. One big wave at just the wrong time and one or both of us could be bashed against a rock and knocked out—or killed.

Clinging to the bigger rocks, I gradually moved away from shore, bracing for each wave. After every one, I turned to make sure Tom was still behind me, still okay. Why I cared, when he'd tried to save himself at my expense earlier, I didn't know. Probably the same reason I'd tried to help Lenny the other day. I just couldn't turn off that stupid nurturing switch.

The next five minutes felt like an eternity. For every two steps forward we managed, the water pushed us back a step and a half. But slowly, slowly, we made our way into deeper water. When I was about chest deep, I managed to move around behind a rock that stuck up out of the water. I motioned to Tom to join me. It gave us a little bit of shelter from the battering waves.

Taking my regulator out of my mouth, I said, "Here. This is a good place to put on our fins. Then we can try to swim."

He stood there, chest heaving, then managed a nod. I considered it a minor miracle that we both still had our fins, and sent up silent thanks and a quick prayer. One miracle at a time. My fins were too big, but I pulled the strap at the back as tight as possible. Then I helped Tom on with his, which at least fit.

I reached over and pushed the button on his vest to inflate it all the way. He'd probably panic if he started to sink. I'd worry about actually diving once we were away from the jagged rocks.

"Okay, let's go. Follow me," I said, and put my regulator back in my mouth.

I waited for the next wave to break, then took advantage of the backwash as it went out to come around the rock and let it carry us further from shore. When I saw the next wave coming, I ducked down, motioning for Tom to do the same. It still pushed us backward, but not as dramatically as when we'd been on the surface. This just might work.

The moment that wave receded, I leveled out and kicked my fins as hard as I could, trying to get well away from the rocks before the next wave could reach us. A few more yards and we'd be past the breakers, which should make for easier going.

I glanced back but didn't see Tom. Grumbling, I had to let the next wave carry me backward, undoing all of my progress. There he was, still clinging to the rock. I motioned to him again but he shook his head at me. Was he hurt? I moved back around behind the rock where I could stand and took my regulator out again.

"What? What's wrong?"

"I mwama sfay eer," he said around his mouthpiece.

I pulled it out of his mouth. "What?"

"I said I want to stay here. It's the safest spot we've found. Maybe they'll give up and leave after a while, and then we can go back."

"Well, I guess we can at least—" A loud crack interrupted me and made us both jump.

"What the?" I turned to look back toward shore and saw three figures still there, one pointing at us. There was another crack, this one even closer—and this time I saw sparks from a nearby rock. "They're shooting at us!"

"Okay, I guess that was a bad plan," Tom said. I was relieved that he didn't sound as scared as I'd expected. Maybe, like me, he'd worked past that first rush of terror. I hoped so.

"As soon as the next wave breaks, follow me," I said. "Swim as hard as you can. We need to get out past the breakers and away from these rocks—and out of range from that gun."

I didn't know if Phelps was a bad shot or if he was just trying to scare us. Both, I hoped.

The next wave broke, and this time Tom came with me around the rock and out toward open sea. It took two, three more waves, with us ducking down for each one, before we were past the main line of breakers. The water was still rough, with whitecaps breaking all around us. Too rough for talking. And the current was still pushing us toward shore.

I stretched my fins down as far as they'd go and discovered I couldn't stand. I took a deep breath, then pulled out my regulator just long enough to say, "We're going to go down. We'll be safer there."

Tom started shaking his head, but I didn't have the energy to argue or explain. Instead, I reached over and let some air out of his BCD, then did the same with my own. We started to sink.

Tom sort of half screamed through his regulator and flailed his arms. I grabbed one arm firmly and patted it, then took his hand. It seemed to calm him slightly. He stopped screaming and kicking and started breathing again.

It was pitch dark below the surface, but only a few feet down we hit rocks again. I guided Tom's hand to hold onto one, then I grabbed another. The current was still strong, still trying to force us in toward shore, but now we had some leverage.

I considered working our way deeper, but then realized Tom would have no idea how to equalize to keep his ears from hurting. Best if we just stay here. But for how long? Our air wouldn't last forever.

Now that we were out here in the pitch dark, the current tugging hard against our grips on the rocks, I realized that my plan of swimming around to the calm side of the island was worse than desperate—it was impossible. If Phelps and the others didn't leave before our air ran out, we'd be dead just as surely as if he'd shot us.

As the minutes passed and my fingers started to go numb, I started to wish he had.

I tried to distract myself by thinking about what Lenny had let slip earlier. Apparently Melanie Melampus had managed to fake her own death after all. So where did her sister come into all of this?

I shifted my grip slightly, feeling my energy ebb as the adrenaline that had driven me this far started to wear off. I tried to check my air gauge, but it was too dark. Anyway, I was pretty sure my fingers would give out before my air did.

A nudge on my arm made me turn, but all I could see was a dark shape in the water—and an outline of Tom's arm, pointing upward. I looked up and saw what he was pointing at: a light, bobbing on the waves, not far off. A boat?

Maybe we'd been given another miracle after all. No matter who it was, they had to be a better bet than waiting here to die or going back to be shot. I groped at Tom's vest until I found the button to inflate it, then inflated my own, swimming as hard as I could in the direction of the light.

Tom reached the surface before I did, but I was right behind him. It was definitely a boat—but it was farther away than I'd thought. Still, neither of us hesitated in swimming toward it. I only hoped it would stay put until we could get close enough to shout.

I tried to switch to my snorkel to conserve the air in my tank, but the ocean was far too rough. After getting seawater in my snorkel—and mouth—for the third time and coughing so hard I nearly threw up, I switched back to my regulator. Just as well I hadn't suggested Tom use his snorkel.

My arms and legs felt like lead after struggling against the ocean for so long already. At least the water wasn't too cold, especially with a wetsuit... Something brushed against my thigh, and I let out a yelp through my regulator.

I twisted around in the water, imagining sharks and even worse things in the black water, then realized it had been Tom's fin. Still, that surge of adrenaline wasn't without effect. I felt a renewed burst of energy, and I put it to good use, kicking and stroking toward the light of the boat. Was it my imagination, or was it starting to move?

Panicked at the idea of the boat leaving, I dropped my regulator and shouted as loudly as I could. I managed a couple of good yells before a wave hit me in the face, making me splutter and choke again. Beside me, Tom slowed, then took his own regulator part way out of his mouth and hollered, too—then put the mouthpiece right back in. I couldn't really blame him.

I took a couple of deep breaths through my regulator, then kicked upward as hard as I could while attempting another shout, to keep my head as far above the water as possible.

"Here! Over here! Help!" I screamed, before I had to shut my mouth as I sank back down into the waves. Was the boat turning? Coming this way? No... Yes! Yes, it was.

"Hello?" A man's voice came across the water toward us. "Is someone out here?"

Tom and I shouted, "Yes!" simultaneously, and he apparently heard us, because now the boat was definitely coming toward us.

I sagged with relief, allowing myself to just bob on the surface and breathe, waiting for rescue. At least I hoped it would be a rescue and not yet another person working with Melanie/Michelle and company. By now I almost didn't care, as long as whoever it was got us out of the water.

As the boat got close, I saw that it was a small one, about the size of Van's dive boat and built along the same lines. I hoped that meant it would have a ladder, which would make it a lot easier for us to climb aboard.

While I rested, Tom kept moving toward the boat and reached it while it was still maybe thirty yards from me. It apparently did have a ladder, because I could see the figure aboard moving to the back of the boat to lower it, along with the faint splashing that had to be Tom swimming to the same spot.

Wearily, I started swimming forward again. I didn't really think Tom would let the boat leave without me, but I wasn't willing to take the chance.

I'd nearly reached the boat by the time Tom was climbing the ladder, apparently with substantial assistance from the man on board. He'd have had to be told to take off his fins, I realized, plus I was pretty sure Tom had never climbed up a boat ladder before. Definitely not with a tank on his back.

"All right, you sit right over there," I heard a voice saying as I approached the ladder. A familiar voice, I was almost sure, though it was possible I was hearing what I very much wanted to hear.

"I heard someone else out there—a woman." I was almost sure about the voice now. And a moment later, I was close enough to see him.

"Ronan?" I called, nearly weeping with relief.

Then I saw the gun in his hand, pointed at Tom.

# CHAPTER TWENTY-ONE

"NO. OH, NO," I moaned. Then, completely overwhelmed to discover, after everything else, that Ronan was one of the bad guys, I started to cry.

"Wynne?" His voice sounded eager, even happy. "Wynne, is that you?"

I was afraid to answer, but even more afraid not to. "Yes. Yes, it's me."

"Oh, thank God!" he exclaimed, coming to the ladder and peering toward me. "But who?" He turned back toward Tom, the gun still in his hand.

"It's Tom." A tiny hope that I barely dared to acknowledge flared up. "Who did you think it was?"

"Tom? Your ex?" He went back to Tom and pulled off his mask. "Oh, man, I'm sorry. Let me help Wynne up, and I'll explain."

To my amazed relief, he put the gun down and came back to the ladder. I could see his teeth gleaming in the moonlight—in a smile. "Do you have your fins off?" he asked.

"Yes, here." I handed them up, and then he was helping me, almost hauling me, up the ladder.

I was so exhausted, I was more than willing to let him do most of the work. The moment I was up, he surprised me by wrapping me in a bear hug. Maybe he was just relieved. I certainly was, and maybe that was why I hugged him back.

Before I could decide, he half guided, half carried me to the bench beside Tom so I could sit and get the heavy tank off of me.

"What are you doing out here?" I asked, pulling off my mask and unclipping my vest. "And why did you have a gun?"

"I came by boat in case Michelle or anyone else tried to escape by water when they realized they were trapped," he said. "Look." He pointed back toward shore.

I looked and saw lights—flashing red and blue lights, and several sets of headlights. "Who else is there?"

"Haliakis and the FBI and the Aruban police, I imagine. At least, that was the plan, and it looks from here like it worked. We won't know for sure until we get back to shore."

"You got my message, then?"

"I did. And I'm really, really sorry I didn't check my voice mail sooner. I could have told you it would be a trap, especially once I found out it was Phelps's room that note was delivered to."

"But how—" I started to ask when Tom interrupted.

"Look, can we do all the explanations later? I really want to get into something dry. And have a good, stiff drink."

Ronan laughed, which was more than I was up to just yet. "I don't blame you a bit, buddy. Yeah, let's get back. We can talk on the way."

He powered up the boat—I realized now that it really was *Van's Vandal*—and swung it north, toward the tip of the island.

"There's no place to put in along here, so we'll go around the point and dock at Palm Beach," he explained. "That way we can get you both into something warm and dry before we go meet the others."

It sounded like an excellent plan to me.

"Okay, I told you what I was doing out here," Ronan said when I joined him at the helm, still wearing my wetsuit for warmth. "What were you two doing in the ocean in the middle of the night? Where did you get the dive gear?"

"They brought it," I told him. "Phelps, or I guess it was Lenny, had the idea to make it look like we died in a diving accident."

"It's a miracle that you didn't," he said, staring at me for a moment.

I realized he was right. I'd gotten my miracle. I sent up another, belated prayer of thanks.

Ronan continued as though he hadn't heard. "That surf, those rocks—there's a reason only the most advanced divers ever do this side of the island."

"If you hadn't come, I'm sure they'd have succeeded," I said. "Even if I'd figured out that the police had come, I don't think we could have made it back in through those rocks without getting killed. My whole body is one big bruise from the trip out." I looked down at my bleeding knees.

Ronan reached out and squeezed my shoulder. I thought he was about to say something, but then he seemed to change his mind and faced forward again. Another wave of exhaustion hit me, and I went back to sit by Tom, who was leaning against his tank and vest, snoring.

I envied him. Tired as I was, I knew I wouldn't be able to sleep tonight until everything had been settled. And I suspected that was going to take hours.

AS IT TURNED out, I was wrong on one count. When Ronan cut the engine, I jerked awake to discover I'd dozed off against Tom's shoulder. How embarrassing.

My other prediction was correct, though. By the time Tom and I had changed into dry clothes and had our numerous cuts and scrapes bandaged, Agents Truman and Walters were waiting for us, along with Argus Haliakis and the chief of the Aruban police force. It was going to be a long, long night.

The Royal Aruban opened a small conference room for our use so that the police and the FBI agents could take statements from us. Over the next two or three hours—I lost track of time after a while, despite endless cups of coffee—I learned almost as much as I told.

"Was I right?" was my first question as we all took our seats around the conference table, Ronan on my right and Tom on my left. "It was Melanie Melampus after all, wasn't it, and not Michelle Alvares?"

"You were right, Ms. Seally," Mr. Haliakis answered before anyone else could. "I recognized her right off—along with my cousin Loxi. Did you say he was calling himself Lenny? He used to work for Mr. M but quit after...well, a few months before Mrs. M disappeared."

"He's your cousin?" No wonder they looked so much alike. "So he quit after Mr. Melampus's conversion?"

Agent Walters, across the table, mumbled something I didn't catch.

"Yeah. We never did get along. He's a few years older and used to bully me when we was kids. I guess him and Mrs. M both felt the same way about Mr. M getting religion."

"I don't know about that last part," said Agent Truman, "but it's true that your original guess was correct, Ms. Seally. Melanie Melampus admitted her identity after Mr. Haliakis recognized her, and it won't be difficult to verify that. I apologize for our earlier skepticism."

No apology from Walters, I noticed.

"So...what about Michelle Alvares?" I asked. "Where is she?"

There was a silence, during which I thought both FBI agents looked uncomfortable, and then Ronan spoke.

"From what Gus, er, Mr. Haliakis and I have been piecing together, it's looking like there might never have been a Michelle Alvares."

"Never—" Maybe because I was so tired, I couldn't seem to wrap my mind around that at first. "You mean...Melanie made her up? But the newspaper stories—"

"Were all interviews with Melanie," Ronan said, and Agent Truman nodded. Walters just glowered. "If you remember, no one else ever saw Michelle."

"And the first Mr. M or anyone else heard about her was pretty recent," Haliakis put in. "I'd say right about the time Mr. M pulled out of his more, um, unconventional businesses—" he glanced at the FBI agents— "and changed his will to leave most of his stuff to charity."

"Instead of to Melanie?" I was starting to understand, even with my brain in low gear.

Agent Truman cleared his throat. "Yes, well, we can puzzle out all of the details later, when we have more of the facts. Right now, I'd like to get statements from Mr. and Ms. Seally and Mr. Gale, here—who somehow seems to have been left out of what we were told earlier."

"Yeah, I noticed that, too," Haliakis said, but now he was grinning.

If I hadn't been so tired, I might have blushed. I did wonder what all of this would do to Ronan's chances of getting that million dollar bonus, but I wasn't *quite* brain-dead enough to ask right then. I hoped I'd get a chance later.

The interrogation started in earnest then, Agent Truman asking most of the questions with an occasional query from Walters and the Aruban police chief, whose name I never quite caught.

Tom didn't have much to add to my account, beyond his conversation with Phelps earlier that evening. However, he looked more and more horrified as I gave my own rendition of events, starting with my first finding the ring and continuing through tonight's near catastrophe.

"Maybe I should have called you tonight myself," I said to Agent Truman, "but when they threatened my daughters—" I broke off in sudden horror. "My daughters! What if Melanie or Phelps get a message to whoever they have in Indiana? What if—"

"Not to worry, Ms. Seally," Mr. Haliakis said. "I've already talked to Mr. M, and he'll make sure no one touches your girls."

"From Miami?" Tom spoke for the first time in almost an hour. "How can he do that?"

It was Walters who answered him. "I imagine Melampus still has connections, no matter how he pretends to have gone straight. Eh, Mr. Haliakis?"

"I wouldn't know, sir," Haliakis replied, giving nothing away with his expression. "The important thing is that the Seallys' kids are safe."

"Well, I'll be going home tomorrow—or rather today," Tom said. "So I can make sure of that."

It was nice that he cared—or said he cared—but I couldn't help trusting Stefan Melampus's ability to keep the girls safe more than Tom's. "I'm glad to hear that," was all I said.

"I assume you're coming with me. After all this, I'm sure you've had enough of Aruba."

As much as I wanted to see the girls again, to hug them and reassure myself that they were safe, I shook my head. "I still have a few days left of what was supposed to be a vacation. I plan to use them to relax, and maybe get a bit of a tan."

"But—"

"Mr. Seally, perhaps you and your wife can have this discussion later," Agent Truman suggested. "Right now, I'd like to finish this interview and let everyone go get some sleep."

Tom nodded, though he shot me a disgruntled look, along with a frown for Ronan, who hadn't said a word.

"All of you realize that you may be called upon to testify, should any of these cases make it to trial?" Truman asked then, looking at Ronan and Haliakis, as well as Tom and me.

"Do you mean that any of them—Phelps, Melanie or Lenny, er, Loxi—might get off?" I asked, startled.

Truman shrugged. "It's always a possibility. In a situation like this, I'd call it a probability, given their connections and that we only have two witnesses, and no one was seriously hurt. Phelps may get disbarred, but that's not a criminal proceeding."

"But he tried to kill us!" Tom protested.

"Yes, but he didn't succeed. And he managed to ditch the gun you both say he had—probably threw it in the ocean. Even if it turns up later, it'll be hard to tie it to him. We did find the ring on him, at least."

"And what about Melanie?" I asked. "Isn't she guilty of insurance fraud, at the very least?"

Ronan touched my arm. "I hate to tell you this, but even in the most flagrant cases—which this is—convictions for insurance fraud are really rare. Especially when the perpetrator never collected, which she didn't."

Again I wondered about his commission. But all I said was, "That just seems so wrong. But at least her showing up alive will void Stefan Melampus's murder charge."

"Yeah, his house arrest will be lifted by midday tomorrow," Walters said, clearly disgusted. "We'll probably never nail him now. For anything."

I exchanged glances with Gus Haliakis, but both of us managed to keep from grinning.

Agent Truman frowned at his partner, but didn't disagree with him. "Well, I think that's everything, unless you have any more questions?" he asked the police chief.

The poor man looked half asleep. "What? No, I don't think so."

We all stood, shook hands all around, made sure everyone had everyone else's contact information, then went our separate ways.

I'd never been so tired in my life—at least, not since getting the girls through their last bouts of all-night childhood illnesses.

Out in the lobby, Tom again tried to persuade me to leave with him on the first available flight. "The girls will expect it," he said.

"They won't. They've been very supportive of my taking this trip. I'll call them both tomorrow and take them to dinner when I get back. You can take them out tomorrow night, if you want, and if Darlene doesn't have other plans."

"I told you—" he began, then apparently realized I was baiting him. "Good night, Wynne." He headed for the elevators.

I waited a moment, not wanting to ride up in the same car, and realized Ronan was still standing there, a few paces away. He looked at me questioningly, and I managed a tired smile.

"So, what will this do to your big bonus?" I asked him. "I'm sorry if I screwed that up for you by almost getting killed."

He chuckled and came over to me. "It's too soon to tell, but I hope you'll believe me when I say that the thought of losing you scared me a lot more than the thought of losing that bonus."

That was nice to hear, but I was in no state just then to deal with any ramifications underlying his words. "Thank you, Ronan. But I can't—"

"Hey, no strings, no expectations. I know you're not ready for that just yet." He glanced toward the elevators, where Tom had just disappeared. "I just wanted you to know."

"Thanks," I said again. "I hope I'll see you again before I leave Aruba."

"Count on it. Now, go to bed and don't set the alarm." He kissed me lightly on the cheek, turned me toward the elevators, and gave me a tiny push.

Zombie-like, I made my way up to my room, staggered through my bedtime routine, then fell into a coma-like sleep without dreams, as far as I could remember.

.  .  .

THE BEDSIDE phone woke me ten minutes before noon. I rolled over, still groggy, to answer it.

"Wynne? It's Tom. I'm booked on a two fifteen flight, so I'm leaving for the airport in a few minutes. Are you sure you don't want to come with me? I checked, and there are still seats available."

"What? Oh. No, I'm sure. I couldn't be ready in time even if I wanted to. Your call woke me up."

"Oh, um, sorry." He sounded more irritated than contrite.

"That's okay. I didn't plan to sleep this late anyway. Have a good flight."

"Yeah. Maybe we can talk when you get home?"

"Right." I hung up without committing to that conversation, but there was probably no avoiding it. I still wasn't ready to forgive him—that would take a lot more growth on my part. But I could make an effort to be civil, at least, for the girls' sakes.

That reminded me that I needed to call them. I'd forgotten to plug in my cell phone—it was still in my purse, which Agent Truman had retrieved from Tom's rental car. I assumed he'd gotten the car back as well, though I couldn't remember if it had come up last night.

I plugged my phone in and made both calls while it charged. The girls and my mom were all fine, and all still confused. I told them Tom would be home that night, gave them a very sketchy synopsis of recent events, leaving out the scariest parts, and promised to go into detail when I returned home in a few days.

That done, I showered and dressed so that I could go in search of sustenance. My stomach was growling—not surprising after my early dinner, an enormous amount of exertion in the water, and no breakfast.

Ronan was in the lobby when I reached it. "Hey, sleepyhead," he greeted me. "I didn't want to call your room and risk waking you, so I've been waiting here for you to return to the land of the living."

"Thanks," I said. "Tom wasn't so considerate. He called to say he's catching an early afternoon flight. Just as well, though, because I'm starving."

"Then let's get you something to eat," he said with a grin.

The hotel dining room was the closest option, so we headed there. "Have you ever been around me when I wasn't hungry?" I asked. "I promise, I'm not this way at home."

"You have a really good excuse right now," he pointed out. "And diving has been involved most of the other times, too. Besides, I already told you I like to see a woman enjoying her food."

Embarrassed, I lapsed into silence until the server came to take my order—which consisted of a dinner-sized portion of shrimp marinara over linguine and a salad. Ronan ordered a sandwich.

"I've already eaten," he explained, "but it seemed polite to keep you company."

We spent the meal talking about travel—places we'd been and places we wanted to go. Ronan had seen a lot more of the world than I had. It was as though we'd agreed not to discuss the events of the past few days. Or maybe we were both just talked out on that topic, after last night's marathon interview.

As I mopped up the last of my sauce with my fourth piece of bread, Ronan's cell phone rang.

"Yes?"

A voice on the other end spoke, and he sat up perceptibly straighter in his chair. "Already? I see. Yes, sir. Yes. Of course. Ten minutes, then."

The look he gave me as he hung up was a little dazed. "That was Stefan Melampus. He's here on the island—in this hotel, actually— and would like to meet with both of us right away."

I set down my napkin. "Stefan Melampus? Here? How? Already?"

"That's what I said. And yes. Apparently all restrictions on his movements were lifted early this morning, and he had wheels up on his private jet within the hour. We're invited to his suite on the top floor."

Ronan signaled for the check, and I was so distracted that I let him pay it, even though I'd eaten more than twice what he had.

"Can I stop by my room on the way up?" I asked as we left the restaurant. "Just to—I don't know—check my makeup and stuff?"

"You look fine," Ronan said with a smile that made my cheeks tingle. "But if it will make you feel better, sure. He said ten minutes, and it's been less than five."

"Thanks. Let's head up, then. I promise not to delay us more than a couple of minutes."

We took the elevator up together and got off on the fourteenth floor. It occurred to me as I keyed open my door that this would be the first time Ronan would see my room. Had I stashed my dirty laundry out of sight?

I went in first just to glance around for anything flagrantly embarrassing, but luckily there were no bras draped over chairs.

"Nice," Ronan commented, coming in behind me. "Very nice."

"Yeah, after my first room was broken into, they gave me this one—probably so I wouldn't raise a stink about their security." I checked my face and hair in the mirror on the back of the closet door. Maybe a touch of lip gloss?

"Um, about that." Something in Ronan's tone made me turn to face him. He was looking almost sheepish.

"What?" I asked.

He raised his brows and shrugged, gesturing around my suite. "I, ah, guess you have me to thank for such luxurious digs. I was the one who broke into your room that first night. Looking for the ring. I meant to tell you before, but—"

"But you wanted me to trust you?" I'd nearly forgotten that Ronan had been one of my prime suspects early on.

"Well...yeah. And you can, Wynne, really. I mean, I didn't even know you then. Now, I'd never—"

"Ronan, it's okay. And I'm glad you told me. But it doesn't really matter. Not now." Okay, I probably wouldn't have thrown away all of my undies if I'd known it was him. But I definitely wasn't telling him *that*.

He looked at me for a long moment, as though trying to gauge my real feelings on the matter, then finally managed a faint smile. "I'm glad I told you, too. But now, we really ought to head up to the eighteenth floor if we don't want to keep Stefan Melampus waiting."

## CHAPTER TWENTY-TWO

IF MY ROOM was luxurious, Stefan Melampus's was off the scale. Ronan and I were shown into what was undoubtedly the Royal Aruban's largest suite by Mr. Haliakis, who greeted us both with a big smile.

"Bet you're both feeling better after some sleep, huh? I know I am. That was some wild night last night."

"Gus," came a voice from behind him—a voice I'd heard only twice before but would never forget, a voice as smooth and rich as premium dark chocolate. "Don't keep our guests standing."

Haliakis stepped back. "Oh, sure thing, Mr. M. Come on in and have a seat, guys. I'll get some drinks."

We entered the main living area of the suite, which was about twice the size of my living room at home, and Stefan Melampus came forward, hands outstretched.

"I'm delighted—enchanted—to meet you in person, Ms. Seally. And Ronan, it's good to see you again."

He was even more handsome in person—tall, dark, with a distinguished graying at the temples, impeccably yet casually dressed. And he had a charisma, a vitality, that hadn't been evident in the pictures, but was almost overwhelming up close.

"Mr. Melampus—" I began.

"Stefan, please," he said, taking my hand and actually kissing it, with Old World charm. "And dare I hope I may call you Wynne? A particularly apt name, I must say."

I swallowed. "Of...of course." I hadn't thought about the homonym of my name since college.

"Not fair," Ronan said, shaking Stefan's hand in turn. "Now she'll never look at me again."

Stefan laughed and waved us to a couple of plushly upholstered chairs. "I doubt you need to worry, Ronan. The sort of thing you two have been through this past week tends to create a bond. Ah, Gus—lemonade? Perfect. Thank you."

Haliakis handed around tall glasses that were fancier than anything I'd seen in the hotel. I wondered if Stefan had brought them himself. And the lemonade tasted like it had been made from scratch.

"I came here as quickly as I was able," Stefan said, sitting down across from us. Haliakis faded into the background—quite a feat for such a gorgeous young man.

"And took us by surprise," Ronan admitted. "You must have been in the air almost the moment the papers were signed."

"Very nearly." Stefan chuckled. "But I felt it was important to personally reassure Wynne, at the earliest opportunity, that her daughters are indeed safe. I regret terribly that they were put at risk, and I take full responsibility."

"Thank you," I said. "But really, I can't see how any of this was your fault. My finding that ring was pure coincidence, and all the rest—"

"Was orchestrated by people who wished me ill," he finished. "Which does make it my fault, at least indirectly. If I had no former associates capable of such evil, you and your family would never have been in danger."

I still didn't agree that he was to blame, but I didn't think I was going to argue him out of that conviction. "At least everything seems to have worked out all right now," I said.

"Praise God," he replied, without the least bit of self-conscious-ness. "I'm exceedingly thankful not to have your, or anyone else's, injury or death on my head."

"Amen," said Ronan with a grin.

Stefan raised an eyebrow at him, and the grin faded a bit. Then he turned back to me. "I would also like to apologize for doubting your word when you told me you'd seen Melanie here in Aruba. It appears that she was quite creative when she orchestrated her disappearance."

"Yes, how *did* she do that?" Ronan asked. "The quantity of blood alone—"

"The blood found in areas likely to be tested was indeed hers. That spread down the side of the yacht, however, apparently was not, though more tests will be attempted. I imagine she had assistance in that scheme from someone more knowledgeable about criminal investiga-tions. After reading the transcript I was faxed from last night's state-ments, it seems she and Loxi Haliakis were, ah, closer than I imagined."

There was a tightness about Stefan's mouth as he said that, and my heart went out to him. I knew what it was like to be duped—betrayed—by a spouse. At least Tom hadn't tried to frame me for murder.

"What about Agent Walters?" I asked then, as much to change the subject as because I was curious. "He kept trying to get me to give him the ring, and I think it was so he could make it disappear."

Stefan lifted a shoulder. "Agent Walters and I have a bit of history, from prior incidents where I, ah, may have eluded prosecu-tion where it was deserved. His zeal in this instance was perhaps understandable, though his methods may not have been by the book. Without proof, however..." He let that trail off and I realized he was probably right. All I had was suspicion, not proof.

"As for your finding Melanie's ring in the first place, Wynne," he continued, "I already told you what I believe about coincidence. I have no doubt this has all been part of a greater plan. Not that that mitigates my debt to you.

"Which brings me to my other reason for meeting with you both," he said, rising. "I believe in paying off my debts promptly."

I glanced at Ronan, but he was watching Stefan expectantly as he went to a desk in the corner of the room, picked up a file folder, and came back.

"Ronan," he said, "though our agreement was for something rather different from what occurred, your assistance was crucial both in flushing out Melanie and her accomplices, and in keeping Wynne safe. Here's the bonus I promised if you succeeded in clearing my name."

He pulled a check from the folder and handed it to Ronan, who glanced at it, swallowed visibly, then put it in his shirt pocket.

I stared. So it was *Stefan* who had promised Ronan that bonus and not the insurance company? It made sense, but I planned to discuss that little bit of deception with Ronan later. I also might ask to see that check, since I'd never actually seen a million dollars before.

Ronan turned to me then and said, "Our earlier deal holds, you know. Twenty percent of this is yours."

"That's commendable, Ronan," Stefan said, "and definitely your prerogative. But possibly unnecessary." He turned to me with a smile.

"Wynne, Gus has given me a thorough report on everything that has occurred, and I've done some research of my own as well. I'm more than willing to give you a check identical to Ronan's, but I believe you might benefit more from a different offer."

I opened and closed my mouth a few times before anything would emerge, so overwhelmed was I by the thought of my very own million dollar check—not that I'd feel comfortable accepting it. "Offer?" I finally managed.

Stefan inclined his head, which somehow seemed more sophisticated than a nod. "Offer. One you are perfectly free to refuse, if you wish. As it happens, I've recently come into possession of a nice little dive shop in the Florida Keys that is in need of a proprietor. In lieu of a check, I'd very much like to give you title to that shop and its contents, along with whatever funds will be necessary for you to begin operating it."

"I...I don't know what to say." And I really, truly didn't. But the idea of moving to the Keys, owning and operating my own business, caused an undeniable flare of exhilaration within me. To have a purpose again...

"Of course, I would also put a substantial sum into a trust for your daughters, so that their futures would not be jeopardized by the inevitable vagaries of running a business," he said, as I remained dumb. "Or perhaps you feel it would be too stressful for you to leave Indiana and the home and people you've known there?"

I started shaking my head. "Uh, no, actually, I think a fresh start someplace entirely different may be exactly what I need." I met his eyes—dark chocolate, like his voice—and managed a smile. "But I'm guessing that's exactly what you figured out from your, ah, research."

He returned my smile. "It did occur to me that an opportunity for a change might not come amiss right now, yes. Will you accept my offer?"

I hesitated, thinking of all the reasons I should refuse, or at least delay a decision. Stefan Melampus had—allegedly—been a crime boss, after all.

"I can assure you, Wynne, that there will be no strings attached whatsoever," he said then, correctly interpreting my hesitation. "And also that I acquired this shop in a completely legal manner. You need not worry that you might be accepting, ah, 'dirty money.'"

"I didn't...I mean...I should talk to my daughters, my mother, about it. I should see what the real estate market in Indianapolis is like right now. I should—" But my whole life had been built around *should*. No more.

Lifting my chin, I looked Stefan in the eye. "Yes. Yes, I accept."

"Excellent. There is one other thing, Wynne, though it may be none of my business. I understand that you've stopped attending church in recent months."

That was some thorough research! "Um, yes," I admitted. "Tom, my ex-husband, was an elder there, and—"

He raised a hand. "I'm not asking for an explanation. I simply hope you won't allow the actions of a few misguided people to turn you away from God. When you move to your new locale... We all need help, Wynne."

I realized I'd done exactly what he said. And the only one I'd hurt was myself. "Thank you. I'll remember that."

He smiled broadly. "Good. As for the dive shop, I'll have all of the paperwork ready for you by the time you return to Indiana."

Stefan stood, indicating that our interview was over. Ronan and I did likewise.

"And now," he said, "I suggest you enjoy your remaining time in Aruba. Have Ronan here take you out on the town. He can afford it."

We shook hands all around again, and Ronan and I left the suite. I'm pretty sure I didn't manage anything coherent besides "Thank you" before we were alone in the hallway. My brain was much too full of the possibilities that lay ahead.

"So," Ronan said as we headed back to the elevators. "You have a few more days here to simply enjoy. What would you like to do first?"

I thought for a moment. "First, I'd like to stop by my room again. I need to change."

"Change? You look great. Are we going swimming or something?"

"Maybe later."

I didn't say anything else until we reached my room. I pulled a plastic bag out of the closet and went into the bathroom, where I took off my tank top and replaced it with the shirt from the bag:

the NO FEAR t-shirt I'd bought the day I'd been certified as a diver.

Surely, after everything that had happened, I had earned the right to wear it. I grinned at myself in the mirror, then went out to join Ronan, ready to dive into my future—whatever it held.

———

## AUTHOR'S NOTE

Until recently, it's been a little known fact that in between my historical romances and my young adult science-fantasy books, I wrote a mystery novel—though as I was writing it, I considered it more of a humorous, suspenseful women's fiction novel. I wrote it mainly for fun, hoping to rekindle my joy in writing when I felt burned out after fifteen historical romances. I'm happy to say it worked! So well, in fact, that I went on from there to write my **Starstruck** series.

In republishing *Out of Her Depth*, I was able to make a few updates (it was written over a dozen years ago) and give it a new cover I feel better reflects the story than the spookier one the original publisher used. I'm eager to hear what my readers think, as it's somewhat "off-brand" for me—though definitely still "sparkling romantic adventure"!

With so many books out there to choose from, I thank you for choosing and reading *Out of Her Depth*. If you enjoyed it, I hope you will consider leaving a review in my web store or wherever you buy or talk about books to let other like-minded readers know they might enjoy it, too. And please do drop me a note to tell me what you think!

## ABOUT THE AUTHOR

New York Times and USA Today bestselling author Brenda Hiatt writes novels of sparkling romantic adventure spanning Regency England, Americana, contemporary teen science fiction and more. Which ever you pick up, you'll find excitement, romance and, always, an uplifting happy ending. In addition to writing, Brenda is passionate about embracing life to the fullest. She enjoys scuba diving (she has over 60 dives to her credit), Taekwondo (where she's currently working toward her 4th degree black belt), hiking, traveling...and reading, of course!

For two free short stories and the earliest news about Brenda Hiatt's books, subscribe to her newsletter at:
brendahiatt.com/subscribe

*Connect with Brenda at:*
brendahiatt.com

www.ingramcontent.com/pod-product-compliance
Lightning Source LLC
Chambersburg PA
CBHW060811190726
48285CB00002B/629